A Voice of Her Own

A Voice of Her Own

Becoming Emily Dickinson

A NOVEL BY BARBARA DANA

HARPER TEEN
An Imprint of HarperCollins*Publishers*

Emily's schedule at Mount Holyoke Seminary (pp. 150–151) and the menu
(pp. 153–154) are from *The Letters of Emily Dickinson,* edited by Thomas H. Johnson.

HarperTeen is an imprint of HarperCollins Publishers.

A Voice of Her Own: Becoming Emily Dickinson
Copyright © 2009 by Barbara Dana
All rights reserved. Printed in the United States of America.
No part of this book may be used or reproduced in any manner whatsoever without
written permission except in the case of brief quotations embodied in critical articles
and reviews. For information address HarperCollins Children's Books, a division of
HarperCollins Publishers, 10 East 53rd Street, New York, NY 10022.
www.harperteen.com

Library of Congress Cataloging-in-Publication Data
Dana, Barbara.
A voice of her own : becoming Emily Dickinson : a novel / by Barbara Dana. — 1st ed.
    p. cm.
  Summary: A fictionalized first-person account of revered American poet Emily
Dickinson's girlhood in mid-nineteenth-century Amherst, Massachusetts.
  Includes bibliographical references (p.   ).
  ISBN 978-0-06-028704-7 (trade bdg.)
  1. Dickinson, Emily, 1830–1886—Childhood and youth—Juvenile fiction. [1. Dickinson,
Emily, 1830–1886—Childhood and youth—Fiction. 2. Amherst (Mass.)—History—19th
century—Fiction.] I. Title.
PZ7.D188Vo 2009   2008010289
[Fic]—dc22   CIP
                                                                     AC

Typography by Michelle Gengaro
10 11 12 13 LP/RRDB 10 9 8 7 6 5 4 3
❖
First Edition

For
Julie Harris

There is always one thing to be grateful for—
that one is one's self & not somebody else.
                    —E. Dickinson

Author's Foreword

As I immersed myself in the poems and letters of Emily Dickinson, some of her favorite phrases found their way into the manuscript. I have included a list of these phrases, along with the page numbers on which they appear, at the end of the book. The poems in the text are not hers. They are my impressions of the kind of poetry Emily might have written in her early years. Emily had a unique way of expressing herself. This has been honored. However, in the interest of clarity, a few unusual grammatical uses have been omitted. Details appear in the Author's Notes at the end of the book.

Emily E. Dickinson.

As I tasted the gingerbread a thought took its place in my brain. No trumpets—just the being there—the arrival unnoticed, by me at any rate. It had been a Large Day—the rushing, the concern, the drama! And yours truly standing in the road—mute—my beloved Carlo at my side and the wagon that would carry us away.

Prologue

I t was too dreary, the last of our family's possessions piled by the side of the road as if Gypsies had relinquished squatter's rights and were moving on to points unknown. Father had the situation well in hand. He stood by the wagon, instructing Horace and Little Pat as to how things should be loaded. There was an appropriate order—make no mistake about that—some to the front and some to the back! Certain things were to be placed above certain other things, which were to be placed below. Presumably, this had to do with weight, but one could not be sure. There were surprises, such as the parlor settee finding its place atop the small kitchen table with the narrow legs. It would appear that efficient stacking is no small matter. With Father there is a way to do things and there are many ways not to. No questions asked!

There had been much Hurrah over the move, what with Father's determination to return to the Homestead, the endless renovations, Austin's soon-to-be-built house next door and Mother's anxious state regarding the wallpaper—not to mention Vinnie's concern about the cats. I caught the excitement some, along with a sinking dread. When moving day came all I could feel was a locking back to stone as a nameless fear possessed me. I was leaving my Pleasant House on Pleasant Street— my Home for fifteen years—no small thing when one is twenty-four.

"The table first and then the chair," said Father, raising an index finger.

Horace backed up with Vinnie's chair, while Little Pat swung the end table up and over the edge of the wagon. Fanny twitched an ear. It was November, so it wasn't because of a fly. I put it to boredom, but one never knows with a horse.

I wondered where Vinnie was. Helping Mother, I presumed. My sister is two years younger than I am. Her "proper" name is Lavinia, but I don't call her that. I sometimes wonder that we could have come from the same well. I honestly don't know where I came from until I think of Austin. My dear brother—two years from me on the older side—surely began his journey from that selfsame place, wherever it was.

Carlo lifted his nose. He stood at my side, my constant companion, a dog as large as myself. Father bought him for me shortly after my return from Mt Holyoke. Seven years of Love! He is golden red, with hair like mine and a head as large as Mother's pillow. He is Newfoundland mostly, with a pinch of something else, Saint Bernard is my guess. Father says we can never be sure and I tend to agree with him in this instance.

When at last the wagon pulled off, Carlo and I watched it go—all the way to the corner, where it turned and disappeared from sight. How long we stood outside my white fence I don't know. I see it now, latched tight, my yard off bounds to such as me. We stood still—lost. I, at any rate, felt thrust forth without my skin. Carlo looked up at me, his eyes deep with questions, as we began walking our way to the Homestead, over the hill and across the field, because he would take up too much space in the wagon.

The cats survived the ride to Father's House—I shall always call it that—with little incident. However, moments after we arrived they were nowhere to be seen—and Vinnie running to and fro calling, "Drummydoodles!" "Roughnaps!" "Tootsie!"

I ignored the situation and went about outside with Carlo to inspect the newness. The cupola on top of the roof was a capital addition. How I would have loved that when living at the Homestead in younger years. There was also an added part of the house to the side and back, and green shutters and freshly painted yellow brick. Now that was something to see!

The yard had beautiful trees. Some I remembered—most certainly my favorite oak—but many I had no recollection of. Whether they were there when I was nine and looked so differently now as not to be recognized, or whether they were new I cannot say. Behind the house stood the barn. A weathervane had been placed upon its roof with a lacy ironwork flag to indicate the wind's caprice—two red orange balls on a thin rod, a featherlike iron twig slanted at the top and letters to indicate the four directions. It brought me comfort to see it, a reminder of the Larger World—Circumference without edge.

Through the woods at the end of the path to the west, Austin's house was to be built—Austin's and dear Sue's. I was delighted with the nearness of the site, a two-minute walk at most. Carlo padded along the path, pursuing I knew not what. He sprang around quickly, heading back in the direction of the Homestead. A squirrel had been the reason.

The November wind was strong. It had begun to snow. It occurred to me that I should follow Carlo. I would explore inside. As I approached the back door I noticed Father, muffler all about, tossing crumbs to a group of waiting birds. Caretaker supreme! He can be exceedingly tender.

There was much fuss over finding the cooking things. Despite Father's detailed loading plan they were nowhere to be found, and Mother and I searching everywhere until it seemed they were to be lost forever. Vinnie was on her cat search and good for no one, unless you count the cats. At last the cooking things were located in a crate behind the stairs and Mother went to lie down. The house felt dark. I walked from room to room unable to settle my brain. I decided to bake some gingerbread. The simple act might be of comfort, I reasoned.

Carlo lay by the stove in a deep and thankful sleep as I creamed the butter, whipped the cream, mixed the two lightly, sifted the flour, soda and salt together, added the ginger, and combined them with the butter, cream, and molasses. The dough was stiff as I pressed it into the cast-iron pan. Twenty-five minutes later—gingerbread! I never cease to wonder at the marvel of baking! Carlo lifted his head as I pulled the heavy pan from the oven. I let it cool a bit, broke off a small piece from the corner, and sampled it. That's when I noticed the thought.

So much has happened since I stood in this self-same kitchen. I want to keep it forever.

Carlo watched me chew. His eyes were deep and full of longing, but he didn't move. He knew how it went. He would have to wait until after supper for his portion.

Later that evening I showed Carlo his new sleeping place—*my room*! At last he could sleep with me—my own room, no sharing with Vinnie! I wished he could sleep on my bed, but that presented several problems, not the least of which was his size. Had we managed to arrange ourselves with mutual respect for the other's well-being, doubtless morning would find one of us in a heap on the floor, and that was bound to be me! I considered risking the inconvenience for the joy of going off to sleep, an arm around his softness, but were I to find myself shivering on the floor as the sun stole through my window, Father would be angry. I would have to lie about it, and I have never cared for that. It leaves me without a place to put my feet.

Carlo and I climbed the stairs. I could hear Vinnie's voice coming from the far end of the hallway, presumably addressing the cats: "... *Very* bad! You must come when I call you!"

I was tired from the day's adventures, if one may call them that. I tried to list them all but soon fell into a gray place and lost all sense. I missed my Pleasant House, my orchard, my elm tree, my front door stone. I could not find myself in all the letting go.

I looked about my room. I was pleased with the four tall windows, the high ceiling—higher than my Pleasant Street ceiling by far. There was my bed, waiting, the quilt already on. Mother must have put it there before her evening headache.

Carlo sighed and lay down on the straw mat. I moved

to the window. Outside, the sun was almost down. And the colors! Oh, the glory of that well-known surprise—that show of Nature's majesty! So much had happened since my eyes had fallen on that selfsame scene. When I think I left a child and returned a woman—in name at least—it freezes my blood.

I stood at the window. As a child I had shared a room with Vinnie on the east side of the house built by Grandfather Dickinson. Grandfather lost all his money founding the Academy and the College, so he had to rent out part of the Homestead to another family. Now we had the house to ourselves. I had the corner room, with windows south and west.

I looked across the hayfield to the Pelham Hills beyond. How often as a child I had seen the orange and lavender fade on those very hills, my eyes wanting to hold the colors and never let them go. It had been fifteen years since I had looked out those windows. The gingerbread thought returned.

Where are the years now, the weeks and the days? Gone forever?

I went on thinking about how fine it is to have memories, to know where one came from and what one did with one's life.

How grand it would be to hold all my time on this Earth in my brain, to be recalled at some silver time when memories are one's dearest friends.

A song was in my mind. I don't know why. It was one I had made up as a child. How old? There is a question. Four perhaps, or five. The song was a play on Words, my dearest friends, unless you count Carlo, which of course I do. The first verse went through my mind.

> *Staircase, Watchcase—*
> *Staircase, Watchcase—*
> *All the little Sailor Boys*
> *Go marching down the Street—*

Someday I may know what I meant, and maybe not, but what of that? One thing is certain. I already knew one doesn't have to rhyme.

I opened my valise. My pencil and paper were on top of my clothes, waiting for me. I sat on the edge of the bed and began to write.

Part I

Girlhood

"I wish we were always children."

Stoneless Place

❧

March 1840.

My nine-year-old legs swung nervously back and forth beneath the table as we sat in the dining room, having our morning meal. Father's face was pulled tighter than usual, his lips so thin, it looked as if he had no mouth. That was not a good sign. I could feel my heart beating rapidly in my chest—a humming-bird when the cat comes near the bush. Father is given to dark storms within that grip him without warning—to me, at any rate—pulling him back inside his skin until he all but disappears.

My mind raced over everything I had done that morning in search of the culprit deed. I must have done something wrong. Father wiped his dry, straight lips, one sweep across, with his napkin.

Oh, no!

I knew what it was. Each morning we gathered in the parlor to address an eclipse—the one not seen—called our Lord. I can see the black Bible spread open on Father's knees, his striped trousers, the thin, worn pages, the Scripture declaring its Hellfire Truth. That day I had yawned—and at the worst possible moment.

It was my yawn!

I looked at Austin. His head was bent, his eyes closed. Or was he staring at his hash? Vinnie was of similar demeanor. I had hoped for contact with some member of my regiment, but it was not to be. Mother stared at her teacup, her still and waiting fingers barely touching the handle.

Could it really have been my yawn?

I was no longer certain. Father has his notions, but a yawn within the family's private world would not likely tempt such strong displeasure. And Father is especially lenient with me. I don't know why. It brings me guilty pleasure.

Mother sat still as a statue.

Did they fight?

I had never heard them fight, but often felt the heft in the room when they were not of the same mind. When that happened I feared a fight and wished it too, to clear the lead.

Father stared at the grandfather clock on the far side of the room. He had taught me to tell time by that clock, or so he thought. I knew better. I had understood not one word! The concept of time would simply not take its place in my brain. Father seemed so proud of me, happy too, and proud of himself for taking the time to teach me. He thinks of himself as a generous man and I do believe he is, but the evidence hides in a deep place. I had found it that Time Teaching Day and was not eager to let it go.

Mother lifted her teacup. "Emily, eat your breakfast."

I picked up my fork and moved it through my cold and waiting hash. Father was still staring at the clock, his eyes blank, as if he could not see, nor cared to. He was "behind his eyes," as we called it. "Father's gone behind his eyes," Vinnie used to say. She told me once she wanted to get in there and be with him. Austin said it was impossible and I've found that to be true.

My chest felt heavy. I could barely breathe. I would have given anything for an end to the silence. I tried to think of something to say—anything! My mind was blank. Father set down his napkin. I thought he was about to speak, but no luck was to be had in the matter. All at once, Vinnie's prize cat, Roughnaps, rushed through the room in a great swoosh of tail and scampering paws.

How daring! None of us would do a thing like that, though we might wish to.

"We will be moving to a new house."

Father's declaration landed like a stone. Mother set down her teacup.

"Our new house will be on North Pleasant Street," Father continued.

"It's lovely," said Mother. She took a thoughtless sip of tea. "It's near the Northrups."

"I don't care about the Northrups!" I exclaimed.

"Emily!" said Father, his displeasure with my outburst far from secret.

Vinnie's lower lip quivered the way it did when she needed to cry but did not dare. Austin was quiet, his dark eyes locked on Father.

"Mother is right," Father continued. "The house is lovely."

"What's wrong with *this* house?" I asked.

Father had no answer for that, at least none he cared to share. His face took on the serious expression I knew so well. It was a sign to leave all contradiction on the far side of the road, better yet in another town! "It has been decided," he stated with firmness. "We move next month."

Silence into silence—and deeper still—heavy with distress. Vinnie was crying now. Large soundless tears rolled down her cheeks and stuck to her chin.

"Don't worry, dear," Mother said, then added vaguely, "It will all work out in the end."

"No, it won't!"

"Emily!" corrected Father.

I looked at Austin, who was smoldering as only he can smolder—eyes like daggers.

Why won't he speak?!

I was on my own in the battle.

"Our new house is across from your school," Mother offered. It was a fact of questionable relevance, as I would be attending a new school in September, on another street entirely.

"I don't want to move!" I shouted. I don't know why I felt so strongly on the matter. I can only say that I did. Change has never landed well with me.

Father looked stern to the point of his own discomfort. I was hardly behaving like "the best little girl in Amherst." He fancied me as such. It was too awful, really. I had so many dark thoughts. If he only knew!

"That will do, Emily," he pronounced.

I ran from the table, out the door, into the yard, around the house, past the oak tree, and down the hill toward the garden. My breath was coming in broken sobs. The wind stung my face, blowing my short hair back, then forward into my eyes, sticking to the tears, making it hard to see. I hate not to see.

I ran along the flat stones. They become smaller partway down the slope leading to the grass of the Stoneless Place above the narrow steps. I stopped at the first step, collapsing in a heap of tears on the cool, flat surface. My

15

world had split apart and I, a tiny fragment, spinning in the space of the unknown.

I think it was not as long as it seemed before Austin was at my side. "It's all right, Emily," he said.

"No, it's not!" I cried, bemoaning my fate.

"Don't be stubborn."

"Go away!"

"I'm trying to help."

"It's not working."

"You know how you are."

"And how is that?"

"Things are terrible one minute and glorious the next!"

"Leave me alone!"

"The terrible times don't last."

"Neither do the good ones!"

"Don't be contrary, Emily. Your stubbornness will get you nowhere."

My breath came in jolts of life—gasps—as it did when I swam too long in the pond. Austin sat next to me on the stoop.

"Why didn't he tell us?" I asked.

"He did."

"Before! Not now, when the day is upon us!"

"The day is not upon us," said Austin. "The day is not for weeks."

"Weeks is sudden when a thing is unexpected. He should have told us before!"

"It's not the end of the world," said Austin.

"How do you know?"

Austin looked at me, pausing a moment before summing up my character. "You're too young to be morbid."

"What is the proper age?"

"Thirteen."

"Fine," I said, ignoring his ill-timed attempt at humor.

"At the youngest," he added. He was smiling by then. I was smiling too, but inside myself and careful to keep it a secret.

"Father says we can take the cats." It was Vinnie—who else? She had joined us on the steps, holding Roughnaps, wide-eyed and suspicious from all the confusion.

"Is that all you think about?" I asked.

"Not all." It was pitiful how small she was and going through such a large change. I reasoned if it was hard for me to leave the only home I had ever known at nine, it would be worse for a girl of seven. At times compassion fills my selfish heart, which amazes me and delights me very much.

As it turned out, Austin had his own dislike of the thought of moving. He did not confess to it that day, but later told me it was a blow to his sense of security. He said he had always assumed the Homestead would be in the family for generations, passed on through time like an ancient castle, complete with a moat. He also liked the yard.

Vinnie carried Roughnaps inside to tell Tiger Boy and Snugglepoops about the move, leaving yours truly and her brother to our own vices. We sat in comforting silence. I knew of no one in the world with whom I felt the same ease in quiet space. After a time, Austin followed a friend down the road to do something. I don't remember who the friend was, or what they were going to do. Austin had many friends and none of them wanted to play with me, a fact that caused no small amount of pain. It was not so much because I wanted to play with them but because I wanted to play with Austin, and when given the choice, Austin chose his friends. Off they would go to places unknown, leaving me alone in all my glory, unless you count Vinnie, which I did not. Two years is a long way down when one considers a sister who is only seven.

I looked about the March yard. Soon a robin would be coming down the walk, the daffodils would be swaying in the breeze, the tulips would be up and proud and the trees would be dressed in all their finery.

I can't leave now! My friends are coming! They will miss me!

It was really too much. There I sat on the top step at

the end of the grass of the Stoneless Place and below me, the four long, narrow steps to the garden. There are five steps all together. I wondered about the Stoneless Place. I loved that spot. Stones, stones and more stones and in between—no stones at all. Was it Nature did it? Was it the work of men? Was it a woman, lone and able, clearing a soft place for the pure want of it?

I would have to say good-bye to my Stoneless Place and to my steps. The steps were good for jumping games, better with company, most especially my "particular friend," Abby, but if Abby was not handy and Vinnie unwilling, I could play alone. The rules were various and changeable, a fact that bothered my more literal-minded sister. But I was fair. I never tricked her. Well, I did once and felt the worse for it, but otherwise I did not change the rules in the middle of a game to suit my personal advantage, though I thought of it. I never considered such willful dishonesty with Abby. My dear Abby! Abby Wood. She lived just up the hill—a step-walk away—with her uncle, Luke Sweetser. Now there would be distance between us—a walk of many minutes!— inconvenient when sudden fancies for moments shared might strike. I had known Abby forever to my waking mind. Orphaned at three, she had come to Amherst to live with her uncle.

The wind was blowing hard, its March custom, yet I

had not the mind to move. The larger move was all my heart could bear. A bird came down the path. She did not know I saw her, leastways not that I could tell. She may have caught my watchful glance only to hurry later to the nest, spreading the nimble tale of how a girl sat on the step looking "oh, so lost." Then all the other birds would wonder at the loneliness of humans.

A Wooden Way

✿

The day before we left the Homestead, my feet went a wooden way. There was no life in them that I could tell. I walked across the yard as in a trance, so sad I was to be leaving. I was angry as well but sought to ignore that fact, which is easier said than done. I had to say good-bye to my friends—the grass and trees, the flowers, the birds. I would see no bees that day as they were deep in their winter rest. I hoped they might come to Pleasant Street to visit my flowers there, for I was sure to have flowers. I could not think of life without them.

The forsythia looked finely—great blazes of yellow along the fence—and the pink cherry blossoms were budding. One could see the red fog on the trees in the distance. The bushes were budding too. Mother's tulips were crimson. Who would water them now? And the daffodils, just ready for picking, if one cared to disturb them. The blue daisies stood proud, their bright yellow centers announcing the strength of the unassuming. And there was round-lobed hepatica, deep purple pansies, not to mention the crocuses, the yellow coltsfoot and the tiny blossoms of the whitlow grass. Soon there would be asters and showy lady's slipper, but they would not be seen by me.

I sat beneath the large oak, my back against its strong trunk. The sun was hot and no leaves yet for shade. I made no move to get my bonnet. I pictured it resting on the hook by the stairs. As I had come into the yard to ease my heart in its impending tear from Home, I cared not to tighten the chains by going back inside. My mind was in a dark place. I felt as if I was moving from Safety to Danger, from Life to Death almost. I cannot say what made it so.

I went around to the back of the house. There was the barn, one giant's step from the house, the animals quiet within.

Thank God the animals are coming with us!

It was hard enough to leave my plant friends without adding the cows and horses into the bargain. We would, however, be leaving the barn well, which was fine with me. I did not have to fetch the water from that Siberian outpost. That was Austin's job. Father would never permit Mother or me to do it. Father always instructed Austin in no uncertain terms to watch out for the cattle lest he be hooked or stampeded by our docile companions. Now, that does seem far-fetched if you ask me.

When I reached the back door I stopped. There,

a little to the left, was my Flower. Mother was the gardener then. I learned a great deal from her about the likes and dislikes of our various charges in matters of when to plant, when to water and preference of location as to amount of sun or shade. All of Nature's people have minds of their own. One does well to learn them.

I stood looking at my Flower. I had planted it entirely by myself, choosing the spot with care. I had considered digging it up and taking it with me, a plan which Mother did not recommend. "It will die," she warned. "The transplanting will overtax its tender roots."

Like Mine.

I did not share this thought with Mother as I knew it would upset her. Mother has always been frail, with headaches, neuralgia, mysterious pains and bouts of low spirits. Many times we don't know what ails her. Perhaps her mind is far from the answer itself, a likely reason for her to leave the rest of us in dark as regards her situation. This Day Before Moving Day, Mother rested on the lounge under a woolen blanket.

I knelt by my Flower. "I have to leave you," I told it. Tears were pushing at the back of my eyes. I don't like leavings. I thought of my first leaving then. Vinnie had just been born. Mother was not well and so it was arranged for me to leave. Mother must have felt overwhelmed with a new baby and Father away so much. I was the expendable one. I recall a carriage ride. Aunt Lavinia. A cloak across my face. Darkness and cold. Flashes of white fire through the cloak and a crack to split my ears. A thunderstorm? I longed for Mother, but I was a good girl.

"HELP!"

Vinnie was calling from the kitchen window, and I squatting in a manner most unbecoming a fashionable young lady, boots caked with mud, skirt brown with dirt from my excursions about the yard.

"HELP!!"

Vinnie had been calling after me much of late. It was always about some great Hurrah that when looked at squarely was nothing more than a "tempest in a teapot," as the saying goes. I think Vinnie was scared of leaving Home, as scared as I was, only more so, being so small.

"ROUGHNAPS HAS A BIRD!"

I hurried into the house as fast as I was able, being so vexed at the news as to give not one ounce of thought to the mud on my boots, and more importantly to Mother's certain reaction to the telltale signs the same would leave upon the floor.

As the kitchen door slammed behind me, I realized I had entered a veritable hornet's nest—great shrieking and scurrying about, as Roughnaps, the monster bird murderer, was rushing, body at a slant, toward the parlor, a poor half-dead bluebird in his mouth and Vinnie chasing after him, screaming and threatening the worst and then, "EMILY, HELP!" and Mother rising from the lounge, holding the woolen blanket as Vinnie chased the detestable creature through the front hall.

That was the precise moment when Father chose to arrive from work, straight and important, with cane and hat and black briefcase in hand.

A feeble "Hello, dear," from Mother; "it's the cat...."

"EMILY, HELP!" from Vinnie.

"He has a bird ... it's nothing," said Mother. "It will all be over in a minute."

Father stood motionless, erect, disapproving.

Scratch, scratch and a great scraping of cat nails across the recently polished floor. There was a great rush of air about my ankles as Roughnaps hurried past, the innocent bluebird dangling from his jaws. I myself wanted to kill Vinnie's prized, fang-toothed ball of fluff. I detested his murderous game.

"Stop him!" I screamed at Vinnie.

Father set down his briefcase.

"We don't scream in the house," said Mother, a comment clearly meant to show Father he needn't question her disciplinary techniques.

"He's murdering a bird!" I shouted.

"That's unfortunate," said Mother, "but we don't scream about it."

I do.

Father looked important in his office clothes. It was good to have him at home, however briefly. He had recently been away for the better part of a year with the legislature in Boston, a fact I resented, the truth be told.

I tried to express myself firmly, but quietly, as if I were a respectable young lady. "Vinnie simply must stop that cat," I explained. "It's not fair." At this point Rough-naps headed for the stairs, Vinnie on his tail. "Get your cat before I kill him!" I screamed.

"Emily!" A sharp call from Father.

I wanted to plead my case, but Father's mind was busy elsewhere. It seemed unsuitable to call it back. Mother held tightly to the blanket, watching Father. She looked a pitiful figure. "How was your day?" she asked.

"Good enough." Father hung his hat on the hook by the door.

There was a great scuffling from upstairs.

"DON'T GO UNDER THE BED!"

Father stared straight ahead, looking "dead as a door-nail"—a favorite phrase of Mother's.

I could not remain quiet. "Why does he have to murder innocent birds?"

"Emily . . . ," said Mother.

"And if he's going to do it, he should go outside where none of us can see him. I think he does it for spite."

"I doubt that, Emily," said Father.

"I don't."

"The subject is closed." There was a dry and serious pause.

A door slammed. It was General Mack, the father of the family with whom we shared the Homestead. He passed through the kitchen on his way to the stairs, a tall man who sold hats. I was used to sharing our house with strangers and paid him no mind. Father looked at Mother. "How's that cold?" he asked.

"Better," said Mother.

It did not appear so to me. Mother had spent the afternoon on the lounge in the parlor, complaining of feet "as cold as ice." She made a sad and dreary picture bundled there, her blanket about her tiny frame, the shutters closed, the room near empty, as much of the furniture had already been moved to the new house. Whatever her situation—neuralgia, a cold—moving makes it worse. Mother has never cared for travel.

Father looked at her. "Don't go out, just the same," he instructed. Father is always at us about our health. "Don't go to church in the snow," "Don't go to school in the wind," "Don't let the cattle hook you when you go to the well," "Don't let the woodpile fall on your head" and the old standby, "Don't be anxious." That was hardest to obey amidst the infinite sea of dire warnings. My favorite could not be surpassed in the measure of fear it inspired in our tender hearts. "Don't fall out of the carriage as a wheel may roll over your body and kill you!" How's that for lifting the spirits!

"Would you like your paper?" Mother inquired of Father. Why she referred to it as "your" paper I cannot say, as we all, excepting Vinnie, read that same *Springfield Daily Republican* and Mother knew it. I put it to an attempt on Mother's part to honor Father to an inappropriate degree. At any rate, as Father did want "his" paper, they retired to the parlor, leaving me free to hurry upstairs to check on the progress of the Gruesome Bird Murder.

The house was too quiet.

What's happening?

I was soon to find out. Upon entering our room, I saw Vinnie, half under the bed—only her legs could be seen—and not making one sound. "Did he kill it?" I asked.

"I think so," came the small words from underneath the bed.

I bent down to look. It was black as pitch.

"He won't give it back," said Vinnie.

It was some moments before my eyes adjusted to

the dark. There was Roughnaps, crouched in the farthest corner beneath the bed and growling a deep-throated growl, the poor dead bluebird locked between his jaws!

"It's dead," I said.

"Poor bird," said Vinnie.

"Poor bird is right!"

It was very sad indeed. I do believe Vinnie was more upset than I was. She loved the bird *and* the cat, while I loved only the bird, which made my anger straight.

That night I went outside to say good-bye to my Flower. It stood small and proud, its petals a brilliant purple in the light of the April moon that shone down from above Father's Oak. I sat on the cool ground— just being there. I cleared some little stones away from the stem and smoothed the earth around the Flower with my hand. It was truly a miracle, my single Flower, with a mind of its own and a destiny inside, just as they had been inside the tiny seed I had planted a few short weeks before.

I made up a poem then. It was to my Flower. I sometimes wrote poems as a child—not many, but some. They marked important Circumstances, not Large perhaps, but always containing significance in my child's mind.

My Flower keeps the largest Friends—
It blooms outside my door.

For company—the Sun, the Sky—
And Earth Forevermore!

I spoke the poem to my Flower, feeling its pleasure
and the breeze and the moon and the stillness of the
night all around.

Vinnie Snores Loudly

My new house was white, friendly and made of wood. I was pleased with it almost immediately, it being far from what I had expected. I had seen the house from the outside and thought it small compared to Father's House, but inside there was plenty of room, with lots of light. It was North of the Village Center, a short walk. Its back faced North, putting the house "side to the road"—not facing the street as I had come to expect from a house. Its position was irksome to me, but in time I came to take pleasure in the Circumstance, as it relaxed the approach to the front door. It gave my mind a sense of easy in and out. With Father's House—or the Homestead, as it is most often referred to by others—once you are in, you are in. Once out, one questions the certainty of a safe return.

Outside there was ample space for a garden, grapes and a wonderful orchard. Austin, who has always loved flora, had plans to plant a grove of white pine trees—not a large grove, but one to claim notice. Father said, "Such planting of trees is a large task for a boy of eleven," but added, "Austin is no ordinary young man." I have found this to be true. It was not long before the beautiful grove began to take shape—and each of us the better for it.

Inside, one straightway noticed the floorboards. They were as wide as two footsteps if I put my feet toe to heel. I wasted no time in trying this. In the barn there were boards as wide as an elephant's footprint! The wood must have come from an enormous tree that gave its life to shelter our oblivious cows.

A disturbing fact about the house was that it bordered the cemetery, and not only that, but the selfsame cemetery where Grandfather Dickinson was buried. He had died two years before and I, then merely seven, could not get my mind around it. The event of his death claimed a lasting place in my brain—Father bent by the stairs in the hall—Mother kneeling at his side—me, watching, wondering. "Grandfather died," says Mother, but does not look at me.

The day after we moved into the new house, it rained. I stood at the window, looking out at Grandfather's resting place, the molded grass dotted with gravestones, somber and reminding. The cemetery looked deserted—fog and the gentle rain upon the stones. I would see many dear to me carried to that place. I imagined them, pale and silent, within the darkness of their eternal chambers, protesting not the six-foot journey below the sod to

Nowhere. Will I really be dead one day? Will I cease to be? And what of Heaven? Is it really all they say? It seems to me I shall never go there, shall never cease to tread New England's soil, and yet I know I must. I think I shall never understand Death until my head be a dreaming laid—dead—and then I shall have no one to tell, as all about me will know. Little point in telling *them*!

That first night Vinnie snored so loudly, I had a mind to sleep in the bushes. Had the weather been warmer I would have. April in New England is a frosty affair. I was exceedingly restless that night, shoving Vinnie several times with deliberate purpose and shaking the bed. To be fair about it, I don't believe my sleeping difficulty was entirely due to Vinnie's snoring. I missed Father's House, the only house I knew. It seemed to me that I had *no* house but lay in a strange bed, in a strange room with double-step planks on the floor and a cemetery outside the window. I missed my Home, my Sanctuary, my place to belong. I was used to Life, my old room, three steps from my bed to the bureau, pitcher on the right, lamp on the left, twenty-one stairs to the downstairs hall, parlor just there, my tin box on the shelf beneath the window, my Treasures inside. I used to carry them to the kitchen and line them up on the kitchen table by the stove, window at my back. My circus animals liked to be placed high up on the whatnot in the corner by the hook for

Mother's apron. No hook now, no whatnot, no window at my back. And where was Mother's apron? Nothing in its rightful place, most especially *Me*!

When at last I fell asleep I had a dream. It was this.

I am in Father's House but he is not there. I am alone. His things are everywhere—his briefcase, his hat, his cane, his waistcoat, his watch, his newspaper—strewn about. I try to walk, but my legs are snagged by his belongings. My legs are numb. I can't breathe. I feel I will faint. I want to sit down but there is no room. On the table is a half-finished bowl of Father's favorite pudding. I feel hopeless and lonely. He is gone and there is no room for anyone else.

I want to paint a picture of Amherst as it was that first summer in the new house. The very center of the Village was—*is*—the common. Cows graze here unaffected by worldly concerns. There is, however, much mud and far less grass than cows prefer. This I can state with utmost certainty as I have so often been witness to their far-off expressions of loss as they stand in the mud among the occasional white birch trees, accepting their fate.

The common is a lengthy stretch of land that goes from its north end, not far from my house, all the way to the College, the main attraction of the Village and I daresay much of New England as well. Two three-story buildings, plain and made of brick, stand facing the west on College Hill, a steep affair with no trees. Adjacent to these structures and higher on the hill is the Chapel.

West of the College stands our church. It is a Sunday walk of no short consequence when the church bell summons the God-fearing citizens of Amherst to worship. We had a new minister then, a Reverend Aaron M. Colton, who was likely to be preaching a sermon on such weighty topics as "Is There No Balm?" and "The Road to Forgiveness," matters most certainly worth a Sunday thought. Our previous minister, Josiah Bent, had died in November. He had been looking tired for some time. It may have been from the degree of vigor with which he chased after the pitiable people of Amherst, trying to persuade them to become Christians. As one can be born into a family of Christians but not actually *be* a Christian until claiming Christ as one's own portion, that very claiming is a matter of utmost importance. I have never understood this. I have always felt I *was* a Christian. Why the need to *become* one?

In my opinion Reverend Bent had gone on to his reward as a result of having traipsed about the Village in all weathers with a committee of church members— presumably Christians themselves—conversing with other members of the church—presumably not yet Christians—on the subject of the need to give one's life to Christ. The effect proved exhausting for all concerned, with Reverend Bent visibly worn down from the whole affair. I find spiritual matters to be of deep significance— far too deep to send committees of frozen Christians into the snow to discuss such things with whomever their fancy dictates. Matters of the Soul are too large for petty intrusions.

Back to the common. A wooden fence encloses its grass and mud and the birch trees—and all around, the dirt roads and shops and various places of business to the north and west and then the houses, white and dignified about the town. The people of the Village must be described as dignified as well—me excluded! These do all manner of appropriate things with their time. *All* go to church, attending the various functions in addition to the services. The men are farmers, merchants and teachers mostly, with a few lawyers, doctors and politicians thrown in for good measure. The women stay at home and dust and do all things pertaining to a smoothly running house. All are "Ladies" in the strictest sense of the word. I shan't ever be a "Lady." I will not join that society of "culprit mice," gossiping over endless cups of tea. I would rather rest within God's deep brown earth than know such calamity! Oh, let me not forget. There are some women not of that stamp. These make hats at the factory—straw hats, no less. Many of these same get their lungs destroyed from breathing in the dust from the palms and die at a young age. It's a shame and if you ask me, not worth the hats.

Our Pleasant House looked finely that first summer. I was gaining a liking for it, which both surprised and delighted me very much. The yard was well suited for games. There was sun and space and welcome shade, a gift from the Elm that stood near the front. One afternoon that first summer Vinnie and Abby and another friend, rough and ready Helen Fiske, set about making up a little play. We often put on shows involving many characters, our favorites being pirates, sailors and helpless maidens quite beflown. This day our drama depicted Nature, the Mother of us all. Our play contained every animal we could think of—no, not *all*, but *most*—our favorite animals, which reflected quite a list. And our audience?—A squirrel! He stationed himself on the trunk of the Elm, just level to our eyes, nose facing straightway to the ground, body long, tail to the sky. As we began, he arched his neck, lifting his head just a little, watching our most edifying drama in what appeared to be amazement, though I'm sure I don't know what it was. You would have to ask him. He did look amazed, however—to me, at any rate—and if he was, who could blame him? Four upstanding young ladies leaping and crawling about the June grass, a deportment highly unsuitable for such respectable specimens of Amherst society!

37

It was an impressive scene, with the cherries fast getting ripe, and behind us Mother's garden—daisies, larkspur, orange pot marigolds and ageratum in small lavender clumps about the ground.

Across the road grazed several friends who added no small manner of interest to that first uncertain summer in our new house. Two horses and three cows, all black and white. How starched they looked, how crisply outlined in the bold June light, as if painted by some fine and knowing hand, the mind behind the hand possessing a most intriguing sense of the joke. Or perhaps it was only the farmer's whim. The two horses stayed together. I don't believe I ever saw them apart, all the while eating their precious grass, heads down, half-moon necks and teeth straight, a flat row, locking the narrow green shoots, tearing them, swallowing them up into the darkness of the Great Beyond. I used to wonder if the grass went to Heaven. It was a childish fancy, yet who is to say?

The horses would sometimes take it upon themselves to run a merry chase, with one first lifting its head. A moment—then the sudden shot across the field, the other tearing a hurried clump of grass before following her sister at a sprightly clip, then stopping, docile and omnipotent, at her side. The cows were philosophic at such times, being of a more sensible stamp. They ignored the reckless ways of their mirror comrades, chewing in endless, languid circles, their gentle ears falling to the sides in peaceful acceptance of Nature's Paradise.

Frying Doughnuts

❧

On July 2 there was to be a Church Fair, a festive event with baked goods and singing and colorful decorations. It was being organized by the ladies and would be held at Academy Hall. The chorus was busy practicing "Angel's Call," the high notes well within my range and Abby's too. Father was away, I don't know where. Boston is my guess. Father is most often somewhere other than here, attending important government meetings as representative of the General Court of Massachusetts and preparing his law briefs. I shall never cease to miss him—deep in my bones, where it matters most. I sometimes feel as if I don't have a father and wish I had one, but when he returns he is well noticed to say the least, as the Household tunes to his every whim. I find this vexing and at the same time a comfort, as I know we are securely under his wing and no danger will come to us. That spring he had been to Baltimore. May was scarcely on when he went south to attend a Whig Convention. I fancied he had gone to meet with a group of gentlemen to discuss man-made hair. Mother set me

40

right on that point. The Whigs are a political party, an odd name for such in my opinion, but I had not been consulted in the matter.

That first summer on Pleasant Street, Father spent quite some time in Boston. He bought ink, but what else he was doing there I cannot say. Oh, yes, I can! He was sending us those horrid religious journals. Vinnie was the lucky one, as she, not reading yet, missed all the gory details of the gruesome occurences befalling those poor innocent children gone wrong. Father was also writing his Be Careful Letters. These same arrive like clockwork whenever Father is away. He leaves no stone unturned in the matter of our safety. Austin and I are always commenting as to the extent of his unfounded concern. Mother bears Father's absence with a quiet persistence that is really quite remarkable, working round the clock to keep the House afloat. A Serious Housekeeper, she is busy with the garden, the orchard, the baking, the dusting—that ever-endless pursuit—rug beating, sewing, mending, the preparation of meals and all other manner of household duties, not to mention church functions and helping the poor. All this she carries off with quiet intention, while suffering neuralgia and various other debilitating complaints.

"Be careful not to bother Mother," Father tells us. "And help her in every way you can."

That summer, as a reward for our efforts, Father sent us a subscription to *Parley's Magazine*, a periodical filled with stories to amuse and edify the minds of young readers throughout New England. I spent many summer afternoons in its gracious company, under the front-yard Elm. One issue had a particularly intriguing cover, picturing a young girl, dressed finely and standing by the stairs, holding a book. I wondered at what appeared to be a basket of laundry on the table to her left, seeing little reason for the artist's decision to include it in the picture. The scene appealed to me nonetheless and so I kept it for several years in the tin box I shared with Vinnie.

The day before the Fair, Mother agreed to teach me how to fry doughnuts. This day holds a strong place in my brain, as close times with Mother have always been scarce. A loving but anxious presence, Mother is either not well or too busy for "unnecessary" occasions of shared adventure. My heart touches that Doughnut Time for rest and peace, to remind my tender knowing that Mother really cares.

That day we had both been ill, Mother with her usual assortment of maladies, and me with pain in my chest and a cough that had been with me for weeks. Abby was sick as well. We are both sick a great deal. This time as usual I had lost weight due to loss of appetite and had been enduring countless bird admonitions from Mother:

"Finish your dinner, Emily," "You eat like a bird" and so forth.

This Doughnut Morning was dreary, as it rained, then stopped, in bouts of leaden grayness, the clouds full and waiting, only to let go another round of soak. Vinnie was in the yard, a fact Father would surely have brought into question had he been at home. A sudden chill could bring on a canker rash, or influenza, or some such unwanted visitor. He was more lenient with Austin, due to Austin's being a boy and thereby more resistant to germs, a dubious deduction if you ask me. Austin was out seeing to his rooster, Albert, leaving Mother and yours truly inside with the cats, who disliked the rain as much as Father did.

Mother stood by the cast-iron stove, a gift from her father, Grandfather Norcross, her hair done up in a pocket handkerchief. "Remember, Emily," she said, reaching behind her waist to tie her apron, "I will teach you how to fry doughnuts on one condition."

"I must never fry them alone."

"Never."

"I could burn myself."

"Badly."

We began to gather the ingredients. Eggs, sugar, milk, shortening, flour, baking powder, cinnamon and salt. "Better not tell Father," I said, retrieving a lemon, at Mother's instruction, from the bowl on the shelf above the sink. "He's sure to warn us of how our fingers will be scalded by the hot oil and melt and fall off into the batter."

Mother smiled ever so slightly. "That's true," she said, "but doughnuts are worth a bit of trouble, don't you think?" Mother has a wit that often goes unnoticed. The reason is her own, as she buries herself beneath a cloak of obedience. One seldom sees her realest Self. God save me from such a Fate! Our realest Self is all we have to call our own.

"I hope he didn't lose the valise," Mother said unexpectedly.

I didn't know of whom she was speaking, much less which valise she had in mind. "What valise?" I asked.

"Father's," said Mother. She was weighing the flour. "The one he took to Boston."

"What makes you think he lost it?"

Mother looked concerned. "He moved to a different hotel."

As that did nothing to clarify the matter, I questioned her further. "And?"

"He had to take it with him to work."

It sounded as if Father had to take the *hotel* to work, but I knew she didn't mean that. Anxiety had brought on vagueness.

"Oh," I said. Mother's ongoing concern about the disappearance of luggage had lost its interest for me, even at the age of nine.

"Someone may have taken it," she said, sifting the flour.

"Why would they do that?"

"It has all his laundry in it."

"That's no reason."

Mother got that distant look in her eye. There is no way of disputing her statements when she stops making sense. She gets afraid and her mind stops. I think one reason Mother doesn't care for travel is her fear of losing her luggage. It is her most well-known trait, that and a dislike of writing. I understand she used to write Father when they were courting and expressed herself well. I myself rarely see her with pen in hand and am often privy to family jokes regarding her reluctance to sit at the desk. She reads little as well, unless you count *The Frugal Housewife*, which hardly accounts for Reading in my manner of the word.

Mother passed me the eggs. "Beat these," she said. "Then add the sugar and continue beating."

I followed her instruction. As the mixture began to thicken, I stopped to watch the way the sugar made the batter froth like an angry sea.

"Don't stop," said Mother. "You must beat continuously."

I returned to my beating.

"I will tell you the most important thing to know about frying doughnuts," Mother continued. She scratched the end of her nose with the back of her hand. "They must be dried for fifteen minutes before they are fried. That way they absorb little fat. And remember, Emily, you are never to fry doughnuts alone."

"I'll remember." I have always tried to be obedient regarding important matters like not being scalded to death by burning oil, but when public opinion takes a route far from one's inner conviction, one cannot value disobedience too highly.

When I finished beating the eggs and sugar together, Mother instructed me to grate the lemon rind while she melted the shortening. I asked her if she didn't think the Church Ladies would consider doughnuts a frivolous dessert for so respectable a celebration. Religion and doughnuts seemed to me "strange bedfellows," to quote that English playwright of some renown.

"Doughnuts will please the children," said Mother. "After all, it is a fair."

"That's true," I said, but did not think the Ladies would approve. Their favorite sport was judging the acceptability of others, their favorite pastime to gossip—the pilfering of precious time. Their minds had long since been given up to the paleness of common dilution. How gruesome to be estranged from one's own Soul, lost beneath the dimity and teacups! Mother is an exception to that mindless brood. She has a mind of her own, however quiet it may be, however timid of being discovered.

We worked in quiet for some time, and I, wrapped in the welcome cloak of Mother's love.

"I caught him!" Austin burst through the door, his disorderly hair full of brambles. Mother and I were used to Austin's untimely declarations and therefore made no attempt to obtain further information on the topic so intrusively brought to our attention. We were certain to be graced with a detailed account of the situation, whatever it might be, without dropping our present occupations in order to chase after it. And so we were! It seems that Austin's rooster, Albert, had gotten excited over an incident with a neighbor's dog, escaping into a thicket behind the orchard, causing no end of chaos, not to mention inconvenience. It was no surprise to us when we were blessed with an accounting of the entire episode, acquiring more edification concerning the habits of roosters in fearsome encounters with dogs than either of us deemed necessary.

"Get these burs out of my hair!" said Austin when he had completed his sprightly tale.

"Please," said Mother.

"Please," said Austin.

Mother wiped her hands on her apron and went to help him.

Otis

The most disturbing thing about that first summer in the new house was unexpected. It was a hot morning at the end of summer. As was his custom, Austin had strewn several of his belongings about the parlor. His slippers, some books and a wooden soldier lay in random fashion, adding a lively touch to the décor. Austin received many hints ungentle to return his things to his room. Father is insistent as regards tidiness. Mother is less demanding, yet her quiet disapproval weighs heavy.

That morning, Father being away, Mother was the one to suggest to Austin that he remove his possessions from their unseemly resting places about the parlor floor. Vinnie watched from the lounge, where she sat with her doll, Matilda, a limp, well-worn girl in a long dress, a sorry figure by virtue of the fact that she had only one eye. "You had better pick up those slippers," Vinnie told Austin as he stooped to obey Mother's gentle command.

"That's what I'm doing."

A higher-pitched voice continued. "And you'd better not forget those books!" That, we were led to expect, was Matilda *herself* talking at the end of Vinnie's outstretched arm. Austin chose not to respond.

"Austin," said Mother, "I need you to go to Mr. Cutler's store." She was in need of ribbon and a certain kind of thread. "Emily, you can go along."

I was well pleased with the plan.

Every time I went to town there was someone I loved to see. His name was Otis. He was a brown horse, with a shaggy coat, long legs and large hooves, who stood in the road in the shade of a little tree. Otis' Tree—I called it that—was the last one in the row along North Pleasant Street, under the D. MACK JR. & SON sign. Otis would stand there, hitched to his wagon, waiting for afternoon delivery time—a patient soul, accepting of his lot. I remember as a girl of three holding Mother's hand as we walked up Main Street, past the houses, past the shops—reaching the corner, rounding it—and there beneath the little tree would be my Otis, waiting with patience surpassing all understanding, his wagon attached, his harness about his neck, his broad hooves flat on the dirt.

I often brought him apples, sugar, a carrot and his special treat—peppermints. When I started at the District School, I was small and very much afraid of so large an enterprise. The night before the first term was to begin, Mother helped by asking what I planned to bring Otis on my way to school. It was kind of her. As I made my decision, fear bolted from my mind as there was no room. Otis was an ever-present comfort to my child's mind. Life held so many changes—too many, it often seemed. Otis was always there. He could always be counted on—my port in a storm.

This August day, as Austin and I headed up the street in search of Mother's ribbon, I carried a peppermint for Otis. It was hot. Austin had soaked a handkerchief in cold water and had tied it about his forehead. His ample hair stood up in several directions. Water dripped down his face and about his ears.

As we approached the corner, I noticed that Otis was not under his tree. I straightway felt a fright. "Where's Otis?" I asked Austin.

"I don't know."

"He's always under his tree."

"Well, he's not there today."

"Where is he?"

"I don't know."

"Guess."

"I can't guess," said Austin. "I have no idea. We'll ask Mr. Cutler."

When we entered the shop, Mr. Cutler was sitting

behind the counter, his head in his hands. "Where's Otis?" I asked.

Mr. Cutler didn't move.

"We need some thread," said Austin.

"He's not under his tree," I continued.

"And some ribbon," added Austin.

"Where's Otis?" I repeated.

Mr. Cutler looked up. "He died."

The world tipped—and I about to fall.

I had learned a sorry lesson. Even the things of which we are most certain may sometimes disappear.

Father was at home next month, when school began. I was awfully glad about it. My new school seemed large and indeed it was when compared to the District School, at which I had previously pursued my studies. Starting at Amherst Academy was a milestone in my girlhood life, an adventure I cared not to embark upon without I had Father. And he was home! How grand a thing! Oh, he was busy with his briefs as always and with his long work as treasurer of Amherst College.

Father's being in residence had its undesirable side— the need to sit up straight at the table, quiet demanded, punctuality required, the early-morning prayers, not to mention the numerous encounters when ill with his ever-present "cold box" full of remedies. At the same time, when Father is at home all is right with the World. He is proud of his children and would most certainly go to any lengths to protect us, I know. When the time is right, one catches a sparkle in his eye that lifts one to the Heavens! It is quite wonderful, really!

That first Academy Morning, Father was precise in his instruction as regarded the subject of Austin walking Vinnie and me to school. Austin greeted Father's announcement with heavy silence. I could see he cared for the arrangement not one bit. When Austin had a mind to join his friends on some occasion, we were *not* to be included. This was clearly such an occasion.

"You will walk your sisters to school," Father repeated, following Austin's telling silence. No one questions Father when he is firm on a matter, and so it was. We would walk to school, the three of us, in perfect safety and obedience to Father's Word.

After breakfast we said good-bye to Mother, who stood next to our wooden baby cradle—a poignant touch. She appeared sad. It may have been due to the occasion of all her children leaving the nest and attending such a grown-up school, but I don't know. Mother feels many things, but rarely tells. Vinnie was too young to be attending the Academy but was let in as an exception by the teacher, Caroline Dutch Hunt, an old friend of Mother's. Father felt Vinnie would be better off with her brother and sister and not "alone" at the District School, and it was arranged.

So there we are at the door and ready to leave straightway when Vinnie takes it upon herself to sit down. Lip aquiver, she makes her point: Roughnaps simply can*not* spend the entire day without her as he has been used to her company throughout the summer, and if she leaves for school, he will not eat or drink any water, and she will not leave him to waste away and dry out during the many hours he would have to spend without her. She is convinced that when she returns, she will find him lying on his side, flat and dead, with his tongue hanging out. Snugglepoops, being older, might have a chance of surviving, but Roughnaps is sure to dry out and die.

At this moment Roughnaps enters the hallway from the parlor and stands, orange and questioning, by the edge of the stairs—motionless—in a pose suggesting curiosity as to what is going on. Father tells Vinnie that her cats will weather her absence with no ill effects because Mother will see to it. When Mother promises to attend to Roughnaps' each and every need, Vinnie's terror is somewhat assuaged.

There had been rain through the night. Although the morning sky was clear as glass, the mud was deep. Our boots *squoosh-squoosh*ed as we made our way along, slowing us down considerably in our efforts to arrive at school on time.

Across the street was our old District School. Children laughed beneath the familiar tree in front, taking no notice of our little band trudging past, as if we had never laughed beneath that selfsame tree, never been the ones to strive at recess in the field behind, as they would do some short time hence.

Father said the walk to school would take five minutes. I was still in the dark regarding my ability to read a clock, and with no reason to doubt Father's word on the matter, accepted the statement as fact. Nothing is far in Amherst, not scientifically at any rate. I must say, however, that the distance from Home to my new school felt Large inside, where the meanings are.

Vinnie was quiet as we walked, no doubt wondering whether her beloved Roughnaps, the guiltless bird murderer, would survive the morning. Although he might currently be devouring an innocent sparrow, or otherwise engaged in some equally gruesome of his thoughtless pursuits, I wished the cat no serious harm. He was but an honest creature, making his way as best he could throughout this troublesome land alone, as we all must do in the end.

The gentle hill felt steep, the mud sucking back each boot on its way up for air. And then it started, a pointless and intense topographical review, which went like this.

"No hill here," Vinnie announced as we began our gradual yet by all means obvious climb toward the corner.

"There *is* a hill," I argued, some little miserly voice within grabbing at my own supremacy. The moment I heard myself contesting the fictitious proclamation, I thought the better of it. Some thoughts are better left unspoken, yet it is often hard to tell which ones they are.

Vinnie stopped, feet planted firm, mud to the top of her boots. "It's a grade," she said.

I stopped, turning to face her. "It's a hill."

Vinnie looked me squarely in the eye and then, at penalty of death, "It's a grade!"

"It's a hill," said Austin, coming to my defense. "It's a hill and we have no time to argue about it."

"You are wrong, brother," Vinnie said, "very wrong and very tall."

"What has that got to do with it?"

No answer from Vinnie.

"Let's go," said Austin. He was getting impatient.

"No."

"I'm not leaving you in the street!"

"Maybe you are."

"Let's go!"

"It's not a hill."

Seeing the seriousness of our situation as regarded the possibility of tardiness on the first day of school, I reached for my most democratic self. "We are both right," I said in as reasonable a tone as I could manage. "It is a grade *and* it is a slight hill."

"That's true," said Austin.

Vinnie paused to think about it. "Emily is right and I am right."

"Yes," said Austin.

"But I am more right than she is."

Austin looked at me. "Can you accept that?"

I thought for a moment. I wanted to speak the truth but also wanted to get to school on time, so I had to tell it slant. "I accept that she said it and that it's what she believes," I said. That did it, thank God, and we continued along our way.

When we reached the corner, I remembered my Boltwood Lion. He used to be pictured most elegantly on a sign that hung just there, in the center of Amherst, for all my remembered life until I reached the age of seven. It was really quite amazing the way he had been painted with a human face, except for the breadth of the nose and the two dark triangle ears that pointed to the sky. He looked right at you and lay by a tree, his two front legs before him like human arms, complete with elbows. Between his paws was some meatlike thing of flesh, a scarlet surprise, and blood dripped from his jaws! The words AMHERST HOTEL took their place above—BOLT- WOOD below. The offhand way the lion held the meat, the bloody jaws and riveting gaze all conspired to cap- ture my girlish imagination. Abby found him gruesome. None of my friends liked him one bit, but I adored him. My Boltwood Lion!— So daring, so bold, so red!

At the corner we were joined by Helen Fiske and her younger sister, Ann, a gentle little girl. Ann is Vinnie's age, having beaten her to the cradle by two months. Helen beat me to that place by two months as well, an orderly foursome. Ann differs from her sister most dramatically, being delicate and somewhat shy. Helen is of a hardy stamp, always ready for a wrestle. Ann had her own concerns that day as regarded her cat, Sooner, informing us that on Sunday last she herself had stopped believing in God.

"Why?" I asked.

"My minister told me Sooner won't go to Heaven, so I'm not going and I stopped believing in God."

"Why don't you stop believing in your minister?" I asked. It seemed the most logical choice, to me at any rate.

My Tenth Birthday

It was a sprightly fall. I enjoyed my new school very much indeed, it being "forward thinking," as the term goes, in many respects. It had recently opened its doors to girls. Classes were held on all three floors of the building, the second being the one most often inhabited by Abby and myself and Vinnie and all the other "delicate flowers." Small boys sometimes joined us there, but the larger boys were kept apart. There was one exception to this—"Speaking and Composition," an enjoyable class held once a week on the third floor. Here both sexes assembled in a large space with an arched roof and many windows. Ladies and gentlemen together—how daring!

Besides school, the fall offered many treasures, all set within the celebration of the trees—Mother Nature's flaming show! There was the Ploughing Match in October, followed by that Grateful Day, Thanksgiving, with Mother's Feast—her gentle and unnecessary fluttering, the shiny apples, the cider cake—from Mother's personal "Bible," *The Frugal Housewife*, page 71— and most wonderful of all, the laughter, Father's included! Holidays never cease to put Father in the highest of spirits. There is a special comfort in Home that transcends all. I must include here Vinnie's new cat, Pussy, a pliant individual whom Vinnie enjoyed draping about her shoulders like a shawl.

Last, but by no means least, one cannot forget the inspirational and most edifying sermons delivered with admirable regularity by Reverend Colton on many varied subjects, including charity, obedience, love—unfortunately, not of the romantic kind—and redemption, a lecture to chill the blood.

Before I knew it, it was December 10—*my* birthday! When I awoke, I was greeted by the most beautiful snow! It must have fallen silently throughout the night without telling a soul. Only the birds knew and the groundhogs and the snakes, maybe. We other upstanding Amherst citizens had been told not one word about it and missed the whole event, being far away like stones on our pillows. When I looked out the window, there it was—Snow! And the sunlight so bright I had to shut my eyes from the pain and the glory of it. A blanket of the whitest snow covered the gentle hills and slopes of the cemetery, untouched by travelers, with the exception of a feather-light line of bird tracks, the crisscross news left by an early chickadee, a tufted titmouse, or a small woodpecker. The gravestones, those patient reminders—past waiting now—quiet, with snow like rounded white caps on their heads.

School that day was longer than I could bear, and all the while my mind on the many fine presents I was sure to receive. How greedy I am and not a bit proud of it. How unsuitable for the "best little girl in Amherst." Abby gave me the dearest little pressed clover inside a folded paper with the words "Abby and Emily—Particular Friends." That loving remembrance carried me through the morning.

At home we have a custom for birthdays, which is to celebrate with the five of us alone. We never have parties with strangers roaming about. I have always enjoyed our unusual habit and wonder that others can bear the intrusiveness of lightweight connections at such important times.

That year Mother made my favorite meal. It was a dainty chicken—not stuffed—served upright, a merry idea. The cooking is not swift as the chicken must be soaked in milk for hours and browned on the coals.

When we finished eating, it was time for the much-anticipated gifts, and fine they were indeed—a flower press and a calico apron, just as I had hoped! Vinnie gave me several yards of embroidery thread, which was startling in its collection of the boldest colors, perfect for my new sampler. Austin gave me the most beautiful pocket handkerchief with the smallest Daisy embroidered on with a careful hand in yellow, straight from the field to my heart.

Just as we were about to rise from the table, Father pulled a book from behind his back, having hidden it throughout the meal in an extraordinary display of inert composure. My heart raced. I took the book, holding it as if it were gold. Never had I seen a more beautiful cover! There was a dog, large as a bear, golden red, in shafts of light, with the most soulful eyes. Next to him stood a girl, the top of her head reaching just to the dog's shoulder, and all about, red, green, orange and blue, and gold leaf to complete the event. It was the story of a small girl and an enormous dog who go from a quiet garden life to the sea, where they have many adventures. What a Large thing to do! How thrilling the first league out from land must have felt! What was the dog's name? Thurston? Torbold? I can't remember. Whatever his name, it don't affect the story any. He always comes to the girl's rescue. I longed for such a companion.

That evening Austin and I had one of our Night Talks upon the kitchen hearth. All proper folk, having heard the 9. oclock bell, were under cover, a fact adding in no small measure to the excitement. We used to have these talks quite often, and I think there is nothing in this world I loved more, unless of course you count Roughnaps.

That was a joke.

This night as usual the others were long in bed, the cats secured in their basement lair—Tootsie complaining in halting stanza regarding his dank surroundings and no Vinnie to sit on—and Austin and I in all our glory upon the hearth going on about the Universe, an enjoyable place to be if one considers the alternative.

"Why do the stars look still?" I asked.

"What do you mean?"

"If our Earth is spinning on its axis and not only that, all the while circling the Sun, why do the stars look still?"

"It has to do with distance," said Austin, looking very wise.

"What sort of distance?"

"*Our* distance, our perspective, all such things that frame our mind's view of the truth."

I pulled my shawl about my shoulders, my arms about my knees. "But if one rides in a carriage, let's say, what one looks at appears to move, though it may be quite still."

"That's true."

"Why don't it seem the same with stars?"

"It does."

"It don't to me."

"The stars are so far away as to appear to move *very* slowly."

"They don't appear to move at all."

"They move. You just don't notice it." Austin took a sip of cocoa from his special large china cup. "If you looked at the Big Dipper now and again at midnight, it would appear to be in a different place."

I suggested trying the experiment, but Austin felt that by midnight, I, being only ten, would have fallen asleep and that he had, as he put it, "things to do in the morning." I did not believe him about the "things to do in the morning." It was my feeling he himself was tired but, being proud of his advanced age of twelve, did not care to admit it.

"I think there is more to life than we can see, don't you?" I asked.

"Where?"

"I don't know, but it's there. What we see is not everything."

Austin took another sip of cocoa. "Probably not," he agreed.

"Where is Heaven?"

"What do you mean?"

"I mean *where* is Heaven?"

"Where is Heaven?"

"Is it on the other side of the stars?"

"Heaven isn't *there* in the way you mean it."

"What way is that?"

"As if it were on a map, or at the end of the street."

"Is it there in *any* way?"

"Don't let Reverend Colton hear you ask that."

I remembered our esteemed minister's sermon some weeks before, the one that told of the wickedness in our hearts and the need for redemption. I had been awfully vexed about it. "I cannot accept that all the fine people of this world—every last one of us—was born a sinner," I exclaimed. "What about the animals? Were they born sinners as well? All the valiant dogs, the placid cows, the sheep, the birds? Can they be sinners too, or are they considered too insignificant to be members of the fearsome equation?"

"I think it is only man who must repent." It appeared that women were to be excluded as usual from serious matters, yet on this point it may have been to their advantage. "Animals don't count," Austin added. There seemed to be little or no sense to the whole business. I felt the desire to take refuge from such weighty concerns and closed my eyes. They hurt, from being tired, I surmised. We sat in quiet, full and loving, no need of proof.

After some time I spoke. "What do you think of our portrait?" The picture had been commissioned by Father some months before and rested on a chair across the kitchen, waiting for Father to have sufficient time to hang it. Painted by a certain Mr. Bullard, it showed the three of us children in uncomfortable clothing, looking out from the canvas with identical pairs of eyes. I remember how scratchy my white collar felt as we stood still to be painted. Vinnie wore a fancy blue dress. Mine was darker and plain. Mr. Bullard knew me well, though how I cannot imagine. There I was, holding a flower and a book. Now that tells my story!

Austin was studying the portrait. "My cheeks are too pink," he said. "I look like a girl."

He did not look like a girl despite the pinkness of his cheeks, and I told him so. However, I pointed out that in my opinion the portrait caught little of his masculine roughness. "The mind is there," I told him, "but not the muscle."

He appeared relieved.

"I like the way I am holding a rose and a book," I mused.

"It suits you."

"I shall write books," I heard myself say.

It was a girlish fancy—as a child might say "I shall wear fine dresses" or "I shall travel about the world."

I didn't know I meant it.

Girl Friends

Spring brought many pleasures. First off I started the piano in earnest. I practiced every day and even began to make up songs, which delighted me very much. My new flower press was handy. It is possible to press flowers with books, but one must use quite a stack. The books must remain in place for two days at least, so you are out of luck if you want to read one.

And of course there was school! I loved all my teachers! I also loved all my subjects, Composition and Recitation being my special favorites. We were obliged to write a composition every other week and deliver it before the entire student body Wednesday afternoons. Abby and many of the other girls did not care for writing and certainly did not want to read their compositions in front of five hundred students, most of whom were boys, but this was my meat!

I have to laugh when I remember the composition of a young man named Porter, whose Subject was—and I quote—"Don't put all your eggs in one basket." It went like this. "If a gentleman is walking with a cow and sees a lady with a dog who has no ears, don't put all your eggs in one basket." I told him if he wanted us to follow his story, he had better not put all *his* eggs in one basket.

My compositions were varied and of great interest to myself as well as to the many fortunate listeners. One was about Vinnie's cats, as models of propriety gone awry; another about a trip to sea and many aboard ship being already dead, a fact revealed in the last sentence only; another about the journey of a bird migrating from New England to South America only to discover that her mate was never to arrive. That was a sad one.

The cemetery was a busy place that spring. One Saturday I stood looking out my window as the latest funeral procession headed up the hill toward the freshly dug grave. It was poor Mr. Wentworth from Main Street, who Sunday last had occupied the pew ahead of us at church, with his baby daughter, not three years old. The sun was bright, a show of disrespectful cheer on so serious a morning. Mrs. Wentworth carried her tiny, fatherless daughter. Her son's anxious hand grasped her black skirt.

Questions filled my brain as I stood by the window, surrounded by the heft of the unknown.

Where is Mr. Wentworth this fine morning, and only days from Sunday church?

Consumption was the culprit. I do not understand Death and fear it very much.

I backed away from the window. The starkness of the sun's insistent rays burned my eyes. Or was it unrest?

Do I have consumption?

I have this thought very often, but tell no one, as I fear it will upset the apple cart. I had consumption as an infant. Father used to take me to the mill as they say breathing in the grist will cure it. But that don't help the lesions one bit, no matter what they say. Father never mentions consumption. Even when I am ill for months with an ax in my side and a cough that don't quit, he says not one word. Perhaps he fears I have consumption but does not speak of it as he imagines to name it would be to make it so.

I stepped closer to the window, watching as the mourners gathered about the coffin, formal—wooden— ceremonious—numb. Reverend Colton read from his Bible. His lips moved, but all was silent in my bedroom world.

Do I have consumption? Is it lying in wait only to blossom into Death at the will of a guiltless God?

I asked Abby about it and she said there was no way of knowing for sure, but her feeling was I did not have it. I prayed she was right.

Two things pleased me most that spring, my friends and my hair. At the risk of offending modesty I must say my hair is soft like the sunlight, fine like a baby's and golden, with a touch of red. It was growing longer. One day soon I hoped to wear my tresses done up in a net cap, as many of the older girls were doing. I had no doubt many Whiskers might turn in my direction when that came to pass, as I would be a comely sight to behold.

Last, but by no means least, I had such wonderful friends! Abby was closest of the close; and there was Helen Fiske; Emily Fowler—an older girl; Harriet Merrill, whose mother ran, of all things, a boardinghouse; and my dear cousin, Sophia Holland, two years older than me and very wise. Sophia was unlike anyone I had ever known, gentle and fair and as delicate as a porcelain vase. I sometimes thought she would break. Our times were quiet walks and long sits on the hill, reading, each a different book, together in the truth of Nature. Sophia was shy. At times her tenderness broke my heart. And there was Jennie—or Jane Humphrey as she is scientifically called. Jennie came to Amherst to attend Amherst Academy. The plan had been made between our parents that Jennie would live with us for some brief time. I had been looking forward to her arrival with curious anticipation. I loved her straightway. We shared a bed and would always run from as far away as possible and jump onto it. We never climbed into bed modestly as proper New England young ladies are taught to do. No such ordinary method of retiring for us! The run, the jump, laughing, rolling off, jumping again! Mother gave us the extra room to sleep in. It was small, yet suitable for guests and the storing of things used rarely.

The cats loved that room. When Jennie and I moved in, it became necessary to lay down the law. We even put a sign by the door. NO CATS it said in bold letters. Although we placed the sign at cat's eye level, it was meant to inform Vinnie of the seriousness of our position in regard to the matter. The cats would on occasion get in. Tiger Boy was the worst offender. He would often be perched atop the largest box, staring at us with proprietary eyes as we entered in search of a little private comfort. Then Vinnie would be called to come and get the intruder before Jennie and I would shut the door and fall on our bed, arms outstretched, flat on our backs and the breeze through the open window playing across our bare arms and legs.

The ceiling needed painting, but the molding was proud. I use to wonder what it had witnessed in its many years above human pastimes. I liked to count the grapes and the leaves in their chain about the top of the room, a grape, a leaf, a grape, a leaf, two grapes, a leaf, two leaves. And all the while Jennie and I having our girlish fancies—how a certain "you know who" had been watching a certain other "you know who" throughout the entire afternoon's recitations and failed to recognize her own name when called by our illustrious teacher, or some such lively escapade, and then we could go on and on until it was time for supper!

It was May, with church activities abounding. There was the Sale of Useful and Fancy Articles—a merry phrase!—the Christian Women's Annual Bake Sale and Embroidery Display—one waited breathlessly all year for that!—the Junior Benevolent Church Members' Evening and the Parish Society Fair. Neither Jennie nor I made large contributions to these events, but Harriet Merrill devoted every spare moment of her time to the Parish Society Fair—and she high on a ladder, dressing Mr. Sweetser's hall with Evergreens!

Abby and Jennie and Cousin Sophia and I enjoyed long talks in the afternoon after school. Our favorite spot for these secret exchanges was the front door stone. One day Vinnie was tracking the cats while Mother as usual was engaged in housework, her hair in the customary pocket handkerchief, pursuing some urgent task or other—polishing a section of the attic floor, or pulling last year's leaves out of the eave spout.

"Emily Fowler's brother is ill," I said as we sat on the front door stone, and a little robin just near, hopping along the walk toward Mother's garden.

"They say it's serious," said Sophia, her long, pale hair lit by the sun.

"What a large name he has," I mused.

"Webster," said Jennie, considering the name. "It is large."

The yard looked finely, the cherry trees in bloom, the white lilies and the slender honeysuckle no longer able to hide their delight in spring. Jennie spread her dress about her legs and I, thinking it a capital idea, did the same. As our dresses rustled, the timid birds in the cherry tree said "chirrup" and hopped away.

"Do you think Helen likes the way William stares at her?" I asked.

"Yes," said Abby. She appeared to have no doubt.

"She tells me she doesn't like him, but I don't believe it."

"Neither do I."

"Why don't you believe it?" asked Sophia. She was always one to give others the benefit of the doubt.

"I can see it in her eyes," said Abby. "She likes him. You can tell."

I expected Jennie to agree with us, but she said not one word. "You seem awfully quiet on the matter," I told her. "It wouldn't surprise me if you fancied him yourself."

"Me??" Her mock surprise told a merry tale!

I noticed two yellow eyes staring at us from the far side of the walk. It was none other than Tiger Boy, who was lying in the grass, his body covered so that all one could see was two black pointed ears and two yellow eyes. I hoped he didn't have his mind on the robin.

"I think Abby fancies him," said Jennie, "if you want to know the truth."

"I do not!" said Abby.

"Time will tell."

"Time will tell nothing!" Abby sat up tall and sudden. "I can tell you at this very moment I do not fancy William!"

"So you say!"

"Perhaps she doesn't," ventured Sophia.

"I don't!"

Jennie was in a silent dither at that point. Attempting to hide the truth of her amorous leanings, she turned the subject to yours truly. "Perhaps Emily fancies William herself," she accused, staring me hard in the eyes.

I kept my composure. "I prefer Josiah," I explained, calm, unruffled.

"Don't you find him short?" asked Abby.

"Height doesn't matter," said Sophia.

Vinnie came around the side of the house, carrying Snugglepoops, a large cat for so tiny a girl but Vinnie has always been strong. "Tiger Boy ran away," she said, her lower lip trembling.

"No, he didn't." I pointed across the walk. "Look over there."

Vinnie turned and spotted the yellow eyes. "Tiger Boy!" she screamed. She ran toward him, Snugglepoops held tightly in her grasp. "Bad cat!" Tiger Boy was not about to accept the criticism and bolted off into the woods.

"Now you've done it!" Vinnie yelled at me.

"I know what we have to do," Jennie said with sudden resolve.

"What?" said Abby.

"We have to make a list of the boys we like."

"Now he's gone forever!" cried Vinnie.

"No, he's not," I said. "He only went to kill some birds."

"And it has to be in order," said Jennie.

"A Whisker List!" Abby exclaimed.

Vinnie carried Snugglepoops inside as we set about making our list. We decided straightway it was to be kept in utmost secrecy. We would ask Harriet Merrill if she would like to add names to the group, explaining our condition that no one would speak of the list to another living soul. We supposed Emily Fowler, being a good five years older, might be too mature for such trivial pursuits and Helen Fiske would consider us foolish, but Harriet would love it.

A farmer was cutting down a tree somewhere in the woods. We could hear the sharp ring of his ax, a dauntless send-off to our plan.

Early Poems and Damnation

I was sick most of the summer. However, once strong enough to lift my head from the pillow, I wrote a poem. It had been on my mind those half-awake days upon the bed, so hot and far away from worldly concerns. I heard a dog bark, demanding of something he felt the right to have. I could hear it in the bark. He—I assumed it to be a male dog—wanted it. It belonged to him. He had lost patience with the situation. His birthright was being ignored. He could be said to be at his "wits' end," a phrase I learned from Mother. As I listened I fashioned myself a part of that dog—not fashioned really. It was not a thinking matter. I felt I was with that dog—*in* that dog—more a sudden happening than a make-believe game. We were one and I smiled all alone upon the sheets and no one there to see. I was at rest and alive at the selfsame moment. It was the grandest feeling! I had very much enjoyed composing my few poems before that day, my compositions as well, but this was different. I was in *my place*.

I don't remember the poem. Wait! I *do*!

He barks to make her understand
That he was born for him—
Not her, nor cat, nor others' way—
Not time, nor tides, nor "shoulds."
—Just he *alone and no one else*
Directs his course by day—
So it will be for all of time—
Until Eternity!

I was proud of that poem. I was getting a sense of saying a thing "just so" and no more. It was a thrill—a secret thrill—as no one knew but me!

Once up and back to the garden, I wrote a poem about Father's shoes. It was an amusing verse. Funny or sad, it mattered not. The feeling was the same. Alive and at rest! A part of all there was and all there was to be. No time and endless time and my certain place in all. I kept the poems in a little box that had a circus elephant painted on the lid. The color was faded, but you could tell the elephant was gray. Its trunk was up and a red banner about its neck. When it was once again time for school, I put my elephant box on the highest shelf I could find. The poems would have to fend for themselves until such time as I could afford them some companions.

While we were at school, our parents received "notices," in the manner of brief reports as to each stu-

76

dent's performance in the classroom. Father read these telltale descriptions out loud, commending us, or passing a critical pronouncement as he deemed necessary. That second fall—after my sick summer, my new poems and my return to "life"—I remember ours all. Vinnie's notice was complimentary, making mention of things like her "enthusiasm" and "quick wit." Austin's was not bad, but not nearly so glowing as those of his illustrious sisters. Father said Austin had far more Dickinson Discipline than was mentioned in the notice, which stated something about Austin's being "a fine lad" and "extremely intelligent" but "not applying himself." Father cared not for that. Mother was not perplexed that I could see, but was careful to say little, so as to appear to be in agreement with Father. She quickly turned the conversation in the direction of her chillblains and a cold sensation in the bones. Mother often plays the invalid to her advantage.

This was my notice. I recall it word for word. "Often absent. A good student. Strikingly original compositions. Needs no discipline. Appears frail." I have little perspective on most of the points, except two. It is true that I was often absent. In fact, I missed an entire term of three months, and me in bed with a pain in my head that was awful. Any light at all was too much to bear and a knife in my chest and a spiteful cough.

That my compositions were original is a fact that

cannot be disputed. Modesty dictates I refrain from elaborating on the matter. However "strikingly original" my compositions were, I leave for others to decide. Father continued to refer to me as the "best little girl in Amherst." I don't know why. It was surely due to no unusual possession of righteousness. When I think of the extraordinarily large number of wicked thoughts inhabiting the dark portion of my brain, not to mention the little miserly ones scampering about my heart, it is really quite terrible. And I not yet eleven!

It seemed to me that many people must have been feeling wicked that year, as there were many revivals going on throughout all of Massachusetts. I wondered if people were feeling wicked in other states as well. I felt that they were but had no way of knowing for sure. Judging by the number of revivals I heard of, people must have been feeling wicked throughout all of New England! A revival, from what I could see, was a great swell of religious purpose to get everyone to accept Christ as their Savior. I thought it should be enough to simply love him and follow his teaching, but that seemed not to be sufficient.

There was a revival in Amherst that year, and as everyone else was going, I thought I would go and see what it was about. I found the main point to be based upon the idea of Original Sin—how we all are sinful at birth and must be cleansed—an idea that has never struck my fancy. As I love Christ, read the Bible, and go to church, I considered myself a Christian, but that is not "scientifically" how it is. One must first receive the call to give one's heart to Christ.

There were many religious activities at the revival—including, but not limited to, sermons, hymns, studies and daily meetings of our prayer circle. There was concern among many of my friends that they might die before becoming a Christian and thereby miss going to Heaven altogether. I myself worried about this very much. For a short time I really did feel as if I had found my Savior. I had a love for God that was quite wonderful really, but I soon lost the desire to pray. The thought irked me and I found myself caught up once more in the earthly joys, which everywhere abound.

At the prayer-circle meetings we were given little books to read containing frightful tales—horror upon horror—Hellfire, Damnation, Retribution and Judgment! The most fearsome consequences of the minor mischievous deeds of fun-loving children were described in vivid detail. I do believe these books did much to dissuade me from pursuing my finer self, that is, from giving myself to Christ. This was a shame as I felt so happy during the brief time during which I fancied I had found my Protector.

Austin and I discussed the matter at one of our Night Talks, and the fire going and the house as still as a stone. "When I think of those little books it amazes me that innocent children don't run screaming from the Lord and all His Mercy every day," I said, wrapping my shawl tight about my shoulders.

Austin spoke like a ghost. "The hor-rors of Re-tri-bu-tion . . ."

"Dreadful! Like those religious journals Father sends us . . ."

"Fingers chopped ooooffff, children burrrning in vats of boiling oooiilll . . ."

"I like the one about the disobedient youth who bites off his mother's nose just before he's beheaded."

"That's a good one," Austin agreed.

I hugged my knees. "And the fearsome pictures! An arm lying in the road . . ."

"Blood dripping down a chin . . ."

"Boys with their feet chopped off . . ."

"Demented eyes, blazing from skeleton sockets . . ."

"It's a wonder we survive at all!"

"We may not!"

"It makes no sense!"

"Nooooooo sense!" Austin was playing the ghost once more, an attempt to scare me, but it didn't work.

"Surely there is mischief in all the children of

Amherst!" I proclaimed.

"Speak for yourself."

"There is and you know it! Why we are not dropping like flies throughout the entire Connecticut Valley I cannot say! God help us, for surely no one else can do it!"

"Noooooooo one!"

"Why does Father send us those wretched journals?"

"He wants us to be well brought up."

"If we live long enough!"

Austin shifted a log in the fire with the iron poker.

"I hope he hasn't read them," I said. "I hate to think he could knowingly inflict such gruesome torment upon his own children."

"Father means well," said Austin, a fact I knew to be true but of small consolation.

We watched the fire in silence.

Abby's Fish

During our second winter in the new house, Father was elected to the State Senate. That meant many long months without him, as he would be in Boston discussing matters of the utmost importance with learned gentlemen and buying ink. Father always bought ink when in Boston. I'm not sure why.

I think Mother worries more about everything when Father is gone, and I don't blame her. It must be hard to run an entire house by oneself. Mother bears it all with quiet dignity and a simple steadfast spirit I don't understand and yet I admire very much—at times, that is. I sometimes wish she would throw up her hands and rush into the wind, calling out the innermost voice of her heart, but that I fear is not to be.

My health permitted me to attend much of the school term, which suited me finely as I loved all my subjects very much indeed. They were Mental Philosophy, Geology, Latin and Botany, as well as Reading and Composition and Music. How Large they sound! And for friends? Jennie was gone then, off to school in Southwick. I missed her awfully. Abby was sick much of that term, missing quite a lot of school. I used to wonder whether being an orphan had any to do with it. Having no parents from the age of three is a fate too horrible to imagine. Could a blow to the heart shake one's will to live? Could it weaken the Soul? Could it open the body to all manner of sickness? I asked Abby about it one day when we were at the pond, looking for unusual fish. "Did you ever wonder at how often we get ill?" I asked. We were on our knees and staring below the lily pads into the brown pond.

"There's one!" said Abby. She meant a fat fish with pop-out eyes, just below the surface.

My mind was not on the fish. Having recently recovered from weeks in bed, the question of excessive illness had claimed a large part of my brain. "I thought you might be weak inside from losing both parents and you so small."

"I don't feel weak," said Abby.

"Never?"

"Rarely."

"I often do."

"What kind of fish was that? I can use it for my report."

"Not if you don't know its name."

"Oh, you know what it is! I know you do!"

"I don't and I have a most important question about Life and Death and the effect of horrible events on the well-being of our bodies."

"You think too much," said Abby.

"And you too little!"

"What fish *is* that?"

I believe we went into the woods then, abandoning all questions to the glory of the trees.

Vinnie was nine that spring and improving as regarded the amount of common sense she displayed. However, her cats still "ruled the roost," as Mother liked to put it, and I must say the phrase applied. Pussy had acquired the dubious habit of climbing up the draperies, while Roughnaps and Snugglepoops ignored her and went about killing birds. Tiger Boy liked to startle innocent humans by staring at them unannounced from various places about the house, his sharp yellow eyes driving an uneasy shaft of knowing into one's very Soul. The top of Father's bookcase was his favorite spot. One night Austin shooed him off by dropping a large book with such a crash that it wakened Mother, who hurried down the stairs overtaken by a terror that a robber was murdering all three of her children with a club.

All in all we managed well enough and yet a balance was missing from the house. At times I felt as I would fall off the side. And then early in March Father returned, bringing gifts for us all—nothing large or unnecessary— just some small token for each, a book, a handkerchief, a bit of calico, some sign that one had not been forgotten.

The night of his return Mother made Father's favorite supper, roast lamb with peas, rice croquettes and custard for dessert. It was a merry meal, Vinnie to my left, then Mother, Austin across and at my right hand, Father. The Special Five! And didn't Father go on about his learned friends in the Senate and how one had sneezed repeatedly during an important vote, bringing on several offers of handkerchiefs, many blows of the nose and so much noise as to demand a recount. Father laughs rarely but when he does one could light the sky by it!

All was right with the world as Vinnie and I climbed into bed that night, and the next day and the next. Then one morning after prayers Father closed his Bible and said that Austin would be sent away. It was innocent enough on Father's part. Austin should spend a year at boarding school, one Williston Seminary in East-hampton. He needed to improve, though in what way I could not imagine. It may have had something to do with his less than impressive notices from the Academy. I disagreed with Father on the subject but remained powerless to affect the situation.

My brother—gone? The only one who understood

me—gone? And why? He could rise to his potential at home in Amherst as well as anywhere, better perhaps, but Father has his own way of looking at a situation. His thoughts are stiff, with many corners. I don't know how Mother felt about Father's decision to send Austin away. I don't imagine she cared for it. With Father gone so much, Austin was the man about the house, a strong arm for her to lean on. I don't believe Mother saw any need to send Austin away. But one never knows how Mother feels.

Before we knew it Austin was gone. The house was a dreary place without him—his coats gone from the hooks, no slippers beneath his chair—and so quiet! I was a sorry figure, wandering from room to room with a face as long as a month of Sundays and a spirit to match.

More sad news that spring. Aunt Lavinia lost a daughter, a sweet little girl of four. The word from Boston saddened us terribly. Mother was most affected. She was already in an anxious state over Austin's departure and would he lose his luggage and would he have enough to eat and who would do his laundry. She had settled the laundry question by deciding to do it herself. She told Austin to collect all his dirty clothes in a bag and send them back to Amherst with whoever might be traveling at the time. She would wash them straightway and return them as soon as possible.

Mother had trouble sleeping after Austin left, tossing and turning throughout much of the night and dozing in the afternoons. We had often to be quiet. Shades drawn. House gray. It was then that I started to have some disruptions of the mind that were quite puzzling. These were of no apparent consequence but unusual in their frequency and in their deep insistence.

The first.

Austin has been gone for several days. We sit at the table for dinner, silent within our blighted lot. Mincemeat and peas, not my favorites. I simply cannot eat another mouthful. Some peas remain. I look at the peas, alone on the plate, their companions gone, swallowed, chosen to live with me while they themselves are forgotten. I feel I simply must eat those lonesome peas. I cannot bear to hurt their feelings. And me, all the while knowing that peas do not have feelings, not cooked peas, at any rate!

It was quite surprising really, and more surprising that I ate them. I could not bear their plaintive thoughts echoing inside my brain!

Another.

Vinnie and I are in our room. Vinnie sits on the bed,

drawing some little pictures—of cats, I suppose. I am planning to join Abby for a walk in the woods. Some wildflowers will be up. I must see the newest signs of spring. I stand, bonnet in one hand, shawl in the other, wondering which to take with me, or whether neither one is necessary. "What do you want me to draw," asks Vinnie, "a chicken or a tornado?"

"A tornado," I answer, thinking it the more lively of the two.

Vinnie commences drawing dark circles of unrest, swirling conelike motions of the arm, as once more I contemplate my choices. Shawl, or bonnet, bonnet, or shawl? After some moments I set the bonnet on the bed and then, in the depth of my center, a fist high between the ribs, a knowing.

If I leave the bonnet on the bed something terrible will happen.

And don't I pick up the bonnet straightway and set it on the chair!

I missed Austin very much that spring. Aunt Elisabeth was with us for a time, which was pleasant. However, she was afraid to sleep alone, which meant I was out of my bed and she with Vinnie, and me in the extra room without my Jennie, and Tiger Boy peering in the dark and no one to laugh with.

The months passed, as they do, regardless of Circumstance. Mr. Washburn took care of the hens, the chickens grew, Mother did Austin's laundry, and Father, when home, looked after the horse. Some skunk made off with a new egg from the coop, and Austin's rooster, Albert, nearly got killed by two others, but survived in the end as did we all.

Sophia

I was thirteen. Austin was home again. Life was more right, but Death was in the air. Always outside the window funerals were passing, a child, an old man, an infant in the tiny wooden box, the freshly dug grave, the soundless tears, the line of black mourners. Grief stopped Time for such as these, while the world went on, the spiders unconcerned, the frogs, the caterpillars and all the moths not knowing, or if they did, not stopping to offer consolation.

First, Emily Fowler lost her little brother. It was a fever took him. They said he spoke of being in a deep well, and no way to get out. Emily's mother died soon after. The shock of losing her boy was too much—that and consumption. I tried to comfort my friend but met with small success.

That same February one more mother was taken. This time it was Helen Fiske and her gentle sister, Ann, who were called to bear the pain. Consumption again was the culprit. When I got the news I walked the gravel sidewalk to their house as I wanted to be of help, but they did not want a visitor and so I left. I took the long way home. The hills were laid out in ribbons—backdrop behind backdrop. The clouds hung between the hills in shades of gray and the fog rested as I could not. It was after three by some and on toward evening. I could see the farthest hills above the fog and below the curtain of clouds above them. Fields, then trees—some pine, some branches merely—then more fields, a barn or two, and then the hills. No sun that day, leastways not to my sorry eyes.

When I reached Home the oil lamp was lit above the gate. Father would be home soon, if Providence might grant us such a blessing. Mother would be resting or in the kitchen baking bread. I felt a chill.

Death could claim them too. And how would I go on?

I could find no answer.

Cousin Sophia had always been frail. Her skin was fair, "see-through" I liked to call it, and her hair—sunlight on wheat, spun from the whitest gold. Her thoughts seemed born in the ether of Heaven. That spring she was not looking well. I noticed a dull look in her eyes and darkness underneath. This worried me. I spoke of it to no one. Perhaps it was to put a distance to my fear, as if its very spreading could infect my friend.

It began with a cough and a headache, then chest

pain, then the sudden fever. I went every day to be at her bed. It was two weeks I went and never missed a day to hold her hand and read to her when she still had Reason. She loved the stories of Dickens. She would lie, her head on the pillow, the linen so white and the lace trim, her eyes half shut, her gold-white hair about her face and a look of contentment, such peace, needing nothing, as the words of the great writer washed her clear. At times she would close her eyes and her head would fall to one side as she slept. That was my clue to stop reading and remain just quiet, holding her hand. Father did not care for my visits as he felt I might catch whatever illness she had. But the doctor said no, it was typhus and I wouldn't catch it, and so Father let me go.

There came a day late in April, when the daffodils were just up and the tulips were beginning, that I shall not forget. I arrived at Sophia's door as usual after school. I knocked. When the door opened it was Sophia's father. He told me I could not go into her room.

"Why not?"

"Her mind has left her."

I felt faint. "She expects me."

"I'm sorry."

"She will wonder where I am."

"Her mind has left her," her father repeated, his eyes dead, like stones.

"Please."

He bent his head. Silence. In a moment he stepped back, admitting me into the hallway, then closed the door. I could feel my heart beating in my throat. "I will get the doctor," he said, and left me alone.

Soon the doctor was in the hallway, his collar open and no jacket and looking tired himself. "I'm sorry," he said.

I tried to breathe.

"She must die."

My breath stopped and my heart—and Time. Then the thunder in my chest—a heart asked to accept the unacceptable—and still no breath, hundreds of tiny bells in my ears—crickets gone mad—hot and cold at once, and beads of sweat.

The voice came from my deepest part. "I must see her!"

The doctor knew it was true, that I must, that it would be my last chance to gaze upon my friend. He nodded. I climbed the stairs to her room on legs not wholly there. I stopped on the landing, Dickens at my heart, a palm's sweat about the leather, the doctor behind me and his words. "You may look in."

The door was partway open.

I bent down.

Dickens on the floor.

I took off my shoes, picked up the book and entered

the room. The carpet was soft under my feet as I walked into the quiet before Death. I stopped at the bed.

Sophia.

She looked so beautiful, her golden hair—spun by Angels—her face lit from within. And a smile! Unearthly beauty!

Are you there?

I could not tell. There some, yet gone too. I sat on the edge of the bed and took her hand. It was cold. Minutes passed. The doctor's voice came from the end of a tunnel. "You must leave now."

No!

"It is time."

I felt him take my arm.

No!

I let him lead me away.

When I saw her in the coffin she was not there. It was only her body, nothing more. I could not call her back. A terrible stillness was over me. Nothing moved. I shed no tear. To weep would be a break too wide. A space so large would lose my Self, and would I have a mind again?

That night I experienced a fixed melancholy. Father told me I would be well in time. Mother told me the same and yet I did not believe them. *How kind they are,* I thought, *how caring, but they don't know how I feel—Leaden, now and forever.* It was *I* who had

Reason. Others did not. Reason told me Life was blank, a temporary show of Pain, nothing more. All was foolish and I apart and still.

Mother brought me tea in a china cup. I had liked the cup in times past, white with trees and houses in muted tones, but now the thought of touching my lips to its narrow rim frightened me. Mother's hand was shaking. She wanted me to raise my head to accept the nourishment, but I could not. The cup was too thin, the saucer as well. It could break. I wanted the strong about me, but the strong was nowhere and so I sent my mother away.

Soon Father was in my room with his "cold box," ministering to me. I had no outward sign of illness, but a tiredness so great that I could do nothing but sleep. A boulder had been set upon me and all my limbs tied down. After Father left I slept for several days. When I began to move about the room, Father made his decision. I would go to Boston. A stay with loving relatives would restore both health and spirits. I did not care to go, but as Father thought it best, I agreed.

Aunt Lavinia and Uncle Loring were most kind, making an effort to include me in all their activities and to keep things gay. I went along, a lonely apparition. I could have been anywhere, watching others do things and wondering why. After some time there were moments when I was not haunted by the vision of Sophia's narrow form in the iron bed, not seeing her sunlight hair, damp across the pillow, or her dead body alone in the wooden box. One afternoon I found myself admiring a slice of Aunt Lavinia's pie. At night I found myself watching the first star, finding it noble. That scared me most. I felt I was accepting the unacceptable—Death, Disease, Decay. I must protest! But I was letting go. I was losing—Lost.

Every day there were letters from Home. Even Mother wrote to me! Hearing from her pleased me very much indeed, especially knowing how rarely she lifted the pen. Can mother and daughter be so different?

Father's letters were edifying in all respects. I must be good and not cause any trouble and not let my feet get wet. Most importantly I should be careful getting in and out of carriages. I must be seated before the carriage moved so as not to be thrown to ground and crushed. That seemed wise.

When visiting in nearby Worcester, Father forwarded a puzzling proposal. I must be sure to visit the Lunatic Asylum. Perhaps he felt that seeing all the poor tormented souls would be refreshing in some way. As it turned out, I passed the sorry place but did not go in. Thank God for small favors! All in all, the trip improved my spirits some. Once again Life held moments of sense, a welcome state of affairs.

Have You Ever Seen
a Naked Boy?

U pon my return, Austin was caught up in efforts to produce large eggs. Well, not Austin himself, rather it was Austin's hens did it. Austin was the supervisor. He measured each egg, keeping a little book in which he noted the dimensions, then proceeded to increase the size of future eggs by feed, temperature, dampness of the coop and amount of sun. He achieved some fine results. It was good to be in the bosom of my family, where all was safe. Life was almost straight.

I found myself to be tired, by reason of travel I supposed and the shock of recently having met Death face-to-face for the first time. I rested some days before returning to school. When I did return, I was in for a Large surprise.

Wednesday afternoon. Amherst Academy. Third Floor. Abby was at home and sick, as I had been. It was my first well day. As I had not been to school in some time, the presence of so many young men and girls in the small space caused considerable discomfort. I sat, straight backed upon the bench, attempting a deeper breathing. *In, out, in, out,* I instructed myself, but found no comfort in the matter. And then, ascending the stairs she came, a girl with composure so remarkable as to be etched in my heart forever, and her hair crowned with dandelions!

I watched her take a seat, so sure, so lovely. I could barely wait until the compositions had been read to approach her. The scramble of the other students leaving was in full force, yet she sat, calmly looking about the room. I wondered at the lack of embarrassment in one new to a school, and all about so many unknown teachers, young men and girls, going about their hurried ways. I would not have been so calm.

"Hello," I said, approaching with unconcealed eagerness.

"Hello."

"My name is Emily."

"I'm Abiah."

"A lovely name."

"Abiah Palmer Root."

"Emily Elizabeth Dickinson." How formal we sounded! I sat next to her on the bench. "Welcome to the Academy."

"Thank you."

"How do you like it so far?"

"It seems nice."

"It is! And nicer for your arrival."

"Thank you."

The room was empty now and just us two upon the bench. "Where did you come from?" I asked.

"Feeding Hills."

"Another fine name."

"Don't you love words?"

My heart skipped a beat. "I sometimes think they are my best friends."

"I enjoy them so much," she said. "I am writing a novel." Well, that did it! I could not have been more impressed had she said she was climbing Mount Everest! "A romance novel, no less!" she concluded.

"How daring! Is it shocking and enjoyable?"

"I hope so."

I thought of my poems, but did not consider sharing the news of their existence as it was not yet time. My secret had to be alone and grow.

Abiah quickly joined our special group of friends. With Sophia gone and Jennie home to Southwick, our special group consisted of me, Abby, Harriet Merrill and another girl, Sarah Tracy, who stayed in Amherst for school only. Now add Abiah! We formed a circle of five, known as the Magic Circle.

I think this time marked a new and deepening importance of my friends in my life. I had always enjoyed them, but that summer when I was thirteen they occupied so large a portion of my mind and heart as to nearly crowd out my family's central position. Not really, but almost. We had fine and secret times. Life was once again catching my interest, a fact that pleased me, while at the same time it caused me concern as I felt Sophia slipping away. Death is too Large a thing to comprehend. I don't believe I will ever understand it.

Two of Vinnie's cats died in the fall. She was awfully upset about it. I tried to soothe her mind, but with little success. Tiger Boy and a new kitten named Tom-Tom made up the sorry lot. It must have been a sickness started with one and the other caught it. There was, however, another new kitten by the name of Noopsie Possum that despite being very sick did *not* die. Sickness and Death are everywhere and yet Father Time marches on. It seems disrespectful the way he disregards Death, keeping apace as if all were well and no one gone forever! Then he goes and brings some new joy so grand as to be forgiven for his random trampling of our human feelings.

My joys were large that fall. I was doing very well on the piano. I mastered some new and difficult pieces, including "Wood Up" and "Weep No More." As I wanted to improve my voice, on Sabbath eves I attended Mr. Woodman's Singing School. I also made Father an attractive pair of slippers.

Afternoons Abby and Abiah and I would sit beneath the Elm and talk, often starting with Books—*Great Expectations*, Shakespeare's *Hamlet* and forward from there. We could go on "until the cows came home," a phrase Mother liked but I never understood, as in my experience cows come early to the barn each evening to be milked.

One October day—it was warm like summer—when Abby had gone on a trip, Abiah and I sat by that handsome tree, our skirts spread out on the grass like girls in a French portrait. Father had just given an illuminating presentation at the Cattle Show entitled "The Report on Horses." One would have expected the report to be about cows, but it was not. I explained to 'Biah, as I often called her, that Father doesn't care for horses and doesn't know much about them and we laughed at how those small points did not deter him from giving his lecture. How glorious to laugh and all the dry, blazing leaves about us, orange, yellow, red and gold—nature's explosion of fire in the color line!

We are on our backs in the starched leaves and gazing at the sky. I watch a black-capped chickadee nearing the woods. I wonder what she will do when she gets there and whether she has a plan.

What mystery propels her weightless form?

"I have news of interest," says Abiah.

I am pulled from my reverie.

"Harriet said that Sarah held hands with Jeremiah at Watkins Mill."

"How exciting!"

"I told you it was!"

"You said it was interesting."

"Well, that's what I meant—interesting, exciting."

"They're not the same."

"You know what I mean."

"Not if you don't say it."

"You carry this word passion too far."

"I don't believe a passion can be carried too far. The point of a passion, as one would expect *you* to know, being the author of a romance novel, is that it has no end."

"Perhaps."

"To be sure!"

Abiah returns to her original subject. "Jeremiah is nothing if not handsome," she says. "I myself would not object to holding his hand."

"And what of your Beau Ideal D.?" He was 'Biah's favorite boy. She spoke of him in codes—and I sworn to secrecy. "Did he say hello?" I ask.

'Biah smooths her skirt. "He did."

"Why didn't you tell me?!"

"I'm telling you now."

"A bit late, wouldn't you say?"

"A girl must have some secrets!"

"Not from her special friend!"

'Biah is thoughtful. "Have you ever seen a naked boy?"

"What?" Her comment has me quite beflown.

"You heard me!"

"Have I ever seen a naked boy?"

"That was my question."

"No! Have you?"

"My cousin."

"Which one?"

"My aunt's boy."

"He's only two," I say. "That doesn't count!"

"That's true," 'Biah agrees. "It should be a boy our age."

"Or older."

"So you never have."

"What?"

"Seen a naked boy."

"No."

"I thought not."

"But I would like to."

"Emily!" she screams, shocked to the very core.

"Wouldn't you?"

"No!"

"You would!"

"No!"

"Where is your sense of adventure?"

We laugh. We roll on the grass, the dried leaves crisp beneath our backs. Later we talk seriously about the subject, deciding we would like to see a naked boy, but only if we could be invisible at the time.

Stain of Death and
My First Bible

I t was a Scarlet time. I was nearly fourteen and wondering and all alone. Why Mother did not warn me I shall never understand. It would have been simple to explain the monthly shame of all women, of old maids and grandmothers, mothers and girls. Yes, girls! The fright can be very great when a terrible bleeding comes and one assumes it to be the mark of Death!

I was the first of our Magic Circle to see Blood coming from that secret place between my legs. No one had spoken of it to me, not Abby, not 'Biah—not any! As it turned out, I was the first to tell them about it, but not until after much distress to myself.

November. A late-afternoon walk from town and already dark. I, alone, with only the light of the Moon to guide me. I am just along the brief strip of pavement where the shops have recently locked their doors for the evening. I plan to conjugate some Latin verbs upon my return home. The assignment being due the following morning, I feel it best. *"Amo, amas, amat,"* I say to the wind, swift in its rustling journey through the leaves of the trees along my path. "I love, you love, he loves—*she* loves!"

I feel a wetness between my legs.

What is that?

I can make no ladylike inquiry into the matter in my present circumstance and so on I go, crossing the road at Main Street, down Pleasant Street toward home. Now I feel wetness to the knee. My heart beats a faster time. It's cold, the wetness freezing my legs and my heart as well.

What is that?

I am home now. I hand Mother whatever package I have retrieved from the village. I cannot remember what. I go upstairs to my room. Vinnie is not there.

Alone, thank God.

I check beneath my skirt and there it is—Blood! Red! Scarlet red and down to my knees! My beating heart picks up its pace and I about to faint from the shock of it. I know where it comes from. No surprise when investigation proves its point.

I am dying.

That night my appetite is gone. I tell Mother I am tired. I want to sleep. She puts a hand to my head. "No fever," she says.

I want to tell her about the Blood, but I don't want to worry her. Perhaps it will stop and never come again. Perhaps I can spare her concern. At the very least I can postpone the torment of her having to care for a dying child. I say nothing more, return to bed, but find it hard to sleep. My heart is beating fast.

What will I do with my bloody underclothes? And the stains on my dress!?

I had taken off my dress, changing it for another. This had brought about inquiry from Mother. I remember the words. "Where is your calico, Emily?"

"Upstairs."

Mother quotes *The Frugal Housewife*—"Hints to Persons of Moderate Fortune," page 89. "Don't be wasteful," Mother says. "Wear each dress until it needs a washing. Your calico has just been done."

"I'm sorry." Hurrying up the stairs. Into bed. A rag between my legs lest more Scarlet and more—and Blood with no end.

The bleeding subsides that night, but I do not trust the quick end to impending Death. When two days or three pass without a return to terror, I decide to tell Mother. I am well. She will be reassured. I am in possession of Scarlet underclothes and a dress with pink stains. These will need explanation. I must speak before they can be laundered.

When I tell Mother about the Blood she says I had the "monthly time of illness" and that until I am very old, or dead, I will have it, as all women do. I am reassured not to be dying but wish she could have found it in her heart to spare me the awesome concern by telling me before. I make up my mind straightway to tell Vinnie and Abby and Abiah and all my girl friends about it so that they be spared my terror. It seems to me that the most private thoughts and feelings a person can have are the ones most often shared by others. It is a sorry state of affairs that one puts up the bars when the best thing would be for those same bars to fall. One sets oneself apart when what one needs most is to know that one is not alone.

My thoughts, that fall, sometimes found themselves in my most private place, that land between my legs, where thoughts are not to go. But go there they did. I was witness to changes I did not care for. First, I did not like the Blood. Bleeding from that place every month without a shred of warning as to the time of day, or the day itself, is not pleasant. Oh, it was exciting to be joining the ranks of womanhood, but inconvenient and not without concern. What if one began the Scarlet Flow at school during Mental Philosophy, or Geology, or, worse yet, while delivering a recitation? I did not care for the changes "down there" in other respects. I had always considered that private sanctuary to be a dainty object, suitable for a girl, simple in its design. Then hair began to grow! This concerned me as it destroyed the gentle smoothness I had come to expect. It was no longer pretty—a sorry surprise!

We were talking quite a lot at that time within our girlhood circle as regarded Love. Everyone was talking about it. Why, we were young ladies! Before we knew it, we would be married! It was too thrilling! And did we dare to consider the "Whiskers staff"? We did! I wondered that there could be room! And wouldn't it hurt? I imagined that private staff to be of ample size. How it could fit was beyond my mind's imagining. This question was never discussed among the members of our girlhood Circle as it seemed too private a concern, to me at any rate. I can only guess at the reasons within the hearts of my dear friends for remaining silent on the matter. It seemed to me that the weight of these unspoken questions brought a certain weight to the air itself.

As if to say "Keep your mind on lofty matters," Father bought me my first Bible. I knew he could not read my thoughts, yet wondered still—

Could he?

Receiving a Bible of one's own is a special event, as one shares the family Bible until considered to be of reasonable age and exemplary character. It was good that he had been kept in the dark as to the degree of wickedness in the mind of his "perfect little girl," or else I would never have received that merry book! It was a most handsome edition, and the fact that it was my own lent a preciousness to the Book that could not be denied. Though I had resisted the hand stretched out to so lowly a bad one as myself, still the matter of religion was and is still one that occupies a high station in my mind. My favorite part of the Bible is the Revelations. How Large they are! What subjects! Wormwood, the Smoky Pit, the Locusts and the Beast, not to mention the Wrath of God! I very much enjoy the Gates of Pearl, the Glory of the City, the Angel with the Little Book, and my special favorite, the "Gem" chapter! Jasper, Sapphire, Emerald, Gold! How thrilling!

There was yet another revival that year, December, I think it was, but I did not go. Young and old alike thronged about in meetings and I attending not a single one! I felt I had been so easily swayed the last time into believing I had accepted Christ into my heart when in fact I had not. Many were saved, however. Most often it was the ones who most vigorously scorned the offerings of Christ's bounty and protection who were most quickly brought to accept his Truth. It was wonderful to see. I felt quick remorse as regarded my power to acknowledge Christ's place in my heart. I hoped most sincerely to awaken one morning and find him there. I prayed that one fine Sabbath day I might be flooded with desire to cast all concerns upon my Savior, that he might carry my burdens, that he might protect me, that he might point the way. I longed to crave his mind and not my own, but such was not the case. I did not desire to give my mind to Christ and could not lie about it. As far as I could tell, the question of Faith had been taken to a land of dubious meaning. It seemed one must behave in just the ways prescribed by others—by men I did not know and did not often agree with. I have always found my place with Faith, but Faith without questions seems a sorry exercise.

Religion to one side, the start to that winter was truly grand. New friends came to Amherst that fall, Olivia and Eliza Coleman. Their father, Lyman Coleman, had come to take charge of the Academy and also to teach Greek and German at the College. They were great girls, Eliza, twelve and frail, Olivia seventeen and in possession of beauty so extreme as to provoke jealousy among all the girls. They were not part of our Magic Circle, but jealousy was not the reason. Olivia was too old and Eliza too young to appreciate our activities, which were many indeed. Though serious matters had deepened our understanding, we often cut a sprightly caper—a roguish band! Harriet was always making a joke, Sarah, calm and lovely, Abby, the studious one, Abiah, adventuresome yet extremely self-possessed, and Me! Modesty forbids comment here.

As the snow fell—and I, fourteen at last—we decided to meet secretly in the woods several afternoons during the week to discuss all manner of things past and current, with ample time given to the contemplation of the future. Imagination knew no bounds. We gave each other secret names. I was Socrates, by reason not only of my infinite wisdom but, just as importantly, of my questioning nature. Abiah was Plato, student of Socrates—me. I had been in Amherst far longer than 'Biah and thereby had much to teach her regarding the ins and outs of the surroundings. And of course, 'Biah was writing a book, as the original Plato had done. Sarah was Virgil. I forget why. Abby and Harriet had names so secret we had, at their request, taken an oath in blood never to reveal them.

At our meetings one was always in for a surprise. "First order of business," Abby would say from her seat upon the large, flat stump of the oak and snow all around.

"Whiskers!" 'Biah would shout.

"Whiskers!" the group would echo, and off we would go! The Whisker List in all its glory! Abiah was the most constant of the group. Her Ideal Beau D. was number one for the entire year. It got so we joked we needn't hear from her. We would go about the circle, each girl speaking the name of her current Whisker Choice, with exclamations, approvals and notes of surprise from all the others. Harriet was always changing her mind. Hardly a week would pass but she would adjust her selection. At one point she even requested the privilege of listing three at the same time, but was denied that opportunity. "Enough is enough," said Abby, and the rest of us agreed.

I fancied two boys at the time. Michael Stubbins was one, a thoughtful soul with light hair, who rode his horse to school. Jake Cutler was another. Jake looked most finely and always carried a book, a custom that attracted my attention. Apparently, however, I did not attract his attention, as he never spoke to me.

Boys were not the sole topic to be covered in our secret meetings. All five of us were greatly impressed by Shakespeare. We secretly called him The Master and soon formed The Shakespeare Society as part of our "inside" Magic Circle activities, reading his plays out loud. I especially loved reading the part of Hamlet and also Thisbe in *A Midsummer Night's Dream*. Too much cannot be said for a little humor.

Lone Suppers

My fifteenth year brought many changes, and beneath, a thorn that never left my side. Austin was once more sent away. I was angry at Father for his decision to banish my brother—*again*! Austin had already spent one term in exile. It was too much! Williston Seminary may be a fine school, but I don't think it deserved to have my brother in its company while his loving sister was forced to bear the long and many months without him.

"Why must Austin be sent away to school?" I asked one evening shortly before his impending departure. We sat in the parlor, Father, Mother, Vinnie, and me. Austin was out in the barn.

Father looked up from "his" *Springfield Daily Republican.* "Children must spend some time away at school," he said.

"I don't see why."

"It strengthens them."

Mother sneezed. She was darning socks.

"They return with added fiber."

The fact did not claim my interest.

Father put down "his" paper and looked at me. "You will leave too, Emily."

I felt a chill.

"When you finish at the Academy, you will spend one year at Mount Holyoke Seminary."

Mother sneezed again.

"Are you sick?" Father asked her.

"I'm fine."

"You'd best be in bed."

Mother ignored him. I imagine she might have liked for me to remain at home.

"Young ladies are fortunate to have the opportunity of college these days," continued Father, "for at least a year."

"Where will *I* go?" asked Vinnie. She sat in the chair by the window, her latest treasure, Noopsie Possum, curled up on her lap. Still a kitten, Noopsie Possum had received her name by reason of her habit of falling into a doze in times of concern. Like me! I was fading into a cushion of Fear, drifting farther and farther away from the room, from Father's knees, his folded-down newspaper, Mother's anxious expression, her pile of waiting socks.

"We'll see," said Father, in answer to Vinnie's inquiry as to the direction her life might be expected to take. Vinnie pursued the matter no further. I can only assume the gloom of Father's disapproval, had she continued to question him, seemed hardly worth it. I too remained silent and made my mind up that it would never happen.

But of course it did. I tried to ease the pain of my brother's absence by sitting in his place at the table, sparing myself the disappointment of looking at his empty chair. His absence was awful. Oh, I did so hope it was awful for him too! I hate not to be missed. Ned, Austin's sorrel horse who can step over a barrel, went off his feed.

Before leaving, Austin had given me his Latin book for use at school. I shared the book with Abby. We sat at the selfsame table, the book between us, our hearts as one. And what a charming book it was—Virgil! A good two inches thick, of the softest leather and the color of a mustard seed. The book was called *The Works of Virgil with Copious Notes*—over five hundred pages! I wrote my name inside the front cover straightway, so there could be no doubt as to whose book it was. "Miss Emily E. Dickinson, Amherst, Mass." That said it!

I enjoyed the study of that ancient language, the root of so many languages to come. So literal, so practical, so cumbersome, with its merry tales of legions traipsing about on all those roads, conquering whomever they saw. Enticing as it was, I must say our teacher—thin neck, large chin; I drew a little portrait on page 215—could at times assign far too much work. I used to fancy writing comments in the margins when the situation threatened to get out of hand. "1 week from Monday—how Mean" and things like that. Abby wrote in the book as well. We both pressed flowers between the pages. I hope they stay there forever, but one never knows what will happen. Forever is a long time.

I find there are times when it's the same old sixpence and nothing new seems to happen, or ever will happen, it seems—and boredom blights my blood. Then come the times when life changes so fast, I feel I never will catch up. Austin left and after Christmas I lost Abiah. With me but ten short months—a part of me—and then no more. I felt I should never adjust to the Circumstance. A certain Miss Campbell's School in Springfield had claimed her, a transfer organized by her father, a Deacon no less and no doubt filled with all sorts of intelligent opinions as regarded the education of proper New England young ladies. It was a time for losing—Austin gone, Abiah gone and soon the breakup of our Magic Circle. Harriet went to Hartford, Sarah went—I don't remember where she went—and that left only two, Abby and me, hardly a circle.

That spring Vinnie went to Boston for a fortnight with Father. I would have gone too had it not been for debility and a lingering cough that bound me to house and bed. Vinnie is a great deal stronger than I, a fact that vexes me and brings about no small desire on my part that the circumstance might be reversed. I possess a truly jealous heart.

I missed Vinnie during her brief excursion with Father. She was becoming a good deal more enjoyable with age. Her life seemed less "all cats," a decided improvement. Although she continued to fuss over each murderous ball of fluff, we had begun having some fine times. Imagination, ever present with us, sported recklessly, capturing with enviable insight the most telling and amusing details regarding the habits of unsuspecting townsfolk. Not a person was free from our razor-sharp perception! "Tompkins!" Vinnie would say in deep-throated ceremonious tone. "Mind you lie by that rock until I return. No food for the wandering!" Tompkins was the smallest dog either of us had ever seen, a shaggy coat obscuring questioning eyes. He belonged to Mr. Enfort, who taught history and coughed whenever he mentioned his mother. Vinnie would cough—"ugh—ugh"—and then, "My mother always taught me to pursue my studies—ugh—ugh! Lie down, Tompkins!"

Vinnie got just the right sound in her voice, just

the right stoop of the back, shuffle of the foot, or waving of the hands that caught each poor unsuspecting individual in all his or her ridiculous propriety. Then I would add my rapier-like wit to the event, forming the precise turn of phrase that none other could possibly have uttered and we were off, rolling about the grass in gales of laughter and nearly no breath left to keep us alive!

Home was a quiet place that fortnight alone with Mother. However, once up from the covers, I did enjoy our Lone Suppers. Mother had named them. I called the sharing of those meals Chicken Time, a phrase borrowed from the old familiar "just us chickens," meaning all others were gone. I don't know where that came from. It was just us two at the table, at whatever time might suit us, no need to sit up straight, no need to fold one's napkin, to watch what one said or how one said it lest it offend our Protector. Mother was most at ease, which I enjoyed extremely.

The days were getting longer, with ample light until 8. oclock at least. After supper Mother and I would finish the chores only to rest in the parlor, I most often in Father's chair with a book, Mother on the lounge with her sewing or embroidery. Sometimes I read to her from the *Republican*. I enjoyed those evenings very much, the quiet and Mother relaxed, for her at any rate, the light slowly fading and the purple and pink of the west, and soon time to light the oil lamp and close the shutters. Mother was working on a beautiful embroidery, a summer scene containing a measure of pastoral beauty as to be quite thrilling. The pattern was entirely her own. It never ceases to startle me when the depth of Mother's spirit makes itself known. It bursts forth from a hibernation so deep, one cannot help but wonder if it ever lived at all. Yet there it is, imagination, power, the will to have a voice of her own! It takes my breath away! And all that soon again to slumber, given up for dead, locked tight behind the narrow walls of convention, of Fear, of thinking only of others and no Self left to do the thinking. Obligation only. No thought abounds—a wooden way of pleasing Father, keeping his house, making no trouble, forgetting her wishes, ignoring her pleasure. The clothes are clean, the pie is hot, but where is she? I longed for her, and most especially so after such an unexpected glimpse into her deepest Self, where we could be—and were—as one. Spare me the agony of "living" as Mother! Grant me a straighter way!

I thought about this quite a bit and soon began a little poem. It told of a girl who could never speak, but only went into the woods and there she could tell the animals what she thought about all manner of things. There she had a voice of her own. This gave her great joy and a sense of purpose. The animals were still and watching and showed no sign of needing her to be another way. When something is most important to me and I do not want to lose it, I gather it into a poem.

The Me of Me

I t was a pleasant summer. Not perfect—but pleasant just the same. The good outweighed the bad. How grand it is in life when one can say that! I found myself writing a few more poems—three, I believe, or it may have been four. Summer inspires my lyrical side—long days, sun and flowers, the song of birds, and peace and bees and poems alone under the tree. One day when I was in the garden and thinking of a poem about a worm I was watching, it occurred to me that I was with my Self. It was a funny poem and nothing to show a brain in the head of the writer but as I thought about it, I and Me were one. That is the only way I can say it. I was surprised to note how rarely I had been possessed of that feeling. One would consider it a birthright, but it is not, or perhaps it is and I was left in the dark. I cannot tell. But there I was among the daisies, my mind on words to capture that one fat worm, its fright at being so rudely uncovered, its haste in returning to the familiar, no-light dark of the underearth—not a moment to spare! I had come Home. I recalled having had that same feeling in lesser measure while writing compositions at school. In a composition one may go on and on about one thing and another and have great fun, but a poem is a like a jewel. It is as it is, and that is that.

I had many classes that summer as school is a year-round affair. Abby and I worked hard and experienced quick gratitude for our wonderful teachers. Professor Hitchcock lectured in Geology at the College. We would never miss a time to hear him speak of mountains pushing up from the Earth, of glaciers and dinosaurs, those great leaden creatures that left their footprints for scientists to marvel at for eons of time. It was thrilling to hear Dr. Hitchcock discuss the connection between science and religion, as the subject of reconciling the two had been of long concern. "Far from opposing each other, science *proves* religion," he said, which had been my opinion since noting the pattern of the seasons and the punctuality of the robin's return.

I wrote several letters to Abiah that summer and received a few in return. I longed for more—at least in equal measure to my own—but that was not to be. Truth can be bitter, but one must bear the brunt. We had much to share, especially as we were both taking lessons "on the piny" as she liked to call it, the real name being "piano." Father had bought me my own! It took its place in the parlor as if it were always meant to be there, dark brown, with the gold letters—HALLET, DAVIS & CO.— and below, in smaller gold—BOSTON. I loved the "dragon legs," carved and ornate. I especially admired the round stool with the garnet cushion. Mother brought down her favorite lamp from upstairs and placed it on the piano on a doily she had crocheted some months before. I loved the lamp's square marble base, the gold pillar crowned with Saturn and the pink globe with the roses.

I could play my piano whenever the spirit moved me, which was often indeed. Aunt Selby was with us for the summer. Not only is she the daughter of our Reverend Joseph Vaille but a fine musician. Good for her! I could hardly contain my delight when she offered to teach me. She suggested exercises from an instruction book by Bertini, which I worked on with admirable diligence. I also played some tunes, my favorite being "The Lancer's Quickstep," which starts as a march, with triplets for one measure only. My favorite part is the switch to the quickstep, where the time changes and the key goes from F to C. A merry piece!

And now for the *best* news! I put my hair up in a net cap! I had envied Olivia Coleman's hair done up that way since I first saw her. I fancied I could look as comely as she with my hair in that selfsame style—a startling supposition. I knew better, but that don't often help one bit! Abby had set me straight on the matter in her no-nonsense way, but when the time came I must admit I looked quite well. I wished Abiah could have seen it. I described it to her in elucidating detail, but it wasn't the same as seeing it. It was really quite amazing to me that a child could stand before the glass of the parlor window, noting her exceedingly ordinary and childlike appearance reflected back at her, then grab the hair with two hands, pile it up and cover with a net cap and a young lady stares back! And don't one see a carnal edge to the picture! Roguish of me to admit it, but Truth will out in the end, so why not now, I say?! It was grand to delight in my appearance. I was certain that by the time I was seventeen, I should have all sorts of admirers—if not before!—and all sorts of merry times selecting my favorite! 'Biah said we mustn't choose too quickly as the enjoyment of many suitors was not a thing to pass over in haste, and I think she was right. I had had my picture made that spring, in the form of what is scientifically called a silhouette, that black shadow cutout that is so popular nowadays. Many praised the likeness. I could only wish the artist had waited some few months until my hair was up!

Almost as exciting as the styling of my hair was my first composition in *Forest Leaves*, the little paper at the Academy. There it was—printed for all to see! We were required to title our papers, a practice I am not wholly in favor of. However, in this case it appeared I had little choice. I called it "The Tea Party." Our assignment was to write on the following theme: "Three or more influential citizens meet to discuss world affairs. Each expresses *his*"—note the choice of pronoun!—"particular point of view. Due Wednesday." You can be sure I raised the issue of the exclusive pronoun contained in the instruction. I asked our teacher straightway whether any of those influential citizens might be female. He said that of course they could be and that it was understood. "Not by me," I told him, adding that he would do well to include both sexes in any future descriptions of events in which both might be qualified to take part. No response from the man was forthcoming.

My imagination brought together the most interesting group of influential citizens. Mother Nature is the gracious hostess. Father Time—ever punctual—moves the party along. Jack Frost—that guiltless robber—chills the proceedings in ample measure. Death—eyes sunken—ever stoic—eats not a thing. For merriment Santa Claus shows up for a brief stop along his renowned route of gracious delivery. We were required to write our name below the title, a tawdry custom in my opinion, but I suppose the teacher must know to whom to apply the grade. Mine, of course, was the highest possible!

As I already felt closer to myself when writing than at any other time—poems most especially, but compositions as well—I always looked forward to our writing lessons. To watch and listen and then to set things down just the way one sees them—there is nothing like it! To step away just enough to see Life straight! Sometimes I quite forget myself when I see a caterpillar making its way across a stone, or a purple sunset, and I think that I am never closer to the Me of me. When I see people go around in some unusual way, it starts a laugh inside, or a knowing so terrible that my blood stops and I rush to my pen and my paper and beg them to take my sight and hold it clear before the sense is gone forever!

I find it remarkable how the mind goes. The summer had been the happiest of my life; then along comes the winter and my mind takes up residence in the darkest place. Or it may be that Dark moves into Mind's domain. I'm sure I don't know which. In two short years I would be off to Mt Holyoke Seminary, my sojourn in the "real" world. I was very much interested in exploring it. However, my feelings on the subject were mixed. Austin would be returning home to enter Amherst College just at the point of my departure, Hearthside Companion and yours truly together once more, our family whole, and then to leave? Life can be untimely.

I was ill much of the winter, which may have had something to do with my dark mood. I find my spirits to be very low when I am ill. The discomfort, the boredom and the fear of Death all conspire to pull me to a dark place. Both Abby and Eliza were sick that winter as well. Abby and I both missed nearly two full terms of school. For my part, I was in bed with cough and influenza and always the fear of consumption. Not only had it been with me as an infant, but there have been many cases of consumption in our family. They say if it's in the family history, one's chances of contracting the disease are enhanced many times over. I also hear that once you have had it, you always have it, only sometimes it's quieter than a mouse guarding cheese. I worried that I might have it and would die. I thought to speak of my fear to Austin. Perhaps he could have offered some encouragement as regarded my situation, but I chose not to bring the matter up as the others might have gotten wind of it and fallen into the abyss. The treatment for consumption is no different than the treatment for influenza, so I said "Influenza!" and went about my way.

No Other Bread

When I was once again able to lift my head from the pillow, I decided to make an herbarium. Many of the girls were making them. Eliza was the champion despite her being the youngest girl. To make an herbarium you need a large book with blank pages—nicely bound, with strong paper—several sheets of yesterday's newspaper, a pair of flower shears or a small kitchen knife, glue and a press, or if not that, several heavy books will do just as well. Along with these, one of course needs flowers and a little book of sorts, containing pictures so one may recognize each and know the Latin names. Oh!—and a Pen! Such a Friend one simply cannot be without!

And off we go!

Cut full sheets of newspaper in half. Lay five cut sheets in a stack. Take your flower and cut it to a size that will fit the page of the book, no larger. Include some leaves and joints, petals, buds and seedpods. Place the flower on the stack of newspaper and flatten, twisting and smoothing the stem and other parts of the flowers with your fingers. Carefully place five more cut sheets of newspaper on top. Place four to five heavy books on top of the newspaper. On the edge of the newspaper write the name of the flower below. Check your little flower book if you don't know same. Alongside the flower name write the date of pressing. Leave alone for one week. If you have a press, use it instead of the books.

After week remove books. *Carefully* lift the upper five sheets of newspaper. Your dried flower will be revealed! Open your herbarium book. Pick up flower. It will be stiff and stand straight up from your fingers as many flowers do not do before pressing. Apply a small amount of glue to the back of the flower in several spots, excluding the petals, which might break. Place flower in the center of the page of your herbarium book, glue side down. Apply slight pressure with fingers. Count to ten. Consult flower book for the correct Latin name and spelling of your flower. Write English flower name on narrow label, with the correct Latin name underneath, then paste label across lower part of stem. A page is done. Repeat process to make a glorious book!

When my health improved sufficiently, Professor Coleman taught me German. Eliza thought I was very brave to study it as she felt it to be beyond understanding. Her father could not convince her otherwise. Father was sure I would forever lose the chance to force my tongue around such demanding syllables were I not to study that very term. Mother wanted me to rest. As always, Father's will prevailed. I enjoyed my German studies, though I am not altogether sure one "enjoys" German. One might rather respect it. German words are so demanding—I could even go so far as to say "punitive." I sometimes have to laugh at their self-important attitude.

My greatest joy that cold winter of becoming fifteen was receiving letters from Abiah. There were not enough to suit me, but those that did arrive were welcome indeed. Most entertaining were the ongoing reports of "The Adorable Mr. Escott"—none other than her piano teacher! Each letter contained detailed renditions of her lessons, including the way Mr. Escott's brown hair curled over the side of his forehead, how he sat on a chair next to her at the piano with *far* too much distance between them, how her heart raced with excitement when he reached out to turn a page for her and how for several bars after the page turn her fingers were so clumsy as not to respond to her mind's design. I never heard much about what she played. Presumably it made little difference.

My other joy was learning to bake bread—Mother and I alone in the kitchen, with Vinnie at school and the cats asleep, awaiting her return. I can see the two of us, sleeves rolled up and laughing and flour all about, Mother's hair covered by a pocket handkerchief, mine done up in its alluring net cap, soon with streaks of flour, foretelling my silver time. It was quite wonderful really and all the more wonderful because Mother and I seldom shared such moments.

As we baked, Mother and I got to laughing over the way Father insists upon judging the Cattle Show when he does not care for cows. Mother felt that a disinterest in cows was an acceptable quality as far as personal taste might travel, though she was, in her own words, "a cow enthusiast." That being said, she had no easy time putting together Father's disinterest in cows with his repeated insistence upon judging each and every Cattle Show in the greater Connecticut Valley. I stretch the point, but not as far as one might think.

That night after tasting my bread, Father made a surprising statement. He said that it was so delicious that henceforth he would eat no bread unless baked by me. Large praise—and Larger Responsibility. Must I be with him always, lest he starve?! Perhaps I should not have baked so well.

Later as I lay in bed and Vinnie snoring at my side, troubling thoughts gnawed at my brain.

What of Mother's bread? Will Father refuse that now? And how will Mother feel?

New Year's Day a gloom settled over me. I sat much of the day in my room, winter's fleeting slant of light barely visible amidst the fog. And my thoughts?

A year gone. So much left undone. Much done should not have been. Resolutions strewn, questions unanswered, plans ignored by inattentive Hearts, desires trampled by Time's relentless march. Old Year, you are gone now and the new one doesn't fit.

There was no funeral that day, only the soundless gravestones—those relentless reminders of the evanescence of all save Death.

Revivals were sweeping through the Connecticut Valley like the plague. Abiah joined the church that year, as did others of my friends, and I on the shore, waving a farewell hand to the boatload of friends and family bound for a place I could not see. Not only that, the place had claimed a piece of their Souls, precious not only to them but necessary to our connection. I was happy they should know "the peace of God, which passeth all understanding," but I could not give myself away— not to anyone! It seems to me that my Self is all I truly have—my one accompaniment to the grave—the most supreme gift of a generous God. The mind thinks its own thoughts—mine does at any rate. It wants to make its own sense of things, not always to follow. It wants to question. How does it seem to me? The question I had as a child remained. *Why would God give me a brain and ask me not to use it?* It made no sense. The mind and its beating partner—the one that so easily may break—are our greatest gifts. I could not give them up! I was only just beginning to know my Self—different, frail but strong, a lover of words, of Nature, of hills and sunsets, girl friends and Whiskers, laughing and music! To spend my days waiting for a Larger time, to give my Self away to anyone, be they neighbor, stranger, Reverend or King—it matters little—the very exercise defies Nature. I fear I may be ungrateful. But to receive a mind and heart and not to use them—*that* seems lacking in gratitude! I have seen the peace behind the eyes of those who have given themselves to Christ in exchange for his protection. I would claim that peace if it spoke in the center of my beating heart, but that has not been the case. I wait and listen.

Grandfather Norcross died in May. Mother suffered greatly the loss of her father—afternoons upon the lounge, blanket over, shades drawn—and I was sent away. Father said it was on account of my poor health, but my frailty was nothing new. I think it was because of Mother's nerves—once again! I did not want to leave. Time at Home felt more precious to me than ever. I would be off to Mt Holyoke before I knew it. No matter.

I went to Boston as Father had instructed, feeling the better for the banishment, a fact that surprised me. It may have been the Chinese Museum did it—all those wax figures in exotic costumes. What fun! And so unusual—especially the Opium Eaters in all their mysterious and highly intriguing ways.

Austin returned home in August. How glorious to have his slippers under the kitchen chair once more and the many coats upon the hooks and most of all to have *him*! The 9. oclock bell would ring, sending the upstanding to bed, as we received our signal—Hearth Time! I wanted to know all about his time away at Williston, what he was thinking and what was in his heart. He would always tell me. No other in the family would tell. We are an uncommon group—closer than close—a Special Five—yet news from the heart is out of bounds. I felt quick joy at being able to share my truest Self with my brother and to know he was doing the same with me.

A Fate Worse Than Death

S eptember 29, 1847.

As if without warning, it is the night before my departure for Mt Holyoke Seminary. Mother prepares my favorite dessert—ingredients being isinglass, fresh milk, chocolate shavings and sugar. Father sits at the head of the table looking a most especially strong protector. He reaches for the bread—*my* bread!

What will he eat when I'm gone?

He spreads the butter.

How will he live without me?

He sets down the knife.

He can't live without bread.

I watch as he chews.

He will be fine.

He lifts his teacup.

I don't want him to be fine! I want him to miss me!

"Stop crunching." Vinnie's words bring me out of

my reverie. "Emily is crunching and I can't stand it."

"I'm sorry."

"It bothers me."

"She's sorry," says Mother, always the peacemaker.

"I hate it."

"I'm sorry!"

"Emily will be gone tomorrow," says Mother. "Let's not find fault."

"Mother is right," says Father. "And don't say 'hate'."

"You will miss her soon enough," says Austin.

"I won't miss the crunching."

"And I won't miss the cats!"

I got her with that one.

After dinner I go up the hill to find Abby. She is sitting on her uncle's porch in a somber mood. I hand her our Latin book. She doesn't speak. I sit next to her on the little bench. "I want you to keep this," I say.

"Thank you." Abby stares at her shoes.

"It's yours now."

Abby looks up. "I will miss you too much."

"I will miss you too much too." We sit in silence. "You must come and visit me."

"How will I get there?"

"I will ask Austin to bring you."

"Do you think he would?"

"He'd better, or he will have me to answer to!"

Abby smiles. "A fate worse than Death."

My tears come over the dam.

My eyes gave me trouble that evening. They were sore and disturbed by the light of the oil lamp. I feared it was the sign of a cold coming on but would not admit it, as I wanted so much to be well for school. Much as I hated to leave Home, I looked forward to the adventure. I was of two minds about the prospect of my further education. I would have to take my examinations upon arriving at school. If I did not pass, I would be sent home. I felt a desire that this might occur, while at the same time, a dread of disappointing Father. I was rent asunder! I longed to explore Earth and all its wonders. I wanted to stay in my room.

I went to bed early. My heart pounded, the sound reaching my ear through the pillow. I felt it was a mistake to be going away. No. That's not how it was. I *knew* it.

Somehow I slept at last. When I awoke I had a soreness in my throat, a throbbing in my head and a tightness in my narrow chest. I decided to say nothing about it.

Father drove me to Mt Holyoke in the carriage. It was a drive of many hours in a gentle rain—down our street, past Mr. Cutler's store, through the town, past the cows in the common, past the church, past the College, south along the road toward the hills, out past the dinosaur pit to places unknown.

Father was silent. I wondered what he was thinking.

Part II

Mount Holyoke
and Beyond

"Don't let your free spirit be chained."

Mount Holyoke Seminary

I could see the red brick building through the fog as Father and I approached in the carriage. It was a large rectangular vision set back from the road behind a white fence. Soon I could count the stories—four—and see the long even rows of square windows across the front. There were many chimneys along the front edge of the roof—seven! And that was just the beginning! There were chimneys in back as well, which were difficult to count as visibility was poor.

I will not be happy here.

The building was too large, too straight, too far from Home.

Father stopped the carriage. I stepped to the ground. My head ached. My eyes hurt. My lips burned as, mouth agape, I took my first breath with feet upon South Hadley soil. Ahead the land was flat, but a gentle hill lay just behind the school and to the right, barely visible through the fog, a welcoming sight in all the straightness. Father came around the side of the carriage with my valise. "This way," he said.

We moved along the walkway and through the gate. My feet went slowly, as if tied down by weights. Before me levels of porches stretched across the length of the formidable structure, narrow spaces from which to view the seldom trees dotted about the yard.

I can't live here.

My heart beat fast. Excitement? Dread? A little of both, maybe.

I was taken straightway to my room by a Miss Whitman, who was second only to the Principal, Miss Lyon, who was otherwise engaged. Father followed with my valise. "Here we are," said Miss Whitman, as we reached the doorway to a small, cold, top-floor room. Inside were two narrow beds, a bureau and two desks. Father set down the valise. Miss Whitman looked at Father. "You can go now," she said.

"Good-bye, Emily," said Father.

"Good-bye," I said, and he was gone.

I felt lost—without my skin. I must have looked pale.

"Are you not feeling well?" Miss Whitman asked.

"Not very," I managed. I was feeling feverish.

"You'd best lie down."

"What about my examinations?"

"Those will have to wait."

I slept for several hours, wrapped in my shawl and

under several blankets. When I woke, there was a girl sitting on the bed across from mine. "You slept through supper," she said.

"What?" I was still partway asleep and not entirely sure of where I was, or to whom I was speaking.

"I didn't want to wake you."

Just then I realized it was my dear and pious cousin Emily Norcross who spoke. She was to be my roommate. I had known this fact for some time. It had eased my concern about coming to the school. She held a small package wrapped in a napkin. "I brought you some bread."

"Thank you." I sat up and took the package she offered, holding it in my lap. We smiled then and embraced. I almost dropped the bread, but caught it just before it fell off the edge of the bed.

"Miss Whitman said you were sick," Cousin Emily continued.

"Yes."

"And that you must wait to take the examinations."

"Yes."

"I bet you wish you could get them over with."

"I do."

"They are not so bad."

Her words offered comfort. Cousin Emily was a senior and in my opinion knew all about everything. "Is it true that those who don't pass their examinations get sent home straightway?" I asked.

"It can happen."

"I hope it doesn't happen to me."

"It won't."

"One never knows. I would hate to disgrace myself the moment I arrived."

"It's too late for that," she said. "You've been here for several hours."

It was good to laugh. I pulled my shawl around my shoulders, then grabbed the blanket as well. "It's freezing in here."

"I know."

"Is it always like this?"

"Mostly."

"I feel as if we're in the Arctic."

"At the very least."

"I'm glad I didn't bring my plants."

"A wise choice. Let me help you unpack." Cousin Emily was exceedingly kind. She had experienced terrible things, having lost both parents to consumption, yet she never failed to consider other people. I was extremely grateful for her presence. A good roommate may be the single most important thing to have when one is away at school. Abiah had told me this and she was right.

My cold improved quickly, a welcome and unusual occurrence for yours truly in the illness line. I was able to take my examinations in three days, applying myself with a determination unknown even to me. I seemed to have left my heart—my very breath—outside the door. A separate faction took up the pen, answering the questions with an ease that was really quite amazing. But when I set down my pen, I was seized by a terror so intense as to chill the blood. It was as if I had been tossed off the side of a ship and me not knowing how to swim. I sat alone in the small examination room at the wooden desk by the window, pen down, work done, afraid and wondering.

How are they at Home? Do they need my smile? Will Father do without my bread?

It was a troubling thought that he might die for lack of it, yet a thought more troubling that he would *not* die, but would live in good health, well satisfied without me.

That night was a sleepless affair, feet cold, pillow unfamiliar. Comfort was not my friend. I longed for my brother, our Night Talks, the slant of his mind, the red contrariness of his hair. And Vinnie! Oh, I missed her too, my bed partner lo these many years. I missed our little dramas. Where was Father's sureness, his steady hand, Mother's quiet way, her meals to warm the heart? Where was my Abby, my 'Biah, my garden, my white House, my piano, my apron, the cows, the common, Mr. Cutler's store, the Pelham Hills in all their glory?!

Light began outside the window. I had not slept at all.

After breakfast and half awake, I learned that I had passed all my examinations. I was greatly relieved. There were three classes, Junior, Middle and Senior. I was placed in the Junior class for review, with a plan to move ahead to Middle Studies as soon as possible. I was glad not to have disappointed Father.

When we left the dining room, Cousin Emily showed me about the school. Everything went on in one building. Over 230 girls resided here and 12 teachers as well, all living, learning, eating, sleeping and dreaming beneath a single roof. As we walked along the main-floor hallway, a woman came toward us from the far end of the passage. I watched the woman approach, a veritable tornado of energy! Cousin Emily tilted her head in my direction. "Miss Lyon," she whispered.

The "storm" greeted us warmly, welcomed me as "one of the new ones" and proceeded on her way.

"She may be the most energetic person I have ever known," said Cousin Emily, when we found ourselves out of ear's reach of our Seminary's lively Queen Bee.

"I believe it."

"She never stops. Her primary concern is that women should be educated."

"An obvious position."

"Many consider the matter to be of little importance."

"That doesn't make it so," I declared as we started up the stairs to our Arctic Hide-away.

As I came to know our Principal, I saw that my cousin was right. Miss Lyon had made the imperative issue of the education of women her life's work, and for that I hold her in high esteem. I soon discovered that my first impression of her was right as well—a tornado of energy! I sometimes doubted she slept at all. She appeared tireless, determined and very much involved in all matters of the school. It would not be unusual to find her in the kitchen, cooking stew! She believed in expanding the mind, in exercising the body, in experiencing the arts and in becoming a Christian.

That evening, after meeting Miss Lyon, I suffered greatly as I was extremely homesick. I wrote Abiah about it. I told her I thought I could not stay another day and would have to return to my beloved Home straightway if I could be expected to go on living. This may sound overly dramatic, but dramatic or not, that is the way it was.

The Dungeon Fear and the
Condition of My Shoes

O n the morning of my fourth day at school I awoke in the company of Possibility. I cannot say why. As I dressed that freezing morning, I had trouble understanding the earlier torment in my brain. My life at Mt Holyoke Seminary had begun!

Here is my schedule, exactly as it was.

6. oclock, rise.

7. Breakfast.

8. Study.

9. Devotions.

10¼. Ancient History—Goldsmith &
    Grimshaw—that weighty tome.

11. Recitation, or Composition—my favorite!

12. Calisthenics.

12¼. read.

12½. Dinner.

1½. Singing.

2. free

2¾–3¾. Piano.

3¾. Sections—where one receives accounts of "exceptions," being one's inappropriate deeds, requiring a *black mark*—decidedly not desired!

4½. Lecture from Miss Lyon.

6. Supper, then silent study hours.

8¾. retiring bell.

9¾. tardy bell.

There were variations as pertained to courses current, such as Chemistry, Physiology, Algebra, Botany and others, but the pattern of the day remained the same.

I threw myself into the activities with no small amount of enthusiasm. Oh, and my beloved Jennie was there as well!—my bed-jumping partner from the golden days of Home! Jennie was a senior, along with Cousin Emily. Both were extremely busy with separate activities, but they were *there* just the same! It seemed as if I would be quite happy after all.

Austin came to visit in but two weeks' time, bringing Abby and Vinnie! What joy to embrace them once more and to hear how they missed me! It is a grand thing to be missed by those you love, too grand almost, for one is in danger of one's miserly thoughts claiming their viselike grip—wanting the far-off beloved to pine. "Be unhappy without me!" the mind calls out. "Find no rose without

I be at your side!" I must confess to hearing thoughts like these echo within my wicked mind and I know they should be whipped! What is to be done with me?

Austin arrived on a Saturday, bringing not only Abby and Vinnie but cake, gingerbread, peaches, pie, apples, chestnuts and grapes! A feast! Mother had selected the items with considerable care, polished the apples and of course done all the baking concerned. What a time we had! I showed my dear ones all about the school and we talked and laughed—oh, it did the heart good! It was an auspicious day. The leaves put all their colors on—a dome of flaming gold!

I watched from the window until the three were gone. When they could be seen no more, I went straightway to my room to count my treasures and to share those remaining with my dear cousin, who appreciated them greatly. After that I decided to blacken and brush my shoes, as Mother had apparently expressed concern to Austin as to their well-being. I had instructed Austin to tell Mother not to worry, that Cousin Emily had all the equipment needed to keep my shoes looking finely and that I would polish them that very evening in Mother's honor.

I missed hearing from Mother. I had warned myself not to expect her to write, as she seldom wrote to anyone. When Father was away, her letters to him were brief. "A few sentences," she confessed to me one day, "and then I don't know what else to say." I often thought that if Mother ever got started, she might enjoy that grand gathering of the humble members of the alphabet to spell a truth, the thoughtful selection of just the ones needed to form the Words to speak one's Voice! Somehow she preferred dusting, or cleaning leaves from the eave spout.

Father wrote frequently—warnings and encouragements along the path of life—as did Austin and Abby, Abiah and Vinnie too. I wrote them back just as often as I could. I liked to play with our names. Vinnie became Viny. Why not? And I was sometimes Emilie. I felt the name to be more romantic. I have always considered "Emily" a serious name. "Emilie" is suited to petticoats and ribbons and dancing in the meadow in May.

I grew fond of my new home. There were many exceedingly pleasant young ladies in attendance. And the food! I never expected it to be so delicious! Cooking for so many girls cannot be easy, but the meals tasted finely. Here is a King's dinner, one representing our usual Fare.

Roast. Veal.
Potatoes.
Squash.
Gravy.

153

Wheat & Brown-Bread.

Butter.

Pepper & Salt.

Dessert.

Apple-Dumpling.

Sauce.

Water.

It was not long before I had a grand surprise. It was a Wednesday—why I remember that fact I cannot say— and as I looked from my window, in the direction of the hotel, there were Mother and Father, walking toward the Seminary! And did they not look the respectable pair! I ran from my room and down the stairs and onto the road, flying—as one with wings—to meet them. I could not have been more delighted, or more surprised, as they had said *nothing* to me about their plan to come.

It was hard to let them go.

And then it happened.

Just when it seemed that all was well and that I really would one day join the others as a grownup and on my own in the Large World, I experienced a terror too Large to qualify. I could tell no one. I felt that to speak of it would make it real, and *that* I could not bear. Did I belong in Father's favorite Lunatic Asylum, the one in

154

Worcester he had so fervently insisted I visit?

Here is how it was.

I am in the basement, where the dining room and kitchens are found. It is just after dinnertime. It will soon be time for singing. We are to receive the music for our fall concert. I hope for my favorite Monteverdi, a merry piece with a strong soprano part.

I set down my napkin. As I stand up, my heart skips a beat, tumbling over the side, then in an instant, bouncing back, catching pace with its appointed rounds. I hold the edge of the table to steady myself. I hear the voices of the other girls, leaving the dining room, chatting amongst themselves—noise only, no words.

What are they saying?

I try to breathe. Can't seem to. I look down at the table—knives, forks, plates and bits of food abandoned.

Collect the knives. Save your life.

Daily I must carry the knives from the first tier of tables, then wash and wipe the selfsame number of knives at night. I pick up a knife. And another. My hands are cold, the knives too heavy. I drop one. I pick it up. I am sleepy-tired. My legs feel heavy. The kitchen looks far away. I can't breathe below my throat.

What is happening to me?

My heart pounds!

What am I afraid of?

No answer save the ceaseless pounding, the name-less dread, the gaping zero at the center of Nothing.

I try once more to breathe, but cannot.

How does one breathe?

Girls push in their chairs, mill about, carrying plates. I think I should ask someone how to breathe. They all seem to know. But I can't speak.

I have to get to the kitchen.

One foot.

Other foot.

One foot.

Other foot.

I cannot!

Heart pounding.

It's too far.

Terror!

Where am I?

Terror.

Who am I?

Terror.

Does it matter?

I don't exist.

All I can feel is the fear.

"Ky-ri-e e-le-i-son!"

Somehow I was with the others, singing. As we

joined our voices in song, the awesome fear began to lift. I cannot say where it came from and that is by far the most terrible part. Even as the Terror lessened, a fright was in my bones that would never be gone, always with me—the Fear of the Fear returning—the Dungeon Fear—never knowing when it would come, never knowing why. These thoughts were in my mind as I sang, and all the while Monteverdi's beautiful music comforting me, fighting with the dark, winning.

But really?

Silent Friend

I was back in my room, under three blankets and shawl on top, exhausted from my Terror in the basement. Soon it would be time for supper. I must go back down to face the Dungeon Fear, wash and dry the knives and hope to get out alive. I told myself there was nothing to be afraid of. It would not happen again. But I did not believe myself. That's when I thought of the peas—when I was young, of needing to eat them all lest their feelings be hurt, lest they feel abandoned. It was more than childish fancy. I *had* to eat them to avoid disaster.

I pulled the covers tight about my chin. I was tired, but could not sleep.

Will I ever sleep again?

I thought of the day I had been unable to leave my bonnet on the bed. It was no game. Once again I was avoiding disaster. And that was my thought in the basement. Disaster was coming.

I did not have the Dungeon Fear that night, for which I was most grateful. I felt I must get a grip on it, lest it throw me to the wind. The most terrible part of the Dungeon Fear is that when it comes I cannot find myself. The fear is so great as to dispel all knowing—even the knowledge that I exist. And that is the worst.

I will write a poem.

I remembered the sense I had when composing verses that I was with my Self—that sense of knowing who I was, of having a voice, of *existing*! One must realize that one exists, or life is a dreary tale at best. I thought of my elephant box, my childhood reminders within, those poems that brought me to my Self: the dog demands his birthright, the worm craves the moist black earth, a place for Father's shoes, my flower with the grandest friends. In my brain I was *there*, writing them, feeling the joy of connection to my *Self*. When writing those poems, I had had that connection more than with anything—like breathing deep on a summer day, laughing with Jennie, or digging in the garden—only more!

I lit the lamp. Cousin Emily was fast asleep. I took up my pencil and paper.

I cannot remember more than the first line. "There is a fright so awful, it gathers meaning up." The line pleased me. And best of all, I was *there*! The edges of a poem serve to hold a fear or joy or other and make it governable. They hold a thing in such a way that one may see it and not be overcome.

159

Later that week Miss Lyon gave a lecture entitled "We May Become What We Will." While I enjoyed the sense of possibility in her viewpoint, it did not entirely correspond with my own. I raised my hand. "What if a poor child were crippled and willed to be the fastest runner in the world?" I asked. "I don't see how any measure of will could be of assistance in her determination to run the fastest."

I don't think Miss Lyon was pleased with my query. She said I had raised an interesting question but had missed the point she had so carefully attempted to make. I was by no means sure of what that point was, so in that respect I suppose she was correct.

That first lecture served as a send-off to the numerous ones to follow, all given by Miss Lyon on the weighty subject of Religion. If the Seminary had a basic purpose in the mind of our fearless leader, it was to turn all its well-brought-up young ladies into Christians. I daresay the pinnacle of excellence might be attained by first off accepting Christ into one's heart and after that becoming the wife of a missionary. The first of these events was by no means against my better judgment, assuming that I in all honesty felt the calling to do so, but the idea of traveling to some far-off place to smile at members of a differing society while hoping they might trade their well-established ways for those of my husband was by no means an appealing thought. I would sooner converse with the daisies!

Every day we were called upon to give ourselves to Christ before it was too late. The matter was of no small concern to me, as I felt an emptiness growing inside my heart, a split from the other girls, who seemed to have an ease with life that I had not been granted. Were I to give myself to Christ would all be assuaged? I did not think so, but more important still, I was not moved in that direction. Father had often praised the Puritan Ethic—self-reliance, hard work, economy and a refusal to accept any way of life that would take away the responsibility of deciding for oneself what was true. Why would I give myself to Christ to decide for me?

Each day one was certain to see at least one notice in the hall, announcing the all-important lectures for the day, such as DEPRAVITY, DEATH AND DAMNATION AT 2¼ OCLOCK, or THE MORTIFICATION OF THE IMPENITENT AT 3. It was a veritable battlefield through which one was required to pass if one desired any peace whatsoever!

In addition to the lectures we were divided into two groups pertaining to our status as regarded becoming Christians. Miss Whitman met with those who were already Christians, along with those who had hope of becoming same, Miss Scott with all the impenitent. I was of the latter. We were not forced to accept Christ into our hearts, yet one felt the pressure most keenly to seek the salvation of our Souls. Here I encountered difficulty, as the idea of Original Sin had never made sense to me. There were several other Christian precepts—in addition to Original Sin—that troubled me as well. I recall asking who it was wrote the Bible. When being told it was "Holy Men . . . moved by the Holy Ghost," I found the answer puzzling, to say the least. Who were these Holy Men? And who was it exactly they were moved by? Were there Holy Women? I heard much about the "Father and the Son," but where did I come in?

In my meetings with Miss Scott and the other impenitent girls, my thoughts returned to these questions. I sat tall, back straight against the rungs of the unforgiving chair, hands clasped in lap, attention on the earnest face of our teacher, the cadence of her words, those Bible passages on Human Depravity and the miserable Eternity that lay beyond for such as we, yet in the corner of my obstinate brain I remained unmoved. I felt the longing, the sense of being left behind, of missing what mattered most, and still the nagging voice:

Hold fast to what feels true.

When others with "no hope" began to go over to the other side, accepting Christ as they were expected to do, I felt their pity. They wondered that I did not feel strange holding back when so many had moved to the Comforting Arms of our Noble Savior. It did feel strange, yet it would have felt stranger to be dishonest. There was a different soil on which I found my feet, as when listening to Professor Hitchcock at the Academy. At those times my heart took flight—to open sky—to Possibility—to the existence of things unseen. His phrase "science *proves* religion" unlocked a frightful jam in reason, and I could breathe.

We were all thoroughly delighted at the prospect of Thanksgiving! Much as I loved the excitement of Mt Holyoke—the girls, the teachers, the acquisition of edifications regarding the history of Sulphuric Acid, the application of proper grammatical usage and many other points of intellectual improvement too numerous to mention—there is no place in the World to compare with the sanctity of Home. The time was to be treasured, especially as we would be denied such luxury at Christmastime. That "Pagan Festival," as it was described by our virtuous and exceedingly energetic Principal, would have to pass unnoticed, by us at any rate. No stocking on my bedpost, bulging with thoughtful surprises. Not this year.

I was in the midst of writing another poem. We had been reading *Hamlet*, and I, swept away by the plight of that sorry Dane, had been toying with some verses that had sprung from an unknown corridor of my brain. The poem lived on two small scraps of paper that I kept in the pocket of my favorite calico. I had written two other poems that fall, those having found themselves at last, home in all their Spartan glory, in the top drawer of my chest, beneath the handkerchiefs. Poems are too personal to be strewn across the landscape in random fashion, to be stumbled upon by whichever disinterested party the wind might design! The first poem was the one about the Dungeon Fear. The second was a Valentine. Born as it was months before its time, it waited, needing to come into itself. Some poems appear at once, complete, as if by reason of their own design. Others need time to change and grow as I help to edge them home. The *Hamlet* poem was to travel with me to Amherst that Thanksgiving—a silent friend, constant through all the coming and goings of the unexpected.

The Wednesday before Thanksgiving Austin came for me in the carriage. He would be taking Cousin Emily and yours truly home. The rain poured down that day, the wind howled and the brooks rushed, swelling to over-flow their expected beds, but nothing could dampen our spirits.

When the carriage stopped in front of my own dear Home I thought my heart would burst with the glory of it—and there to greet us, Mother, all tears, and Vinnie smiling, blue shawl about her shoulders. And let us not forget the cats! Pussy, tail high, wove about Vinnie's feet. Roughnaps and Snugglepoops sat staring from the darkness of the Hallway, eyes wide, suspicious, as if we might be out to steal their peace. Noopsie Possum was not in evidence. No doubt a nap detained her elsewhere.

Austin carried our valises upstairs. As could be expected, there was all manner of fussing from Mother—were we wet, were we tired, were we hungry and did we want some tea.

"Yes, to all!" I told her.

What extraordinary days, those four at Home! Father was in fine form, regaling us with stories—including one about a group of neighbors who had banded together in search of a goat who had escaped from one of their barns, only to be found some weeks later, sitting on the owner's front porch with a boot in its mouth. The boot belonged to another in the group, who had been searching for it with no success and had not a thought in the world that the two disappearances might be related. Father played all the parts, including the goat, who under no circumstances could be convinced to give up his treasure!

Thanksgiving morning was clear and *freezing*! I could only imagine what it must have been like at school, high up in my Arctic Chamber! Mother told us that her feet were "as cold as ice" and the pump handle was "frozen solid"! Mother had raised the handle high to keep it from freezing—*The Frugal Housewife*, page 16—as she always did in winter before retiring, but with all the excitement of our return, had neglected to throw the horse blanket over the pump, as her "personal Bible" suggested.

We skipped breakfast, going first to church, where we heard a cautionary sermon from Reverend Colton on The Perils of Retribution. Upon our return we had dinner, then calls and visits. Abby, and Mary Warner—new to Amherst, pretty, humble, with exceptional hair—and a handsome gentleman by the name of Bowdoin who worked in Father's office, and of course Vinnie, Austin, myself, Cousin Emily and others spent a most enjoyable evening at the Macks'. It was nearly nine oclock when we returned home.

That night Father wanted to hear me play the piano. Nothing would do but that I play for him, several tunes, to which he listened with evident gratitude. And smiled! Especially when I played my own thundering composition entitled "The Devil." Times such as those are joy upon joy. Father does not often share his Soul.

A sad note at that Thanksgiving time. We learned that beautiful Olivia Coleman—the very same girl who had provoked such jealousy among the members of our

Magic Circle—had died in Princeton, New Jersey. It was Consumption did it. She had been gone a year and a half to that far-off place and I had no idea how sick she was. Eliza had been the frail one. As if that were not enough to bear, our neighbor, Jacob Holt, was stricken with the culprit as well. Austin's rooster had been crowing under Jacob's window for reasons unclear. I was vexed about it but was told it was amusing to Jacob, who could use all the amusement he could get.

Monday came too quickly. I hated to leave Home. I felt I would not be safe away. And what of Father and Mother? I recall my thought as I drove off the carriage.

My smile is small, but might be just the one they need.

A Place to Stand

I will now quote my grammar book, an irksome companion during my stay at Mt Holyoke. The book is called *English Grammar*, a bold assumption if I ever heard one, and is said to have been written by a certain Lindley Murray—or Murray Lindley—I forget which. I quote: "The dash, though often used improperly by hasty and incoherent writers, may be used with propriety, where the sentence breaks off abruptly; where a significant pause is required; or when there is an unexpected turn in the sentiment."

When I think of my love for the dash I fear I join the ranks of the improper, hasty and incoherent writers sprinkled carelessly about the globe like so many errant pebbles. But I love it so—its liveliness, its thrust, its enviable ability to include a thought, yet separate that same just far enough from its preceding colleagues to keep the meaning straight. Its boldness, its daring, its sense of abandon! And the freedom, the effortless flow. Why, it takes my breath away! I doubtless express my thoughts with the utmost impropriety. No matter. It will have to do. One can't have everything, as the saying goes nowadays.

It was not an easy thing to return to Mt Holyoke after the Holiday. Loneliness became my constant companion. I felt I would surely die without I was in the arms of my beloved family. As one might expect, my grammar book was of little consolation. My *Hamlet* poem, however, was. When at Home I had not been afforded the leisure to visit it, but now at night, lessons completed—dashes and all!—I arranged my thoughts on those modest scraps from my pocket. The noble Prince's loneliness met mine—as mine met his. The arrangement afforded comfort. I feel when I am lonely that no one in the universe knows that certain pain—has never known it—and I, a lonely Soul, made lonelier by my false surmise. To know I am not alone—there begins a place to stand!

I was soon back in form as life at school reclaimed its relentless sweep through the hours of my being. Silliman's *Chemistry*, Cutler's *Physiology*, Samuel Phillips Newman's *Practical System of Rhetoric*—these were my Preceptors. And let us not forget Olmsted's *Compendium of Astronomy*, containing the merriest illustrations, not to mention the latest discoveries, although for how long they would be considered "late" I could not surmise.

On marched the lectures, the outstretched Arms of Christ awaiting the surrender of us poor souls with "no

hope," a dwindling group. And the rules! No Throwing
Things from the Windows; No Speaking Above a Whisper
in the Washroom; No Sleeping with the Door Closed—
an odd rule if I ever heard one!—and many others too
numerous to mention. There were chores, walks in the
cold, calisthenics, studies, accounts, meetings, lectures
and compositions. There was singing, practice upon
the piano, reading—*Othello* and the magnificent *female*
poet Elizabeth Barrett Browning. What strong verses for
a woman to write. How brave!

My birthday passed unnoticed—I taking examination in the mathematics of Euclid to mark the day. It
seems birthdays fall in the same category as Christmas at
Mt Holyoke, considered serious days for contemplation
rather than occasions for dreaded frivolous celebration.
I turned seventeen quietly, in the space of my own brain,
with none but that certain well-known mathematician
for company.

Christmas was the loneliest I can remember. We
stayed at school and quiet—a gruesome exercise! Alone
and small at school, I thought of Home. A fire in the
fireplace. Father's slippers by the chair. Candy in my
stocking. Christmas Eve late with Austin and us two by
the hearth. Mother's snow pudding. The currant wine,
the singing. Father's smile. Vinnie snoring on the couch
after dinner and Noopsie Possum upside down, asleep

at her side. Pussy and Snugglepoops washing themselves with their rough tongues. Roughnaps attacking a bit of colored ribbon on the parlor floor and the silent snow falling outside the window, the chickadee on the branch—puffed out—air between feathers to fortify against the cold and Mother on the lounge, feet up, under the woolen blanket. I play a tune on the piano. Father has asked!

It was different now. Silence. Fasting. A Meeting of the Impenitent. The senseless and troubling rule—No Lying on the Quilt. A melancholy overtook me. I missed my family, my Abby, my Abiah. Though Jennie was at school she had no time for her bed-jumping partner, a fact that caused me considerable grief. Cousin Emily's presence was dear and yet I felt, despite her kindness, that no one understood me. The other girls could deal with life. I could not. I had a thinner skin.

The days after Christmas were filled with Meetings of the Impenitent. We were *not* penitent, *not* remorseful for our sins. As the primary sin in question was Original Sin and since I did not believe that I or any other of God's creatures had been born in it, I had a hard time feeling remorseful for something that never happened. No matter. Each afternoon the Impenitent were called to meet with Miss Lyon in Room B to discuss the seriousness of our situation. The topics discussed included, but were not limited to, Hardness of the Heart, Damnation, Choose Ye This Day Whom Ye Will Serve, Excuses Made by Sinners for Not Submitting to Jesus Now, Total Depravity, and The Nature of Sin.

As we neared the time for our winter vacation—it began late in January—our numbers were fading. Each night another would weep, then the walls of reticence all awash, cross to the shore of Everlasting Protection, and I alone at sea, amid the storms of uncertainty, left to fend for myself. When the term ended I was very much relieved. Two whole weeks in the bosom of my Family!

Upon my arrival Vinnie looked more beautiful than ever, her dimensions being the envy of all the girls. She was beginning to attract considerable interest from the boys in her class, a delight to her and a matter of grave concern to Father. Vinnie and I laughed a great deal, outdoing each other with precise, perceptive mimic of many an unsuspecting neighbor. At night in our bed I told her disaster stories, the kind she so admired, making them up as I went along, or exaggerating details from actual events at school.

Mother was not well. I forget what the trouble was—a dullness of mood and something with the feet. We had to be quiet so as not to interrupt her rest. Father had just had a birthday, and not having been with him to share it,

I baked him some delicious gingerbread as a present. In addition I drew him a picture in which he was carrying an extremely large briefcase, and me at the door of our house, holding the bread as he approached. He said he would keep the picture always, if not the bread. That he would eat.

That same night Father told me I would not be returning to Mt Holyoke after the first year. The Seminary program is of three years' duration. Although most girls complete one year only, I thought, being of superior intellect and doing so well in my studies, Father might consider me an exception. Several girls were completing a full two years. But Father felt a year was enough for his "delicate flower." The ease and peace of Home would be best for my fragile constitution. I would end my schooling in August.

I was of two minds regarding Father's decision. I would miss the studies. There is so much to learn in this world and always things one did not know before. I find it exciting to spend days gathering insight into the many wonders all around. And we had fine teachers. I would miss them and many of the girls as well. I would *not* miss the endless Meetings of the Impenitent, nor the lectures on the dire consequences of being left "without hope." There was much to be said for going my own way, in my own Home, with loved ones about and books, my piano, my plants, my garden—all the most precious things of the Earth.

Vacation flew by, affording glorious days with Austin—caught up in reading *The Arabian Nights*—Abby and my new friend, Mary Warner—ever modest—her hair as long as ever I saw hair grow! Some fine Whiskers caught my attention. First, *Thomas*!—the *most* attractive young gentleman I may ever have seen! There was little conversation with us, but always the hope of more and watching to see if he was watching me. I have to say that sometimes I believe he *was*! There was also Bowdoin, from Father's office, with whom I spent several enjoyable evenings, both alone and in general company. Bowdoin is ten years older than yours truly, a fact I find exciting, especially when I consider the attention paid so lowly a one as me.

Back to school and Valentine's Week. No Valentines for me. Not a single one! All the girls were getting them. Well, maybe not *all*, but most, while I—desirable, witty, accomplished young maiden—was totally overlooked. I imagined Vinnie received many Valentines, but did not ask as I feared the truth would be less than encouraging.

Miss Lyon was not in favor of "foolish" Valentines, as she liked to call them, and forbade our sending any.

Most of the girls got around the matter by writing their Valentines early and getting them to the Post Office in secret. I admired their sense of adventure.

The weather was cold. No—it was *freezing*! Soon I felt not well, with sore throat and cough and all those familiar visitors who arrive without invitation and give no sign of future plans.

Awful Shock

❦

My cold grew worse. I made every attempt to ignore the situation as I was enjoying my studies and enjoying some new aquaintances. No one was as dear to me as Abby or Abiah, but I did possess a fondness for several of the girls, which was really quite wonderful. The thought of leaving them and all the activity of school only to return to my bed, with Father's constant ministering of unpleasant remedies, was not one I welcomed. I preferred to remain at school, free of the scourge of dosings from the famous "cold box." A bleak portrait passed before my mind—Me, body flat, face pale, Father ministering, physician prodding, days with no names, "good deed ladies" visiting, Mother anxiously fussing. It was a dreary picture and so I kept my lips sealed.

After examinations were completed I was found out. At that time friends were allowed to visit. Mary—with the long hair—and Abby came to see me, but I was so sick that I could barely enjoy the visit. They could see how sick I was. I asked them not to tell Mother and Father, but my wishes were ignored. Mary told them. It

176

was concern for my welfare made her tell. Saturday next, Austin appeared in the carriage to bring me Home.

The picture my brain had painted was nearly an exact match to the real thing. I spent a full month in the "extra room," free from Vinnie's snoring, but not free from Father's tonics, physician's queries, helpful ladies, and Mother's anxious peering around the door, inquiring as to the state of my cough. I had not pictured the cats. They consider the "extra room" theirs. My presence in their quarters was viewed as a rude intrusion. Noopsie Possum took the whole business in stride, but was the only one, sleeping flat on the floor in the patch of sunlight by the window, waking occasionally for short periods to wash. Roughnaps had an entertaining habit of leaping in the air, boxing at specks of dust that shimmered in the rays of Noopsie Possum's sunlight, while Snugglepoops strode in and out as the fancy moved him. Upon entering, he would stare at me with a put-upon expression, often with a poor half-dead bird locked between his jaws, then slink beneath the bed to complete the evil deed. Pussy sat in the window oblivious to the goings-on, making deep-throated growling noises as she stared at the fortunate feathered travelers who had escaped the deadly pursuits of her brother. It was quite a show and served to help pass the time when I was too weak to read. Oh, but when I felt well enough I met my

Lexicon—those precious Words—with precious time to spend in joyful company! I read *Evangeline* and began a wonderful true adventure, *Two Years Before the Mast*, that being by Richard Henry Dana. I admire his spunk. He said, "No!" to those nasty measles, "I won't have you! Be Gone!" and took to the sea for *two years*! The Ocean winds blew the unwanted intruders away—split them with the force of all the elements, scattering them to points unknown! Blessed recompense!

In a month's time I improved enough to return to join "the snorer," leaving the cats to fend for themselves. Vinnie and I had many good times, my strength returning and me able to tell my famous disaster stories before falling into sleep. Vinnie especially liked the one about the dwarf carpenter who fell through the window of a house he was building and was impaled on the iron spike of a fence below, the spike going into his stomach and out his narrow back. That was my version of a piece in the *Republican* that had somehow escaped Vinnie's attention.

I stayed at home for the duration of the term, enjoying the absence of fever and in general reassuring my parents with my presence. It was a time of peace, with long-awaited spring flowers, yellow violets, trailing arbutus, not to mention liverleaf, adder's-tongue and bloodroot. What gruesome names they have! And always there was the church bell tolling its sad announcement—

Another Gone. The number of rings signaled the age of the dead—relative, neighbor, friend—and always the prayer to keep that black-clothed Angel at length from the nest.

Bowdoin stopped by from Father's office to inquire after my well-being. I was awfully happy to see him. Abby visited too. We had many serious discussions about religion. Abby was about to surrender to those Waiting Arms. She expressed such a desire to be good that it took my breath away.

The day set to return to South Hadley offered a surprise in the form of a sudden storm so wild as to delay the trip. It was Thursday. Why do I remember that? The mind has mysterious ways that I for one shall never understand. But Thursday it was and rain and wind howling and Father's pronouncement that travel would be unwise. Friday was beautiful, however, as if Mother Nature's commotion had been only a dream.

There was considerable schoolwork to make up, I having missed so great an amount while away. But I had done some at home and the rest I worked extra hours to complete. It was warmer now and I enjoyed my quiet room, with oil lamp, water pitcher, washbowl and gentle cousin.

The term passed quickly. News from home included

the sad recounting of our neighbor Jacob Holt's death. Austin's persistent rooster had failed in his attempts to keep poor Jacob awake. So many deaths. And always more. Most memorable in the line of lighter news was the entertaining circumstance of Bowdoin attempting to deliver letters to me from home and being nearly overcome by the hysterical teacher watchdogs poised to discourage any and all contact with the "Whisker Set." The rules were strict on the matter. No visits without prior notification and approval of the watchdogs, brief visits in the parlor in the company of selfsame guardians! It was a good thing Bowdoin didn't have his head cut off, appearing as he did unexpectedly with the mail. That would have been less than paltry payment indeed for his performance of so gracious an errand!

So went my final days at school. I enjoyed the springtime walks in the woods with Cousin Emily, dear Jennie, who had a bit of time for me *at last*, and my many classmates. I often went alone—except for the mountains and the birds, the trees and the sky and the constant stream that runs through the grounds. There was piano practice—one hour a day only—Composition, Astronomy, Reading—that being *King Lear* as well as a merry little book called *The Stone*, and the ever-popular Rhetoric. I enjoyed that class quite a lot, although at times found it to be a somewhat arbitrary business. I looked up the word in Mr. Webster's book. "Rhetoric: The study of the elements used in literature and public speaking, such as content, structure, cadence and style." A succinct appraisal, yet lacking in the mysterious elements that add the "bite." How capital a thing it is that all those words can be gathered under one roof. I marvel at the beauty of it! What Miracles exist that my wondrous Friends can be put together in as many ways as there are grains of sand on all the beaches in all the countries of the world! Words put in certain order can lift the heart and pierce the darkness! God is grand indeed! And so is Mr. Webster! I saw his portrait at school. He looked extremely serious, but perhaps one must be serious for such Large work.

At the end of school—our Holyoke Anniversary—I had an awful shock. We were gathered in the hall. The Reverend Beecher—Edward, to be exact—delivered the address. I looked up to see far across the way—Abiah! What joy! Her letters had warmed me all the year through, but never once did she mention attending my graduation.

Abiah!

My heart raced! I wanted to run and embrace her but could not until the minister had had his say. Moments Eternal! At last he was done. There was a great shuffling, crowding, congratulating. I pushed rudely through the mass of people.

She was gone.

My world tipped.

Did she forget me?

Breath short, heart quick, knees weak.

Does she hate me? Has she ceased to care?

I searched the room and down the stairs and in the yard and down the road. She was nowhere. In a troubled state I ended my time at Mt Holyoke, returning to the bosom of my family where solace has always been a noted companion.

Upon my arrival Home the smells from the kitchen told the tale. I do believe Mother to be the most excellent cook in the entire world. Nowhere can a meal be found to equal hers! And there we were—the Special Five—together at the table! Austin looked so handsome, red hair all ascramble, and Vinnie, demure, eyes steady, quite the young lady. Mother possessed a most peaceful look that day, and I've never seen Father so happy. He smiled! And not only that, he told the funniest stories. One was about a cow that was found looking into the window of Mr. Cutler's store. Father suggested she might have fancied a bit of shopping. Mother got to laughing over that. All of us did and Father more than any. I like to think Father's superior mood that day was due to my return, but it may have been the pudding. Mother's cornstarch pudding can lift his spirits when all else fails.

I expected Home might feel different to me now after having been away at school, but it did not. I felt myself straightway back to the old routine and experienced a feeling of safety and belonging I had not felt while away. I wondered if I had grown up at all being on my own those many months and decided that I had not.

That evening Abby and I sat on the front door stone in the bright moonlight and talked and talked. How grand it was to be with my "particular friend" once more. I told her all about how I had seen Abiah at the graduation and how she had disappeared.

"Are you sure it was Abiah?" Abby asked.

"I'm sure."

"You could have been mistaken."

"I know Abiah."

"Why did she come without telling you?"

"I don't know."

"Maybe she told you she was coming, but you forgot."

"I wouldn't forget. "

"It's possible."

"It's not likely."

The moon was large and low, a round, flat disc of a moon, so bright it hurt my eyes. I squinted to ease the pain. Abby was holding Noopsie Possum on her lap. "Let's think about this," Abby said. "You mean she just disappeared?"

"That's what I mean."

"She wouldn't do that."

"She would if she was angry with me. I asked her to come to Amherst this summer, but she never answered."

"Perhaps she didn't get your letter. She may have been waiting for a response from a letter she had written to you, but it never came, so she thought you were ignoring her."

"Then why did she come to my graduation?"

"Because she wanted to see you."

"Then why did she leave?"

"She wanted to see you, but since she thought you had been ignoring her, when she *did* see you, she suddenly felt afraid to approach and so she left."

"I doubt that."

"It could be." Noopsie Possum was resting in a circle on Abby's lap, and Abby stroking her soft fur. "Letters do not always reach their destination. You should write to her again."

In the midst of a deep drowse, Noopsie Possum took a notion to turn her head upside down on Abby's lap. Chin to the heavens, she purred loudly.

I did not immediately write to Abiah, as I did not

wish to force a response I might not care to receive. Deep down I am cowardly and not pleased with myself one bit, but I am the only self I've got and must make the best of it.

Whiskers

Gigantic events were about to unfold for me, and this humble daisy completely in the dark! Things so Large as to defy imagining ahead on the road, and none less informed than the traveler! We think "such and such" or "this and that" but underneath, where the meanings are, another tale is told. Search the Corridors, question the Corners, ask the Stars and the Truth will out!

Amherst was gay that fall. There were carriage rides, concerts, lectures, promenades, charades, parties, picnics, strolls and hikes—there is a difference in these last two, the former being more of a ramble, the latter driven by purpose—and all accompanied by singing and funny stories, being due most often to the wit of a certain irreverent young lady—me! I must say that I was enjoying life. Home again and Abby and Austin and Vinnie and Whiskers all about!

Abby and I quickly divided the Whiskers into two groups. Those of the first were preferred. Those of the second were handsome and charming as well and only slightly less enticing. I list them below.

1st Group

Henry Vaughn Emmons
John Graves (Cousin John)
Eldridge Bowdoin
Thurston Adams
(Thomas was gone by then, or he surely would have been included!)

2nd Group

Joseph Lyman
George Gould
John Milton Emerson
Henry Martyn Storrs
Henry Root
Brainerd Harrington
The Howland brothers (William and George)

Emmons was a beautiful friend, his eyes black and bright as stars. One has the feeling those eyes have known some distant pain, making life all the more precious. We shared carriage rides that delighted me very much—just us two and the breeze and the *clip-clop* of his horse. What was her name? Flora. One day I showed Emmons some of my verses. He responded with verses of his own, which were pleasant, though not in a class with mine, a thought that both delighted and troubled me very much. Handsome Cousin John loved my music. I would often play for him. I knitted him wristlets and asked him in for wine. His gentle features, perfectly molded in casual yet pristine symmetry, held fascination. His philosophical bent added in no small measure to his general attractiveness. Tall Thurston was Abby's favorite. Although I liked him well enough he did not spark my carnal side as did the others. I am *too* bold!

Vinnie knew nothing of our list. Had she offered her opinion, Joseph Lyman would surely have topped the assembly. Though younger than her accomplished and highly alluring older sister, Vinnie was more outwardly romantic, more in the line of stolen kisses and flirtations behind the barn. Her favorite was decidedly Lyman. "Spoony" was their game, with kisses in the shadows and holding hands. Not that I was denied my share of kisses from other quarters, but Lyman and I were friends with nothing more to report. I was satisfied with the arrangement. We read plays in German, sharing the parts, and Vinnie, long chestnut hair flowing, seated on the red ottoman, holding one or another of her precious fang-toothed balls of fluff. I wondered if she might be jealous of our readings, our long walks and literary discussions. With Vinnie and Lyman it was all romance. That may have been enough for her. Lyman told me one day— we were walking in the woods discussing the merits of Edgar Allan Poe—that Vinnie was the most passionate person he had ever known, a point I found intriguing. I trust he didn't share that bit of news with Father!

In some ways Life upon my return to Amherst differed little from the time before my sojourn away. In other ways it was different. Before, it was mostly talk. Now, it was action! With both Vinnie and myself under one roof—can you imagine such quantity of loveliness?—the door was always swinging and Whiskers going in and out. Dashing young men were in our parlor every evening—and always the currant wine! Vinnie and I made it ourselves. The recipe was Mother's, from of her "personal Bible." Break and squeeze currants. Put 3½ lbs. sugar to 2 quarts juice and 2 quarts water. Put in keg or barrel. After 3 days close bung. Wait 1 or 2 years to drink. Our dashing suitors enjoyed the wine, as did Father, despite his active participation in organizations of temperance.

On the evenings when Vinnie and I did not receive callers we often went calling ourselves. Father was always in a state of agitation upon our return. We were required to be home by nine and except on rare occasions *were* home at the appointed hour, but that mattered little. Agitation was the order of the evening. I think it was that he wanted us not to go out at all. Father would like us never to marry. He has never said as much in a sentence, but by inference his preference is clear. Vinnie "must not be flirtatious." I assume I should not be either, though he has not as yet felt the necessity of saying so. Vinnie "must wear a shawl at parties." Mother is frail and "needs our help at Home." He is "in the habit of us." Bread is the "staff of life" and he will eat "no bread but Emily's"! Where does that leave him should I marry?

One evening we were playing charades at Tempe Linnell's house, the girls against the boys and Vinnie crawling about on all fours, suggesting—or trying to!—"a horse of a different color." Her idea was to whinny, while throwing her head up and down, then sniffing at all the most brightly colored objects in the room. She would crawl to an object, sniff, then shake her head in a disapproving manner, whinny and move to the next brightly colored thing she could find. We were all laughing so hard that we could scarcely breathe! The gentlemen had not one idea as to what she was driving at, and more laughter and more, and then a knock at the door. It was an angry knock, insistent, loud. We all froze. Tempe went

190

into the hall and then came Father's voice. "I am here to collect my daughters."

The walk home was dark and silent. The occasional oil lamp above a gate did nothing to dispel the gloom. Vinnie went straight to bed without a word from Father. I, with no word as well, went into the kitchen to wait for Austin. It was only slightly after nine. We had overstayed our time by but a few minutes only. Not a second of grace for such tardy ones as we!

Austin arrived shortly and heard much on my side of the matter. He was embarrassed for us, being collected like a couple of wayward children. I was awfully vexed about it and needed most especially the comfort of my beloved brother. "Why did Father do that?" I asked as we sat by the hearth with some blackberry tea I had put up. "How could he be so mean?"

"You know Father," said Austin.

"What point are you making?"

"He's not mean, exactly."

"What do you mean by *exactly*?"

"What?"

"If he's not mean, *exactly*, then how?"

"He's not mean at all, really, just determined to have things his way."

"At all costs," I said. "I call that mean."

Austin moved to secure a piece of gingerbread from

191

the cupboard. We were quiet then. A poem came to mind—well, the idea for a poem—a man decides a thing is true because he needs it to be, and missing a small but crucial fact, allows his House to be destroyed in a hurricane.

"Would you like some gingerbread?" It was Austin asking. I was completely gone in the world of my Poem.

"What?"

"Would you like some gingerbread?"

"Oh. Yes, I would."

We shared our "feast," with tea as well, going on to discuss Large matters—Immortality, Life after Life, God within and so forth—the two "lingering bad ones" at rest in the territory of what made sense to our Souls. Feeling as I did that moment, I ventured the following. "I have written a few short verses."

"So have I."

My breath stopped. He had spoken in such a way as to end the subject of *my* verses. *His* were the topic now. My chest felt narrow. I felt as if I had left the room.

"I've written several," he continued.

"Oh."

"Yes, and quite good too, if I may say so."

"So. We both have written some verses."

"I have written many," said Austin.

"Be careful not to get ahead of me," I heard myself

say, deploring my attitude even as I spoke. I felt numb. If Austin showed no interest in my Poems, surely no one in my family would ever care. I decided straightway to put the matter of the exigency of my writing verses completely out of my mind. It was too Large a truth to consider all at once.

Part III

❧

Destiny Calls!

"I reckon—when I count at all—
First—Poets—Then the Sun—"

Ben

I first met Ben when the wild gentian was in bloom, the August before Mt Holyoke. He had come to work in Father's office, a lawyer in the making. Though I spent little time in his presence that first summer, he impressed me greatly. He was older than yours truly by nearly ten years upon the Earth. In other ways he was older by larger degree. I suspected this upon our first meeting and had thought of him sometimes while away at school.

The gentian was in bloom once more upon my return, a punctual harbinger of the season's end. And then October. It had been hot for days. The roads were dusty and a heaviness in the air signaled something unpleasant. We all wondered if the heat would ever end, but weather—as all—will not remain unchanged. The next day a terrible storm came up with thunder and lightning, strong winds and a rain that poured as if it had intention never to stop. Lighting killed Mr. Sweetser's cow. I was awfully upset about it. I knew her, as I often had occasion to pass her on my way to church. She was gray, her round eyes deep and pleasant. She had apparently been waiting out the storm, standing in the middle of the field, when she was struck. Vinnie told me the news. I was coming down the stairs and Vinnie was standing by the stairway holding a cat—Roughnaps I think. "Mr. Sweetser's cow was struck by lightning," she said.

I grip the banister.

"She died."

I feel my mind split from my body and I—frozen—a statue on the step. Vinnie is gone, though I did not see her leave.

Where am I?

Nothing.

Should I move?

More Nothing.

Should I go down the stairs?

Blank.

What for?

And blank still.

Back to my room.

I instruct myself, step by step. *Turn around. Up the stairs. Into your room. Onto your bed. Close your eyes. Leave the World.*

When I woke, the fate of the unsuspecting cow filled my mind. No breath. I felt I did not want to live in a world where an innocent cow could be struck down for no reason. Was there *no reason* for her death? An awesome thought—and I spinning alone in the nothing of Space! Was there *a reason*? *God's reason?* How could that be so? I lay on my bed, knowing nothing, caring less. And then the Fear.

Not again!

The feeling overtook me once more that I did not exist. There was only the Fear.

I will not survive this.

I lay for some moments, beginning, slowly at first, to perceive a simple truth. If I could think of myself surviving or not surviving, then I must exist. There was a part of me doing the thinking.

I want a cup of tea.

I made my way down the stairs on trivial legs. There in the parlor was a man. He rose and I, noticing his grave, gentle eyes, greeted him in unthinking manner, suitable to my station. Father was with the man and Austin. "Emily, you will remember Mr. Newton," said Father. "He works with me in the office."

"Oh," I said, remembering and not remembering—mind trapped in fear. I sat on the lounge. The man sat.

"We were discussing the state of the Whigs," Father explained.

"Oh." It was all I could think to say.

Mother came in with cake and fussing. Were we

cold? Were we thirsty? Did we have enough light?

No. No. Yes.

Mother returned to the kitchen.

"Well now," said Father. A pause and then, "Excuse me." He left the room.

Austin went on some about the Whigs. Things were not good with them. I forget why. Before I realized it, Austin was gone to check on Ned and there we were, Benjamin Newton and I, alone in the parlor and no one there to care.

"How did you like Mt Holyoke?" he asked.

"I liked it well."

"What did you enjoy the most?"

"Reading, Composition, Botany, Geology, Music, Philosophy and Latin," I answered in swift define.

"You have many favorites."

"I do."

"So do I."

"What do you fancy besides the law?"

"Literature first."

"The best!"

"And philosophy."

"We have common fancies."

"With you one can hardly miss." We laugh. Vinnie comes in, looking lovely, smiling. She sits on the little red ottoman.

I wish she would go.

Vinnie looks at Ben. "Did you hear about the cow?"

"What cow is that?"

"Mr. Sweetser's cow."

"Don't talk about the cow," I say.

"It got struck by lightning."

"Don't talk about the cow."

"She died."

"I'm sorry to hear that," says Ben.

"It was awful."

"Don't talk about the cow!"

"Why not?" says Vinnie. "I guess I can talk about a cow if I want to."

"Not that cow. Not now."

Vinnie appears determined to enumerate the many lurid details of the poor creature's untimely Death. I am saved by the cats. It may be the one and only time in my life! Some "set-to" in the kitchen—some merciful dispute between Snugglepoops and Pussy—and Vinnie all but flies from the room.

"Sad news about the cow," says Ben.

"I cannot bear it. Silly of me, I know."

"Why do you say that?"

"People dying every day and I worry about a cow."

"I don't think it's silly."

"You are kind."

"I mean it."

"Thank you."

"I don't think it's silly."

"Neither do I," I admit. "But the force of my feelings overwhelms me. Does not Life appear strange to you? Inexplicable? Unjust?"

Ben nods.

"I can hardly manage it at times."

"It helps when I remember my faith in things unseen." His words hit a resting place in the center of my chest. "Existence is larger than we know," he adds.

"I believe that."

"Blessed Immortality!"

"For a cow?"

"Why not?"

I cannot answer the question.

Frozen at the Bone

❧

Ben was often at the house, discussing legal matters with Father. This delighted both me and Vinnie no end. We vied for his attentions as might be expected of any two such stylish and eligible young ladies. He was decidedly too old for us to set our sights on, but that did not stop the fun and in no way hampered our rigorous imaginings!

One fall evening Ben and I found ourselves alone in the parlor, sipping currant wine and eating black cake. We were on the subject of books. Our common favorites—not common in stature, rather common as in "same"—were Shakespeare, Dickens, the Bible, Longfellow and a new writer by the name of Currer Bell. I had just read the remarkable *Jane Eyre*, lent to me by Bowdoin. Jane—so straight, so true! Not about to belong to anyone save her Self, and save herself she did by sticking to that mental attitude!

"Do you know the poems of Emerson?" Ben asks.

"No," I answer. "I know that a man named Emerson wrote some essays, but have not read them."

Ben takes a small book from the pocket of his coat,

opens it and begins to read. I shall never forget that moment. It is as if the top of my head has come off. My skin is on fire. I am frozen at the bone. I have been picked up and delivered to a quiet spring where things "are" merely. I am Home—home to Myself—that region from which one must begin if one is to find any sort of real Life at all. I am nourished in a few small Words! A Miracle! To banish the darkness, to lift a Soul, to give it wings—its *Own* wings, not thoughts plucked from another's brain, but light and air, safety and rest, Circumference without edge—Infinity! His knowing touched my own—

There is more to life than we can see.

As a child I sensed this. The fact had lived within me—a basement tenant—due in part to the measure of its importance and the risk of its revelation too great, lest its declaration offend.

There is more to life than we can see.

I am trembling now.

"Will you read another?" I ask.

Ben turns a page. "'Give all to love; Obey thy heart.'"

I want to be a Poet!

The thought rang through my Soul! My brain was flooded with the precious knowledge of what some-where it already knew.

That's who I am! That's what I want to do! Now I remember!

It was a deep and inner remembering, like coming Home.

I want to know what Emerson knows. I want to spread that knowing. I want to light a lamp that will never go out!

I hear my own voice.

"I myself write some verses."

"Really?"

"They remind me of Emerson."

What did I say? Who do I think I am?

"How interesting," I heard Ben say. "I would like to hear more about them when time allows."

Ben's lack of surprise at my declaration leaves me room to breathe.

That night in bed beside a snoring Vinnie I thought about my future.

I will be a Poet!

Other thoughts attack.

I am a girl. I will be a woman. It is quite the thing nowadays for girls to be poetical, but women must employ the needle and not the pen.

I think of Elizabeth Barrett Browning.

She did it!

Me, hopeful—and then—

But she has a different father.

I hear the buckle snap.

He may have given her the space to breathe.

Vinnie begins to snore loudly. I poke her in the ribs with my elbow. "What time is the parade?" she mumbles. I poke her again. Thoughts of Father fill my weary brain.

He holds us in a viselike grip, tells us to appreciate fine books but not to read them, to think for ourselves but to follow his rules. He wants his daughters to get an education but not to use it. He treasures his family but is seldom at home. He wants us to think of him only, but can't be found; has a sense of humor, but rarely smiles; wants to be loved, but will not admit it.

The more I think about Father, the less inclined I am to sleep.

There is no way to please him!

I feel the desire to please Father rise up to challenge the joyous discovery of my future Calling.

I cannot let him take my Life!

And doubts now, rising up to claim the Me of me—a drowning of my fire.

But he is my father! Would it really be so hard to please him? What would Father consider to be the ideal qualities for a daughter?

I put myself in Father's mind, considering what an ideal daughter would be. Intelligent, deep minded, thoughtful, bright, witty, sincere, obedient, not frivolous, not foolish. She would possess a sense of humor, an appreciation of nature, a diligent spirit and strength of character. She would be capable and enjoy staying at home. She would be hardworking, self-reliant, selfless, sensitive, in need of his care, frail—so as to secure that need—yet she would never succumb to serious illness. She would not be flirtatious.

That's me.

Vinnie turns over and resumes snoring.

Father's most desirable daughter is me!

The idea troubles and pleases me all in one.

Whose person am I? Mine? His? A little of both maybe.

The thought overtakes me that I have turned into someone with qualities Father fancies merely for the sake of pleasing him.

What about me? *I want to be a poet! I don't want to appreciate poems merely. I want to write them! I do write them! I write in the secret dark—past 9. oclock! Father does not know my wicked side. I like to be flirtatious. I like to flirt with handsome young men, with Emmons and Cousin John and Bowdoin and all the rest! I read the books he tells me not to read! Who is* Jane Eyre *for, if not for me?!*

I am wide-awake now, speaking directly to Father inside my brain. "I hate morning prayers! I hate the punctuality of your mealtimes! I hate the word 'punctuality'! It's fussy and unyielding! Like you!"

The moon's bright rays come through the window on the far side of the room. I'm lost in the blue light. I think of my handsome Whisker friends. I wonder what it would be like to lie with Whiskers. Father's displeasure at the consideration of such a circumstance could hardly be measured. "The best little girl in Amherst" lying with men?! Perish the thought! To hear Father tell it, I am *his* "little girl."

But where does that leave me?

I have no answer.

I must not lie with Whiskers. That way I stay "his."

And then.

Do I want to stay "his"? Is that my mind or Father's? Is there a difference?

I imagine a Great Love where all else is swept away—even Father! I speak to him now—out loud—inside my brain. "I laugh at you! I speak of you with Austin behind your back! Sometimes I wish you would not come home with your tight face! You cover the house with your serious opinions! I don't want to clean the house for you! I want to be a Poet!!"

My heart is racing. No sweet sister lying close, snoring or not, can ease the Volcano within—the news of my Destiny!—the thing I am to do—to *be*—battling for its life!

And yet rising up to overtake my very breath, the instinct to be Father's girl—"the best little girl in Amherst"! My very blood knows *that* way—was caught in *his* desire!

Can inspiration tear survival from its moorings?

I spoke to no one of my concerns but waited for Ben. He visited often, a new world—aflame in all its glory. Ben opened my eyes to many things that he and Emerson believed in—the sense that God was within each and every Soul, not separate on a cloud; the difference of each and every Individual, the importance of that difference; the need to be true to one's Self, to be open to Possibility, to the idea of the existence of things unseen, to glorious Immortality! Eternity appeared dreadful to me, a never-ending sameness under the watchful eye of a censoring God—but Immortality! Ever changing, ever growing, ever new, in the company of God's glorious Power within all!

It wasn't long before I showed Ben my verses. I showed him the *Hamlet* poem, the Valentine to Thomas— no name mentioned!—the poem about the dog (my favorite), the Dungeon Fear, the worm, and the sailor lost at sea. When he finished reading, he sat still, looking down at the paper, mute. Minutes passed. Those minutes seemed like years! At last he looked up. "You are a poet."

He said no more, nor needed to for all of Time.

Carlo

J ust when I think Father must be the coldest, most hard-hearted man in the entire world, he does something so pure as to transport me to Heaven and beyond! Not days after his inappropriate interruption of our harmless, merry little game of charades—and me not wanting to speak to him ever again for causing such embarrassment to myself and Vinnie in front of all those handsome Whiskers—the greatest surprise awaited me at his design.

I was in Vinnie's and my room of an afternoon, resting, as I was not feeling well. I had been experiencing a great tiredness, accompanied by a skin rash and a soreness of the eyes. Any light at all made matters decidedly worse, so there I lay and feeling sorry for myself and too distressed even to keep up with my secret delight in reading *Kavanagh*, that intensely enjoyable book by Henry Wadsworth Longfellow that Father had bought but asked us not to read. What did he expect us to do with it?

There came a knock on the door. "Father here." I

quickly buried *Kavanagh* beneath the comforter. Or was it *Jane Eyre*? My mind is unsure. "I have a surprise" came the voice from the hall. "He would like to meet you."

A surprise that would like to meet me?!—a "HE"??

When I opened the door, there before me stood Father, and sitting at his side a dog—a puppy by the looks of him, yet enormous!—and shaggy, auburn hair, gentle eyes and the hugest paws one could imagine!

"A dog!" I quickly bent down, embracing him all around, burying my face in his shaggy coat.

"For you," said Father.

"For me?" Tears over the dam. "Oh, thank you!" I leaned back, stroking the huge dog's soft head and partway down his sturdy back. "He's beautiful!"

"A fine dog."

"Thank you, Father!" I stood up. The dog stood up as well, watching me, waiting. He knew I was his, or so it appeared to me, and I knew he was mine forever! No tiredness now, no strain in the eyes, no rash. All had gone!

A dog of my own!

He looked familiar. Was this another moment as with Emerson—a glimpse into the familiar future—a Poet alone with her Dog?

"He will be good company," said Father. "Long walks will be good for both of you."

"Is he a Newfoundland?"

"Yes," said Father. "With perhaps a touch of Saint Bernard. A puppy."

"He's enormous!"

"I must return to my briefs."

"Of course."

"He may want water."

"Thank you!"

And Father was gone.

I knelt once more, stroking the dog along his broad back. Vinnie appeared in the hall. "What's that?" she asked, no small degree of horror in her tone.

"My new dog," I answered.

"He's going to live with us?"

"No place else!"

The dog sniffed Vinnie's frock for elucidation. Vinnie appeared to be frozen. "What about the cats?" she managed.

"What about them?"

"They won't stand for a dog in the house."

"They will have to learn."

The dog began to pant. "I have to get him some water," I said, and we were off to the kitchen, leaving a stunned Vinnie to gather her equilibrium about her as best she could.

The dog watched as I took a bowl from the cupboard,

filling it with water from the pump. As I moved to set the bowl on the floor, he backed up. Once the bowl was down, he advanced and collapsed flat on the floor, his large paws on either side of the bowl, his ears in the water. His hind legs were out behind him, pointing toward the opposite walls. I wondered that he would be comfortable in such an odd posture. *Lap, lap, lap.* As I watched him drink, I thought back to the little book Father had given me when I was ten, the Newfoundland, all golden amber, just like mine—Torbold or Thurston or some such name. How large he was, how he loved the sea, how he stayed by the side of that small girl and how much I had wanted a dog just like him! I found myself wondering why I had gotten such a wonderful gift from Father while Vinnie got none. I had no answer.

Later that afternoon, I sat with *my dog* in the yard, bundled up against the cold and all the while marveling at the wonder of my new friend, his shaggy love, his brown kisses, his broad head and tremendous webbed paws. My first order of the afternoon was to pick a name. I thought at some length about what would suit him, but without success. All at once he stood up and headed for the pond, where the woods begin, and—*splash!*—into the deep! Newfoundlands love water. They were originally used on ships in the sea in the North and are excellent swimmers. It must be in their blood from long ago. If there was a wreck, the sailors would hold onto them and the dogs would pull the sailors ashore. They were true lifesavers.

Carlo!

The name appeared in my brain without warning. In *Jane Eyre* I had encountered the name of one of the character's dogs. It was Rivers's pointer who was named Carlo. I had taken an instant liking to the name, finding it steady, relaxed and quite Italian, exotic in an ordinary way. The blessedness of opposites! The name was not entirely suggestive of a pointer, but for a Newfoundland it was perfect! "Carlo!"

My shaggy companion looked up from his occupations in the pool, fixing his gaze upon his mistress. "Carlo! Come here!" He ran—a shambling gait—to my side. Such notice paid, such eagerness to be my friend! "Let me look at you." I leaned back, my arms out straight, his huge head between my narrow hands. I wondered at his enormous size and only a few short months on the Earth! "How can you be so large?" My answer was the lap of a wet tongue on my cheek.

Inside, Mother and I discussed Carlo's sleeping arrangements. Mother favored the washroom. That practical spot was located adjacent to the kitchen and apart from the rest of the house, which pleased Mother in both aspects. It would be warm and also away from any rugs that might prove to be places upon which to collect hair.

"He does not want to be warm," I stated, a trifle pompously. "He is from the North."

Mother maintained her point of view. "There are no rugs in the washroom," she said. "That will make it cooler." She patted Carlo on the head. She didn't need to bend.

"I would like him to sleep with me," I said. "He's very young and just away from his mother and all his brothers and his sisters. He will be lonesome."

"He will get used to it."

I had to think of something. "He may cry at night and wake Father."

Mother responded, "Oh, that won't do."

I knew that would get her.

"That dog is not sleeping in our room!" Vinnie had just joined us in the kitchen. "He is too big, he has too much hair and he drools. I'll bet he snores as well!"

"You're a fine one to talk!"

"I do not snore," Vinnie argued.

"You snore," I told her, "and that is the fact of it. I'm afraid you will have to take my word on the matter, as you will never hear what noises you do or do not make while you are sleeping. That must be left for others to judge."

215

Vinnie did not appreciate my declaration. "I don't care whether I snore or not," she said. "He's not sleeping in our room."

Carlo lay flat, chin on the floor, watching me. I had to find another solution. It was this: Carlo would sleep in the hall outside our bedroom door. If he cried I would get up and be of company to him until he was comforted. Vinnie didn't care for this idea either, but Mother accepted it, saying that when Carlo grew accustomed to his surroundings she felt it best he sleep in the washroom. Austin and Father had less dramatic views when presented with the question. Austin said he didn't care where Carlo slept. In uncharacteristic conduct Father left the entire matter to the women in the family to decide.

That evening Carlo and I walked together down North Pleasant Street—away from town. No need to beckon, no cause to cajole, just the walking, my feet keeping a gentle pace and the sun setting to the left in all its purple glory and my own dear Carlo padding along at my side. After we made the turn to go back to the house, I found myself telling Carlo what I had never told another living soul, not even Ben. "I will be a Poet," I told him. Carlo slowed down, looking up, listening it seemed, striving for the sense behind the words he did not know. "I shall write verses like music and when we are both no longer on the Earth they may be of some small help.

What do you think of that?"

Carlo stopped to examine a bush. Ears rounded forward, he sniffed, inferring a history I could only imagine.

Carlo's First Night.

Yours truly is climbing the stairs with a lamp in one hand, the warmest of shawls about her shoulders and a gigantic puppy padding behind on silent paws and up, up, up the stairs, all amber and curious. We reach the top and turn to enter the bedroom. Vinnie is inside, sweetly on the bed, doing a bit of sewing, darning I believe. "He's not coming in here," she says.

"I want to show him where I live."

"He's seen it," says Vinnie. "Now get him out!"

I put down the lamp, take an extra spread from the closet shelf and move to the hall. Carlo follows, watching my every move. I fold the spread, laying it down by the side of the door, against the wall. "Your bed," I say, trying to make it sound as appetizing as a thing could be. Carlo stares. "Nice bed." I kneel down, patting the spread with the utmost enthusiasm. "Come!" Carlo walks slowly onto the spread and stands. "Good dog!" Carlo stares. "Lie down!" Carlo doesn't move. His look suggests his owner may have lost her mind. He watches as I go back to get another spread, lay it beside the first one in the hall, lie down on the second folded spread and pat the first spread once more. "Lie down." He obliges. "Good dog!" I feel the comfort of his warm body, his softness, his trust. Oh, the glory of it! I gather the second spread about my shoulders and fall into a dreamless sleep.

I am awakened by a pain in my shoulder. Once awake I realize I am cold. I have heard it said that heat rises. If ever I had been uncertain of the fact, that night brought it to my attention. Not even the heavenly closeness of Carlo's body can bring sufficient warmth to our drafty spot upon the floor. I hate to leave him, but leave him I must, returning to the bed.

Vinnie is snoring to the extreme. I shove her several times in hopes of securing a quick piece of quiet during which to fall into that holy space of dreams. Finding that space at last, I sleep, but am awakened by a great crash with screaming and yelping and such a Hurrah as has not been heard in Amherst in fifty years! I leap up to see what disaster has befallen, only to find Carlo and Vinnie in a heap on the floor of the hall and Father in his doorway and Mother in her nightgown in utter dismay! It seems Carlo had shifted his spot from the spread to just in front of the door when Vinnie awoke—rested after all that snoring—opened the bedroom door and stepped into the darkened hallway, directly on top of the sleeping Carlo!

He yelped—she tripped—he jumped—she screamed—he yelped again as Father opened his door to check on the commotion. "What's going on here?" he said, or words to that effect. It was quickly determined that Carlo would henceforth sleep in the washroom.

After breakfast Carlo and I went for our morning walk. The air was cold, the fog low, my companion hills barely visible as they rested, holding their plans for spring. My gloves were no help to my fingers, and my nose—a melting icicle—spoke of the dampness in my bones. Carlo was in his glory as he padded steadfastly ahead to greet the Day.

When we returned home Vinnie was dusting. She darted about the parlor with a rag—and Mother with her hair tied up in a handkerchief to put off the dust, a paltry scene for such a Large Morning.

Fingels Cave and the Knowledge of My Destiny

🌹

Life was new! Everywhere was Carlo, and Carlo was in everything! I exaggerate. Carlo was not "in everything." There were occasions upon which Carlo was *not* in the sleigh. He was not pleased about this, I know, as he had to be instructed many times not to follow us. I can picture him by the gate, surrounded by snow, a sorry figure, eyes not believing what they saw, amber fluff in all the white, getting smaller and smaller as we pulled away.

It was the winter of Fingels Cave. Abby had heard about the spot and simply would not rest until we found it. It was a large cave to the south of Amherst, near the dinosaur bones and said to be haunted. We found it on the coldest day of the year. Father was not pleased with the excursion, but we had a grand time—Cousin John, Emmons and Bowdoin, Abby and myself off to explore the World! As it turned out the cave was *not* haunted. That was our opinion, at any rate, with the exception of Abby, who insisted that ghosts lurked within, as she had heard their hollow voices mourning the loss of onions.

Some great onion famine no doubt, not as yet recorded in the annals of Time.

Valentine's Week came soon. *This* year, being eighteen and alluring to be sure, I received *many* Valentines. I especially liked the little book *Picciola*, from Cousin John. I was no sooner caught up in the glory of so many fine attentions than without warning on came a most unpleasant bout of stomach distress. I was lifeless with pain, sleeping the days away, with Carlo wanting to play and I unable to lift my head from the pillow. I find that colds make one carnal, but I can't say the same for disorders of the stomach. I wonder if the carnal nature of colds with all the time languishing between the sheets is a reason for Father's dislike of same. He and Mother never could tolerate anything carnal. Well, I suppose they must have—at least three times! One wonders how *that* ever came about!

Once well, I again thrilled to Ben's visits. The night of his first visit after my illness was particularly cold, and the wind blowing the snow in great swirls about the house. Father and Austin were not at home. Vinnie was otherwise engaged, thank goodness. Ben has come to see *me*! He sits in the large chair by the piano, Carlo at his feet. I pour the wine. Mother enters with a tray of black cake and all her anxious fussing. "Are you warm enough?" "Oh, dear!" "The wine will help." "Have some black cake."

Carlo lifts his nose. He sniffs. Then straightway up to stand at attention, staring at the tray.

"Sit, Carlo," I tell him.

Carlo sits, eyes locked on the cake.

"He's drooling!" says Mother.

Ben smiles. "I'd say he fancies a bit of that cake."

I set down my wineglass, hurrying to catch the drool with my handkerchief before it reaches the rug. No luck to be had in the matter.

"He might be better off in the washroom," says Mother, setting down the tray.

"He's no bother," says Ben.

"Not a bit," I add in haste, dabbing at the rug.

"He's making quite a mess, Emily," says Mother.

"I can handle it!" Not entirely true, but important to state, as anything less and Carlo would be banished to the outer regions! I stand. "All clean!"

Mother returns to the kitchen. I sit. Ben picks up a piece of cake. Carlo is now staring at Ben, who is about to bite into the luscious dessert. Ben bites, chews—and then? He breaks off a piece of moist black cake for you-know-who! "May I give him a taste?" Ben asks.

"To be sure," I say, and—*Snap!* The cake is gone! I can honestly say I have never seen so fervent a response to anything on the part of man, woman, child or beast!

Ben and I talked much that cold night. And to think he had come calling despite the chill, a thrilling event to my mind and heart! I wondered if I loved him in a carnal way. I thought not, but could not be sure. Most precious to me of all was his tender attention to my verses, his belief in my ability to set down words that lived! I shall thank him forever for that and for bringing me to my *Self*!

Miss Lyon died that spring. All her prescriptions for life surrendered to Death, democratic Death, and in March she was gone. No manner of calisthenics, right thinking, religious determination, proper diet or intellectual stockpile could save her from the intention of the Hooded One. Miss Lyon's death was an awful shock, and there had been more recent deaths to dull the spirit—Jacob Holt and Olivia Coleman. There was another loss to bear, harder, I am ashamed to say, than all the rest. Ben would be leaving Amherst.

"How does one hold the blossoms when everywhere there are thorns?"

I put the question to Austin, at home now and busy with his studies at the College. It was one of our famous Night Talks, Carlo at our feet and deep in his sleep.

"I don't know," said Austin. He looked comfortable in his slippers, but not in his skin. I know that feeling, as if something were terribly wrong with one and not knowing what. I stroked Carlo's amber softness. "Do you think if we gave our hearts to Christ, the thorns would disappear?"

"Perhaps." Austin was clearly of a brooding spirit. I wished to shake him by the collar, demanding his presence, as I so often wished to do with Father.

"You are no help!" I exclaimed.

"What do you want me to say?"

"Something! Not just 'perhaps'! What is that— 'perhaps'?" I was quite beside myself. Chaos was building in my world. My Life had been so simple—not always pleasant—but clear. Now Ben had come into my life, calling the knowledge of my Destiny from deep within those hidden regions of the brain, reminding me of a future unknown to my daily mind, to support me as none other had done. And soon he would be gone. I could not bear it! I watched my beloved brother as he sat brooding in the light of the fire, wishing with the fire of my Soul to share with him my longing to be a Poet, to receive that same encouragement bestowed upon me by my Friend. I disliked reserving parts of myself—the most *important* parts!—from my soulmate brother.

Austin shifted uneasily in his chair.

I must not mention the subject of my poems again. My verses must not be trapped beneath the boulders of my brother's indifference.

"I hate growing up!" I said with surprising force. Carlo woke all at once—the sudden jerk of his head, eyes blurred, nose dry, ready. He watched me, seeking clues. "I cannot do it!" I said. "I don't know how!"

"What do you mean?" Austin seemed distant. It scared me.

"Things were simpler when we were children!"

"What things?"

"All things!"

"I don't understand you."

"You used to!"

"I understand you in general," said Austin. "I just don't understand what you're talking about."

"I don't think you understand me in any way! And I don't understand myself!"

"I can't help you with that." Austin can be so cold. I had never noticed it before. I expect all of us can be unfeeling. I thought my beloved brother was exempt from such human failings, but why should he have been the only one?

Abby Slips Away

⚜

It amazes me how quickly I change. Ben read my poem about Father's shoes and said that it held "depth beneath the humor" and carried "layers of experience in the briefest stroke of the pen." No wonder I felt quick joy at those remarks! His plan to leave Amherst at summer's wane seemed distant to me then, and I, filled with the thrill of his assessment of my work, about to burst with a sense of Possibility. I am truly a mixed bag.

In that same week Lyman took us maple-sugaring. He had enjoyed the task as a boy and wanted to share the fun. A group of us went—Abby and I, Vinnie, Emmons, Thurston and Cousin John—off to meet the Maples!— And Carlo at my side and the sharp air and the breeze, the tiny frogs peeping their springtime report from the swamp, the grass at the sides of the spring, the bits of ice and the snow in mounds of lingering winter. All was right with the world that day, blue sky and Whiskers, Carlo and girl friends and laughter and all the while my Destiny at my back—the wind in my sails!

The next day Abby and I came out the front door in

the midst of an important conversation and me without a shawl or a thought of winter! I watched as Carlo frolicked—if such a thing can be said of so awkward a creature—in the little pond at the edge of the woods. I breathed deeply, eyes closed, chin to the sky. "Oh, Abby, don't you think the world is grand?"

"Fine enough for me," said Abby. Despite her fascination with Fingels Cave, she has always possessed a practical bent.

It was a good day. I would see Ben that night. He had stopped by that very morning, leaving his card in the brass bowl on the narrow table in the hall. "Emily. Will call this evening. Ben." The words were thrilling, especially as I had just written a new poem and simply had to show him. It was a Valentine—a love poem to Carlo!

Abby and I moved toward our favorite Elm, just yards from the house. We were making a kind of escape. We had been seated in the parlor, discussing the important matter of whether Tempe had kissed Gould at the mill, when Snugglepoops took a notion to attack our ankles. Charging with military severity, he pounced, grabbing fiercely, needle claws deep, only to be followed by teeth! When shooed with flailing limbs and shouts of dismay, the "Captain of the Infantry" retreated to base camp beneath the piano, gathering force for the next round. I complained bitterly to Vinnie, who offered not one bit of sympathy as in Vinnie's mind whatever the cats do is second only to the Holy Grail.

Abby reached the tree and I not far behind. The buds had begun to show themselves, their intention strong within. Abby sat on the new grass. "So what do you think?" she said.

"About what?" I had forgotten the question.

"Did she kiss him?"

"Who?"

"Gould."

I sat on the grass next to Abby. A bobolink hopped along the path toward the barn. "Did who kiss Gould?"

"Tempe!"

"Who knows?"

"She said she did."

The sun's rays slanted through the branches overhead. I wondered what might follow the kisses of which Abby spoke, yet wondered not so much as at the majesty of the Sun, that ball of fire, suspended in space, so large that one cannot imagine its size! "Oh, Abby," I said, "how chief a thing it is to be alive!"

"They went to the mill last week. . . ."

"Sometimes I gasp at the thought of it!" As you may have surmised, I was referring to none other than that giant Star and she to Tempe's adventures at the mill.

"What do you think happened?" asked Abby.

228

My mind was far from her query. "Where did we come from?" I continued. "Where will we go?"

Abby sat up tall. "Are you listening to me?"

"Will there really be a Heaven?"

"Of course there will."

"And who will go there?"

"All of us."

"The elephant in Africa? The toad behind the barn?"

"You haven't been listening to a word I've said!"

"Oh, Abby, don't it thrill you *some*? Not even a *little*? Life is so unknown and yet it's all there is. Or is it?" I wanted to share my questions of Life and Death with my dearest friend. Ben had opened my mind to so much that had been inside me since a child and later hidden in the shadows of "supposed to." Others seemed not to be interested in lofty matters—only Austin, and he had been so cold of late, so busy. I pressed on. "Oh, Abby, what do you think of Death? Is it separate from Life, or a part of the selfsame thing, unknown until we reach it?"

"We were talking about Tempe and Gould at the mill."

"I know. But hear me! The wonders of Existence are exceeding Large, yet people make the world so thin!"

"Thin?"

"Oh, Abby, don't you think they do? They take the heft!"

"What heft?"

"They mute the world to shadows and put in too much noise!"

"I never know if you mean the things you say or just enjoy the drama."

"A little of both maybe."

"No doubt."

"Don't you think it's a shame what people make of the world?"

"I don't think about it much."

"Oh, Abby, you must! You have a brain as wide as the sky! And we both know how Large that is!"

"I have other things to think about." Abby lay back in the new April grass, looking up at the branches of the great Elm tree. I could feel her slipping away—or was it me?

I felt a terror then.

"Oh, Abby, don't you see? Why must we cover our senses? Why must we bury the joy of living? It don't seem right!"

"I don't understand you."

"Nobody does anymore. Don't you see? We don't know what Heaven will be—and Earth is so beautiful. I don't think Heaven *can* be better. And what if there *is* no Heaven? What if this is all there is and we waste it?"

"Don't let your father hear you talk like that."

"I don't care! My Puritan blood calls, 'Think for yourself!'"

Abby folded her legs beneath her and smoothed her skirt. I kept on. "Life is so grand a thing. It can boil the blood! It can pierce the bone if you let it!"

"I don't care to have my bones pierced, thank you very much."

"You shall get what God gives you, if he lives long enough."

"Our Great Protector can turn his back on the faithless, you know," said Abby, sounding a trifle sanctimonious. "It is not beyond the possible."

"If our Great Protector is as great as he is reported to be—omnipotent, as the saying goes—surely he can do as he wishes, and if he does not wish to protect us, he ought to have a better reason than that one of his children spoke casually of his fate. If God is such a fair-weather friend, I for one will not put my existence in his hands, however capable they may appear to some. He must be of finer stock to move my heart!"

Abby looked down the road. "You must grow up one day."

"That seems a formidable business."

"It's just what happens."

"When I see 'adults'—as they are called nowadays—I wonder if that is the way. Men with their starched shirts, women with their dimity convictions. Oh, Abby, we must soon be women."

"I should hope so!"

"What is a woman's place in the world?"

Abby looked puzzled.

"There used to be an order," I continued.

"To what?"

"To everything! There was Father's House and Father, Mother, Austin and Vinnie . . ."

"The cats . . ."

"God save us! And school . . ."

"You will get used to life without school. . . ."

"It's not just that," I said. "Life used to have edges."

"What edges?"

"School, friends, my room, my garden . . ."

"You have those now, except for school."

"But all will change!"

"Not all," said Abby.

"We must soon be women!"

"And?"

"Where does a woman's fate take her? To marriage, to an unknown house, good deeds for the poor? Dusting?!"

"You don't want to get married?" Abby's amazement knew no bounds. She could as well have been saying, "You don't want to breathe?"

I opened my arms wide. "I want more!" I felt a longing for I knew not what—for Truth, for Beauty, for the very essence of being, for the trees and the sky, for the oneness of all, for Freedom. "Oh, Abby, I want to run in the air of Nature! I can't be shut in!"

"Shut in where?"

"I feel it, Abby. I feel it coming and it scares me. I look at Mother and I think I would rather die than live as she does. If her girlhood dreams live on, they are locked so deep as can never be touched—may never be *remembered*! Is that what growing up does? Does it turn us into shadows of our younger selves?"

The light was fading. Abby lay back in the grass again, observing the purple sky. A beetle passed by the edge of her skirt. A little bird just near hopped to the side to let the beetle pass, a gracious gesture, and then not moments past an angleworm appeared without warning—to me at any rate. I noticed the creature, not thinking much about it. Not so of the "gracious" bird, who turned his head and with a sudden jerk bit the worm in halves.

Life is barbarous!

Abby stared at me. "You don't want to get married?"

"I think I should want to, but I don't *know*! When I see all the handsome Whiskers, their dark smiles and waiting eyes, I feel I am sure to fall under the spell of one—or many—and to tell the truth, I have—several times."

"I know that. We are not best friends for nothing."

"But marriage! I think it's not for me."

There was a great scuffling from the pond. Carlo had spotted a squirrel anxiously proceeding in the direction of the woods with a large nut. Carlo charged, as well as his great awkward paws could carry him, out of the water and after the frightened creature, who was surely about to be snapped up and swallowed for dinner in a single bite. "Carlo!" I shouted. "Carlo, come!"

He paid me no mind—and me in all my glory running after him, without my gaiters, or a way in the world to catch him. Lucky for him, the squirrel made a sudden change in direction and leaped—flew nearly—nut firm between stubborn jaws, landing on a branch of the Elm. Abby screamed in surprise, jumped up and ran toward the house, as Carlo stopped beneath the tree, shaking himself, sending water in all directions.

When recovered from the great Hurrah, we sat once more, some distance from the soaking Carlo, who stood staring up at the self-satisfied nut gatherer, waiting for the next round.

"Why do you question marriage?" asked Abby.

"Take Harriet Merrill, for instance."

"What is your point?"

"You know what they say."

"What?"

"'She has given her life to her Husband.'"

"And?"

"There is no 'and' about it. That is the phrase at the very center of the dilemma!"

"What dilemma?"

I could not believe my ears. My friend saw nothing amiss? No awesome misappropriation of the very essence of justice?!

I rose up high on my knees, assuming a most unladylike posture. "She has '*given her Life to her Husband*'!" I shouted.

"Don't shout."

"The words shut down my brain!"

"There is nothing wrong with my hearing."

I took a deep breath and sat back on my heels, attempting as best I could to quiet the fire within. "The thought of marriage used to be a merry contemplation. Whom would I choose? What would he be like? The suspense! My mind was a peacock and I with all my feathers out—a rainbow fan! Such vanity! Such presumption! And beneath it, the desperate question— May two live together as one and keep the two?? I have never seen it!"

Abby was quiet.

"To give one's life away is so Large a thing, wouldn't you say?"

No answer.

"It deserves, at the very least, a moment's consideration as to whether it be the wisest choice. But no time is taken, no questions asked. And it is always the woman who does the giving away. Why is that, do you suppose?"

"I don't know." Abby was slipping away from me.

"Oh, Abby, don't you see? It's true! And all of us await our turn to do the same, to give our minds away—our very Selves! There's you and Harriet and Mary and Tempe and Jennie and it don't bother you any! It seems to me when I take it to the bone, our Selves are all we have." I was up on my knees once more, a volcano inside. "Life is too Large a thing to spend it withering in a corner—dusting! If there is a God . . ."

"There is!"

". . . Then I cannot believe he wants that! Why would he give us talents and wishes? Why would he give us a mind if he did not want us to use it? I swear on the lives of a thousand grandmothers, it makes no sense!"

Abby lay back on the grass. "If you tell me you did not enjoy that carriage ride with Emmons last week, I won't believe you. His body next to yours . . ."

"I loved it!"

"The kiss on the bridge?"

"Grand!"

"You would leave all that behind?"

"I don't want to, Abby, but I don't *know*! Look where it leads! Dusting, dimity and teacups?! There must be more!"

"Your *husband*, that's what!"

"I wonder at the word 'husband.' We give our lives to this man, but what of *ours*? What of *our* loves, *our* desires, *our* talents? Must they remain unspoken as this husband plods his 'larger purpose'—wife behind, cooking *his* food, running *his* house, agreeing with *his* thoughts *only*? What of our own?!"

Abby looked away.

"Have you never had these thoughts?"

"No."

The trapdoor opens. Down the shaft. Alone.

At long last my "particular friend" spoke. "I loved our girlhood games, but I always thought of the future. I used to think, 'One day I will have a husband and a family of my own.' Why would you not want that?"

As I felt I had answered her question, there was nothing left to say.

I Beat the Plate to Death

❧

In the days that followed I thought about my talk with Abby many times. My concerns about leaving girlhood seemed to have taken root in my being. It was as if the dread of losing my Self had attached itself to my bones and weighed down my days, covering life's joys with a sense of dread.

In June I experienced an unpleasant surprise. Carlo and I had been for our evening walk, north on Pleasant Street, past the row of houses to the fence along the fields and out. Upon our return I reached for the knob of the back door.

Something is missing.

It was Carlo's ever-present softness against my leg, the warmth of his body sensed through the fabric of my skirt, the brushing past in innocent presumption to be the first inside. I turned to look for him and there he was, sitting squarely on top of my freshly planted daisies! He was panting heavily, mouth agape, tongue hanging, eyes locked upon his mistress. "Carlo, come!" My coaxing was to no avail, as straightway he lay down in the newly turned dirt, my flowers much the worse for it and I the spurned lover, abandoned at dusk. Request for company denied!

I spent a lonely night wondering what I had done that he should not be desirous of my company. The washroom was not by my side, but far closer than an outdoor flower bed! Not only that, he had disregarded my command. This caused an unpleasant turn of mind and heart. I lay beside my snoring sister, adrift in a sea of restless concern.

The morning found my shaggy ally sitting outside the door, waiting for breakfast. He came in to eat, but when finished returned to the yard. For the rest of the summer he came inside for meals only.

Ben left in August. I felt as if my claim to life were cut, and I left without a way to breathe. Who else knew my secret—my Destiny?! None save Carlo. And who cared? I told myself that *I* must care and that would be enough, but did not believe it. Ben left for far-off Worcester to pursue his studies. I felt that if he cared more for me, he would have stayed—a vain thought. Before leaving, he signed my book of messages from friends, mostly gone now. Here is what he wrote: "All can write Autographs, but few paragraphs; for we are mostly no more than *names.*" After signing the words, he told me I was one who *could* write paragraphs. My spirit touched the skies!

But soon he was gone.

What else that summer? Noopsie Possum disappeared, got by some wild creature, no doubt. Soon there was another cat to join the ranks—no, two! Two kittens from Stubbins' barn, Tender Boy and Tootsie, came to threaten the birds. Speaking of threats, the day the kittens arrived Father found *Kavanagh* under the piano cover, where Austin and I had hidden it. Father's displeasure could be sensed all the way to Springfield! Father did not see fit to blame his "perfect" daughter for the misconduct. Austin was the culprit!

At supper that evening there was the incident with the plate. When I set it on the table, Father complained of a tiny chip, remarking that he did not wish to receive that plate again. I felt awfully bad about it as I had been the one to set it before him, but the chip was so small as to pass notice, by me at any rate. I cared not to overlook the matter again so took the plate outside and beat it to death with a hammer!

Shortly after fall arrived in all her orange splendor, we had a jolly climb up Mt Holyoke. It was the first I had felt of good spirits for many months. Our merry group included Vinnie and myself, Emmons, Cousin John, Gould, Abby, Mary and Thurston. Upon our return Father was in a black mood. He told Vinnie in no uncertain terms that the next time she went traipsing about the mountains, she had better make the trip a shorter one. It might have gotten dark. We might have been lost and eaten by mountain lions. I wondered why he expressed his displeasure to her only—as if I did not exist. I wished he had addressed me as well, despite the reprimand it would have meant receiving.

In October Mother's figs won first prize at the Cattle Show. That same day I was visited upon by another Terror. Although there was always the fear beneath that one would come, I had been spared the actual event for many months. This is how it was.

For some reason I have occasion to attend church alone. I am sitting, back straight upon the unforgiving pew, listening to the Reverend's sermon on The Difference Between Right and Wrong. To hear him tell it, some things are of one persuasion and some of the other. One must memorize these same and conduct oneself accordingly. As he speaks I am overcome by an unnerving sensation. Sitting straight—shoes polished, hands clasped upon my Bible—the Reverend's Brimstone fills the church, and I apart from it—apart from all—and the thought . . .

My head is made of glass.

It seems that everyone can look through my face and see my evil thoughts.

241

I don't like church. My back hurts. Mrs. Dudley's hat is ugly. The Reverend is wrong.

The Congregation can see my thoughts, I know. They can see my evil deeds as well.

I should seek redemption. It's quite the thing nowadays.

I feel a chill.

Don't make light of your wickedness. See how bad you are?

I remember my glass head. It not only allows others to see my thoughts, it is a shield between myself and the Congregation, impenetrable. I am outside the group—alone! My thoughts come at once—a timeless flash.

It's happening again. My legs are numb. I can't breathe. Do I exist?

I can't find myself. There is nothing but the Fear. I leave the church and run—half blind—and on and on with legs that hardly bear my weight. I reach the House! Open the door! Up the stairs! Once in my room, I fall on my bed. Soon I am There and I can breathe.

The next day I stayed in bed. The Sun made its arc east to west and I, a solitary figure beneath the covers, weak and worrying.

What is wrong with me?

I had no answer.

Vesuvius Unchained

❧

The winter of my nineteenth year brought many occurrences, the exceptional quality of Mother's figs being outdone by events mounting in cataclysmic array to put that legendary volcano to shame for claiming such grand proportion.

Father left once more to join those "hairless gentlemen" in Boston, leaving Mother to follow her everpresent routine as Keeper of the House. Although aided in this noble pursuit by yours truly and by Vinnie—that dusting tornado of some renown—the burden of responsibility fell squarely upon Mother. Home now, Austin was busy at the College, his last year at Amherst, with little mind for else save an occasional charade. Not that Austin is ever much in the housework department. When asked to lift a bench or shovel snow, he is quick to respond in word, but as for action one must look elsewhere for assistance. I don't blame him. It must be remembered that housework is considered a job for women—a questionable distinction at best.

So there was Mother, bearing the brunt. She could,

however, lay claim to the dubious benefit derived from Father's List of Instructions.

1. Lock the doors.
2. Close the windows.
3. Stay out of drafts.
4. Don't let the children go out without their coats, especially Emily, as they may catch colds which could lead to pneumonia or death.
5. Don't go out at night. (You may catch the croup.)
6. Don't lock the barn door *after* the horse is stolen!

The aforementioned has not been recorded verbatim. It is, however, exceedingly accurate, as my ear for the precision of Father's mind is beyond reproach.

On a blustery evening, upon returning from a late October walk, I opened the door and there was Carlo! What joy as he pushed past his mistress in usual presumption, heading straight for his beloved water bowl. Well, I almost swooned! I surmised that when he finished drinking he would straightway turn to face the door to the garden and stare at its flat prevention with apparent displeasure, but was proven entirely wrong. He lifted his large head and, drooling streams of unswallowed water, backed away from the bowl, proceeding directly to the washroom—where he turned, following nose to tail—and down! I did not repine, oh no!—but got to my knees, arms about his amber softness in quick gratitude! A draft came in around the edges of the kitchen door. I hugged Carlo tighter for the warmth of it. Suddenly, I knew. Carlo hadn't deserted me. All those months he had been trying to keep cool! I cannot describe the consolation experienced at my discernment. To lose the approbation of my dog is a thing too horrible to contemplate.

When Father returned from the Whigs we were together once more. And don't that make a comely picture?! The Special Five. I do not believe there is a combination like it on Earth. Grand Protector, Gentle Nourisher, Dashing Partner in Crime, Sprightly Dusting Companion, and highly accomplished Yours Truly—a roguish band! And mustn't forget Carlo, that Loyal Wonder of Shaggy Love!—The Special Six, together beneath the selfsame roof!

But not for long. One week before my birthday Vinnie left for school in Ipswich. Hard as it was to let her go, it occurred to me straightway that Carlo could now share my quarters, as should have been the arrangement from the beginning. I myself would have welcomed my shaggy companion on the bed, were it not for the fact that we could not both fit. The first night I crawled beneath the covers, he came straightway to the bed, front paws on the spread and looking deep into my eyes. I pointed to the mat. "Lie down," I told him. He turned his enormous head to consider the situation and without further ado complied. Soon he was leading the way upstairs each night, a signal that he quite liked our new arrangement. I myself was comforted no end by his presence. It was a lonesome time—Vinnie away and friends were leaving, too. Abiah was gone and Emily Fowler too and Jennie, off then to teach in Warren—in the far state Ohio. Though Abby had not left in the geographic sense, ever since our April marriage talk I noticed a distance beneath the closeness.

Though lonely, the winter was not without some gaiety. Austin, done with Hume's *History*, had a bit more time away from the College. There were parties, carriage rides with Emmons and Gould—so *tall* and handsome!—at the pauper's door, who cared?—and the candy pulling at Harriet Montague's, where I met a new girl by the name of Martha Gilbert, an orphan awaiting the arrival of her sister.

I received many letters from Ben—all the way from Worcester! These brightened my days! He never failed to inquire after my verses, what jots I had made between the bread and the mending and what plans I had for them. The best, most wonderful surprise was when he sent me an edition of Ralph Emerson's poems! I could not believe my good fortune and Ben's kindness. I was near beside myself! Vesuvius was boiling underneath and soon to be "Vesuvius Unchained"!

The lava was heating up. How to contain my life? I did not know. I was writing more poems. I simply *had to*! Simple verses most, foolish some. It mattered not. I hurried through my daily chores—make the breakfast, bake the bread, polish the apples, adjust the comforters, dust the stairs, darn the socks—then Father's dinner—beat the rugs, heat the tea, and on and on, stopping only to catch the arrows from Infinity—a ragged scramble upon the laundry list—illegible? No time to check! Stuff in the apron pocket for safekeeping until that blessed return to Self! 9. oclock! Oh, glory! Home to my Self! 9. oclock had been the time for Austin and me, our famous Night Talks. There were fewer of those now. Now it was time for my Self and Me! There is a force such times that moves like lava to express the *smallest* thing. It need not be "significant" to fire up the blood, not grand. A bird with beads for eyes, the occasional snake, a sunset—it matters not. Up the stairs! Close the door! Empty the pockets—decipher—tend—leave alone to grow in that still, deep place inside. I cannot tell you where that is. I do know it is plain, true, under all, above all—as weightless as the butterfly's wing!

Oh! Abiah was in Amherst in January! It was just a week, but we saw each other one brief time. I did not ask for explanations and 'Biah offered none, but all was well. What joy! The trouble may have been in my mind.

Mother was ill, bearing another bout of neuralgia and low spirits. I felt sorry for her and at the same time burdened by the care of the household. Armed with *The Frugal Housewife*—"dedicated to those who are not ashamed of economy" and written by a certain Mrs. Child—one assumes she has no name of her own—I did the best I could.

One afternoon Gould invited me for a carriage ride. I would have loved to go with him, but "No," I had to tell him. "Can't go. Mother needs me at home." I was extremely vexed about it. I decided to send him a Valentine in the form of a poem—and he, being literary editor at Amherst and serving on the board of the campus monthly, *Indicator*, had it published! That was not the reason I sent it, but must admit to a fleeting imagining of such an outcome, not entirely without pleasure.

Father was not pleased. He never did condone my interest in Gould, due perhaps in part to Gould's financial inferiorities. I think he wanted me to marry no one, wealthy or no, preferring I should stay at home and bake his bread. At any rate, my first publication only served to make matters worse on two fronts. First off, in Father's mind Gould could not be trusted. Publishing a young lady's Valentine was not to be forgiven. Second, Father made it clear I should not be "flaunting my verses in public" or "wasting my time," what with Vinnie away and Mother ill. Father's reaction was a disappointment, though not a surprise. I regretted the publishing, but not the writing of the poem. Never! I was bursting with the joy of words, of what they could do, of what *I* could do by putting them together in countless ways. The Majesty, the Humor, the Phosphorescence! Answer the Call! Narrow the Charge! No time to waste! Sweep the porch! Beat the rugs! Dust the stairs! Then on to my Self! I would trade my *Self* for Nothing! Yet all the while I felt a gnawing in my brain. Father's sense of things is trapped in my blood. I do so want to please him. His preference flows through my veins and cannot be overlooked.

One afternoon in March I encountered a Scarlet Death. As Carlo and I started out for our walk I opened the kitchen door and there in the snow was a dead cardinal. Well, really, it was what remained of that noble bird—some scarlet feathers, his beak and crimson blood, shocking in its brilliance upon the pristine snow. Snugglepoops out for sport? Roughnaps on the kill?

As we walked, I thought about the bird and what he

249

had gotten for showing his Scarlet Grandeur—a bloody Death! But were we not all slated in kind? Male cardinals were brilliant, while the females owned a muted version of their magnificent mates. Must this be so with human-kind as well? All was not so in Nature. Or was it?

Think of the lion! Consider the peacock's tail!

My mind was not comforted by these remembrances. But then—

The tiger! The elephant! The giraffe!

Visions of species flooded my mind where the sexes appeared of equal brilliance.

We must all be ourselves!

Carlo left to chase after a squirrel, leaving me alone with my thoughts.

It's not fair. Girls are not supposed to take pride in their achievements unless it involves dusting something or making pudding.

Carlo returned to my side, panting heavily. He had been outdistanced by a tiny nut gatherer.

Sue

S pring. 1850. And I not yet twenty.

Things had been bleak and dreary, Mother ill, Vinnie gone, Ben gone, Whiskers busy at college. Austin was exhausted with too much study and no proper time to spend with his soulmate sister. No fancies by the hearth, no laughs before the early-morning prayers to put things right, only Father's gray face—disapproval of my published Valentine may have been the reason—a cold and cough persistent enough to send yours truly off between the covers, eyes too sore to read, mind too dull to write. Was I listening to Father's soundless instructions as regarded my heedless self-expression?

Suffice it to say all had been sad for many weeks before spring graced Amherst with its benevolent splendor. Excitement was in the air!— "Hear ye! Hear ye! The Sewing Society has commenced again!" The world would be saved after all!! Then—longer days, robins back, the cherry trees in bloom in the front yard, Carlo soaking in the pond.

And then . . .

I am washing the dinner dishes, Carlo at my feet. In one hand I hold the gravy boat—delft blue sailing ships, sails unfurled on white background. The water from the pump flows over the narrow, sturdy handle. I hear voices in the hall. I set down the gravy boat, leaving the kitchen to end the suspense. Carlo follows.

When we reach the hall, Mother is smiling pleasantly, shawl about her shoulders, and by the door, Martha Gilbert, the orphan girl from Harriet Montague's candy pulling, and next to her a slightly younger girl, straight, handsome, with sad eyes. Mother closes her shawl about her neck. "You have friends, Emily," she says, always the considerate hostess.

"Hello," says Martha, a gentle soul, who stoops, by reason of anatomy, insecurity or poor nutrition. She gestures to the other girl. "This is Sue."

Our eyes meet. Past, present and future in a single moment. I knew straightway. I would know this formidable, mysterious girl forever, as I had always known her. I cannot say why, but this was how it was.

Soon after our auspicious meeting Sue and I found ourselves in the midst of fast and ever-deepening delight. Our Front Door Stone Talks were many and Fancies in the tall grass, walks up and down the hills and across the fields, through the woods, along the streams, New

England arraying herself in the mantle of new Life! It was the same for me, new Life, new Love—Sue!

Sue was born a few short days after the arrival of her loving admirer. Our first private conversation covered this point and many others. Both her parents had died. She had come from Miss Kelly's School to live with her older sister, Martha, at the Cutlers', and on and on, us two on the front door stone and noble March telling its blustery tale. But we don't care for that. Together we sit, our shawls tight about our shoulders, our bonnets tied. "I feel that I have always known you," I say.

"I feel the same."

My heart tumbles on its end. "You do?"

"I do."

"What is that feeling?"

"I don't know."

"We have only just met."

"But there it is."

"It's as if we had known each other in another place . . ."

". . . At another time."

"Have you ever felt this way before? "

"I have, but not often."

"I as well, though not so strong as with you."

Carlo jumps into the pool. A loud splash, then quiet. Underwater paws paddle in silence. I look at Sue. Her deep gray eyes watch my Shaggy Ally circle the pool, his huge head above the water. Sue turns to look at me. My heart tumbles once more. "You've had a sad life," I say.

"That's true."

"I'm sorry."

"You are not to blame."

"Two parents dead. I can't imagine it."

"That's just as well."

"I think it's well to imagine everything. The world is so full! I want to know it all!"

"You don't want to know about parents dying."

"I do! That is, if you don't mind."

"My mother died when I was six. My father died when I was ten. He was, shall we say, of 'ill repute.' Can we talk about something pleasant? People always want to know about my awful past. I want to know about the future!"

Carlo leaves the pool. He stops, shakes water in all directions.

"What do you like to do most in the world?" I ask.

"I like to write."

My breath is near to stop. "I write as well! Is it not the greatest joy?"

"It is."

"To capture those thoughts from the edge of Nowhere!"

"To get ahold of life!"

"A few simple words may be put in such an order as to jolt the senses! Don't you find that true?"

"I do!"

"One's very truth may be challenged to admit a larger Truth! One's very life may be changed by the order of a few chosen words! Have you ever thought of it, Susie?— May I call you Susie?"

"Why not?"

"It takes my breath away! Emerson can do it! And I will do it too!"

"I believe you will," she says. And don't my heart skip a beat?!

That night I lay awake, Carlo on the mat by my bed— a steady breathing comfort of love—and the moonlight through the window. I thought about my new friend.

A writer! How Large a Circumstance!

How grand it was to feel there was someone with whom I could share my deepest heart. One I could talk to—about anything!—and she would understand. It was too soon to know this and yet I knew it with all my being. There had been only Austin, but he was gone in that way now, uncaring of my writing, busy at college, caught up in his own life apart from me. I could never talk with Mother, not in the deep place where it mattered, not with Father(!) or Vinnie, not even with Abby, or my other girl friends, much as we loved one another. Not anymore. Some subjects yes, but others no. And those of the second group were the most important— to me, at any rate. Sue was different. I don't know how I knew, but I knew. We were much alike, with circumstances so different, her parents dead, mine very much alive, her father improvident, mine the very model of respectability. She had traveled much and I almost not at all. She had no home. I had a Home with a capital *H*!

Carlo gave a moan, adjusted himself on the mat and let out a contented sigh. I turned on my back, quilt about my chin, mind racing in the night.

Sue!

The next day we took a long walk with Carlo to the top of Hendersons Hill. We held hands, breathing deeply and full as we strove. "What do you write?" I asked her.

"Stories and essays mostly," she answered. "And you?"

"Poems."

"I admire that."

"You do?"

"So difficult and precise a form."

"My verses hold the deepest part of me," I admitted. We were quiet for a moment, my thoughts having their own way. A matter had been concerning me very much of late. "Do you worry about the future?"

"In what respect?"

"Women rarely write, you know, and that's what we shall be—women!—whether we like it or not."

"Why can't women write?"

"It's not generally done."

"Women write."

"Not many."

Carlo barked at a circling crow. The bird paid him no mind, taking flight over the meadow below. "Can I tell you something?" I asked.

"Anything."

"It's private. . . ."

"Life is dull without a bit of intrigue. . . ."

"I want to be a Poet."

"You *are* a Poet."

"I mean seriously."

"I spoke seriously. You *are* a poet. You write poems."

"I want Poetry to be my life's work."

"Then it will be."

She sees me!

Blessed relief! How grand it is to be understood for who one is!

Carlo brought me a stick, dropped it at my feet and sat. I knew what that meant, so I threw it. Carlo ran to bring it back.

"I would like to read your poems."

No one had said that, no one but Ben and he was far away. Oh, Ben's belief in me was grand, but Sue's brought all that selfsame fire and *more*! As one of the "fairer sex" Sue could see that a woman *must* write if she wants to—not hide her mind behind convention's way!

I was not alone. The inspiration! The permission! The joy!

Stolen Time

Sue had just appeared, bringing spring without and within, when not weeks after, days maybe, there they were—discs of frozen light, moist and broad—soundless—falling outside my window and the Daffodils bending their heads with the weight of it. Imagine their surprise! That selfsame could be matched only by Carlo's as I swung open the kitchen door to let him out. Why, he stopped dead and stared, wonder showing in the straightness of his back, muscles tensing beneath auburn coat, massive head high. A brief pause as Time appeared to stop, then the pounce, the landing, snow past the belly and the snap—snow in mouth, snow on nose!

The sun blinded me, reflected off the virgin whiteness. I shut my eyes. When light is overbright I feel exquisite pain, my eyes involuntarily shut and I to find some dark for comfort. I wonder if others feel this. There may be something wrong with my eyes.

In a few days the Snow was gone—as is the way with all—and it was back to the same old sixpence of spring, and a fine old sixpence it is, with the singular exception of Spring Cleaning. I prefer dirt. I am fond of mud, especially plentiful in spring. I seem to be of a minority as regards that particular matter, as well as many others.

It was the "Spring of Sue"! I wanted to be with my newfound Love—not to clean! I wanted to tend my garden, to read, to play upon the piano, to *write*! But Father was insistent. "Your Mother is down with neuralgia and your sister is gone. The housework falls to you." It seemed to me it had fallen some time back, as I had been carrying the burdensome duty upon my frail but able shoulders for several months. However, I chose not to challenge Father. I was not pleased with the Circumstance. To add Spring Cleaning to the already dizzying number of household tasks—it was too much! Up with the carpets! Out to the yard! Hang them! Beat them!— I needn't describe the vigor with which that was done! Those *bad* carpets, taking me from my Verses—my Sue! Surely they had to be whipped!

In stolen time Susie and I shared our girlish fancies. She read my verses, and didn't she find them exceptional! She was candid in offering suggestions for improvement, which I appreciated very much indeed. She rarely found the need to offer such suggestions—which I appreciated at least as much, if not more! I knew she was honest.

And I knew she loved me. I cannot tell you how I knew. The greatest things are often indescribable. What heresy for a Poet to express *that* thought! But it was mine and therefore must be claimed.

Susie shared her writing with me as well. The sharpness of her mind was exceptional. Right to the very center she went, no questions asked! She spoke it as she saw it and her vision always her very own. I especially admired her essays. We began to exchange books—some great, some not great but merry—as well as many outrageous opinions on Life, both passing and Eternal. I knew straightway that Susie was a thinker of deep thoughts but was surprised by the level of enjoyment she displayed as regards Life's simple pleasures, good times, foolish things and all those imaginings still alive in so many girls at the grown-up age of nineteen! Before we knew it we had developed a secret language divulged to no one, not even Austin, who was taking a shine to both the Gilbert sisters. And who could blame him?! I found his interest in Susie to be thrilling. The thought that the two I loved more than any in the world might fall in love—why, it took my breath away! Should it happen, I would be sure to feel utterly responsible, not to mention an indispensable part of the entire arrangement!

"What thoughts do you have about Austin?" I asked Susie one morning as we sat beneath the Elm, Carlo in the pond—splash—paddle—and us two reading some book or other.

"I'm reading," said Susie.

"I can see that," I said, "but tell me. It won't take long. Do you like him *especially?*"

Sue kept her eyes on the page. "I think I do."

"You don't *know?*"

Sue, eyes down. "Not entirely."

"What kind of an answer is that? 'Not entirely'!"

"That's all I can say on the subject at present."

"He likes you." I had not intended to share this tasty bit of information, given to me by my brother the night before, but could not help it.

Susie looked decidedly intrigued, then answered casually. "Good." She was embarrassed, I could tell, and not in the *least* disinterested! I determined to let the matter rest for the moment and wait to see what life had in store.

It was a glorious spring. Even Spring Cleaning could not mar its glory; however, there was something that nearly did. The "Great" Revival of 1850! It seems there is no end to the need to save all the poor sinful souls born to this world with no hope of redemption. I alone, it seems, have never felt that certainty of guilt that starts the ball rolling. All around me they were falling like flies.

One evening in June, when the Great Revival Frenzy was at its peak, Carlo and I went to the meadow to walk in the tall grass and sit awhile among the wildflowers by the pond. Carlo did not go into the water as was his usual custom, but stayed at my side. He knew his charge was troubled. "I shall never be a Christian," I told him.

He looked at me, brown eyes deep.

Carlo is not a Christian either. We are two of the lingering bad ones.

Well, *that* thought didn't stick! Carlo bad? It seemed to me we were both somehow all right. I noticed the buttercups all about in profusion. I hadn't seen them when we sat down. I do love buttercups. I want that selfsame flower for my funeral—that is, if I shall ever die—and deep down I know I shall.

The summer brought many changes. Unfortunately, the state of Mother's neuralgia was not one of them. She remained resting on the lounge, occasionally feeling well enough to rise and dust the stairs. Carlo slept outside, the heat once more dictating his whereabouts. Austin graduated and Vinnie returned from Ipswich, lifting many burdens. She brought a feeling of the Festive back to the House and reminded us all not to snivel.

Before August was done there was Large news. Father became a Christian! Yes, the Great Revival had claimed his Soul for Christ. Abby followed into those Waiting

Arms, as did nearly the whole of Amherst, including my Sue. Mother had long since been on the protected side and Austin and Vinnie were on the Threshold. Only Carlo and I remained on the shore of the impenitent. I cannot speak for the cats.

Of all those mentioned I was most upset by Sue's decision to give herself to Christ. Was I jealous? The idea was too miserly to consider and yet I was suspicious of its truth. I had been noticing a possessive strain in my love for Susie, more so than for any other girl. Was that strain rearing its ugly head? I asked my mind the question, but received no answer. Sue and I had endured many serious discussions as pertained to the matter of becoming Christians, during which I never failed to feel judged by her and *not* fairly. It was so unlike her to judge any person—especially *me*! How self-important that sounds. How miserly of me to assume I was the one most especially not to be judged. I am not proud of it, but that is the way I felt and I must live with it. And now I will judge my Susie. For one who enjoys such openness of spirit, she shows a surprising distaste for departing from traditional religious beliefs, a fact that disturbs me very much.

As August proceeded on her perennial march to flame, Susie and I put our religious differences aside, once more sharing fine times, simple, but Large where it matters most. One such time began with a group of girls, Susie's sister, Martha—or Mattie, as we called her—Susie, Abby, Tempe and yours truly, all out for a trip to Mr. Cutler's store. Carlo accompanied us, as usual. After completing our various purchases—I can't remember *any*—we decided on a stroll to the College. With graduation over and so many Whiskers gone from Amherst we were attempting to rekindle the spark of livelier times.

On the way home it was just Susie and me. Susie had taken up the black—wearing only that somber color and none other—some weeks before, at the time of the death of another sister—Mary, who had died in childbirth. It was awfully sad. We walked along the east side of the common, the sun bright, the cows under such trees as could be found. Carlo was behind us, followed by a large yellow cat. I had never seen the cat before and wondered what he might have in mind. He must surely have been a "he." Such size and rough demeanor could point to no other conclusion as far as I could tell.

Susie was extremely quiet. She was of that selfsame persuasion much of that summer and the following fall as well, on account of her sister's death. I was not in the habit of attempting to rouse her from so formal a state, as such endeavors generally served to make the situation worse.

Without warning I heard her voice. "Mr. Stubbins

has pain in his back." And there, some yards ahead, was Mr. Stubbins, employing a cautious gait, shoulders round, bent at the waist and carrying a large sack. "Too bad his brother couldn't have done the errand for him," Sue continued.

"Perhaps he's out of town."

"Perhaps."

We had taken up a favorite game of ours called Observation. We had both been enjoying its basic precepts informally for some time, but shortly after meeting we designed a formal structure to the affair. Artists of any persuasion must *see* life before attempting to express their sense of it. This had been Susie's point to me the day we designed the game. She said the best painters *see*, as do the best sculptors, dancers, musicians and all. It may be said that musicians must *hear*, but consider Beethoven, deaf to sound without, yet hearing within, all the senses alive with the glory of life and the Pain— *seeing* it All! So it is with every artist. And Poets are no exception!

The game goes like this. One person mentions a thing she sees. The small things are best as they are often the most telling. Upon hearing the thing mentioned, the other looks at that selfsame and mentions her next thought. It can build from there, but it don't have to.

Mr. Stubbins turned right on Main Street. "He will need to lie down when he gets home," I said as he passed out of sight, taking his burden with him.

At the north end of the common two cows lay side by side in the mud. Frances was the smaller of the two, black and white, not full-grown, while Clarissa, her white coat brown with mud, had met her lasting weight. They lounged contentedly, their mouths in timeless cross-round chews as we approached. "Frances and Clarissa are in their summer spot," I observed.

"Winter on the rise, summer in the mud," said Sue.

"And peace in the ever-returning familiar." That was my comment. Was it not poetical?

Do Girls Marry for Love?

W hen we reached home it was nearly 2½ oclock. As it was not yet time to cook the supper, we decided to prolong the afternoon in another of our loving talks in the tall green grass. Carlo followed us to the spot, lying down in easy collapse beneath the tree. Susie looked serious all in black and the softness of summer in all directions. My Susie—uncommon, deep, sorrowful, honest, bold—the black magnified these essences with all the power of a microscope. I think it is truly amazing how she came to wear black for three years. One could sail around the world in such a Time!

The black separates her from others.

This was my thought. I did not care for the perception. I felt left out. Susie looked down at the grass.

The black gives her strength.

Sue smoothed her skirt.

It tells her where she is.

Sue swept a strand of hair from her face.

With her sister.

She closed her eyes.

In the grave.

She was so still. The black of her blouse was etched in sharpest line against the summer sky.

The black connects her to her loss.

She leaned back on her elbows.

Unusual comfort, but Comfort nonetheless.

She closed her eyes.

She finds her Self in all the pain.

She tipped her face to the sky.

And where such pain is not—where life goes on and no one knows—one can so easily get lost.

Sue remained still. The Sun beat down on the bones of her cheeks and the rounded lids of her shut eyes.

I would wear white. Not after Death perhaps, but as a way to ground the brain, if the need should arise. Bride of Me! Of Truth, plain, pure, unwavering, real! And Oh! Revelations! Worthy, not defiled! Overcometh! Name mentioned before the Angels!

Susie sat up. Chin to chest she stretched her neck, straightened her head and opened her eyes. We both took a Large breath of Life—in the same moment! Life-giving nourishment, a ground for our Souls, exhaling soon in spacious relief. There was such rest then, such loving Silence. No need to speak, no need *not* to.

Carlo broke the spell by snapping at a fly that buzzed

about his nose. I watched the fly stagger—uncertain it seemed. There is a verse in that! Thoughts took up my mind, grand, troublesome. I felt such love for Susie. I knew she was worthy of my love. I knew her to be in possession of an honest, steadfast heart and that heart close to my own as well. We shared such manner of things—thoughts, opinions, talents, desires, a character far from the ordinary and a particular boldness in the face of convention, to name a few. But why I felt such love I don't know. It was beyond reason when considered in view of the facts. It scared me some.

"I have a question," I said at last. Sue looked at me. "I know that love is love." Sue appeared unsure of what my mind was about. She listened, her eyes upon me, deep and steady. "All love comes from the same source," I went on, "but is there a line of difference?"

"What sort of line?"

"A place where the fabric changes?"

"The fabric?"

"The depth, the purpose."

"Love is its own purpose."

"I suppose. But there are different kinds of love, wouldn't you say?"

"Oh, I think so. In fact, I know there are."

"How do you know?"

"I just know. And so do you. We haven't lived for

nineteen years for nothing."

"And here is another question."

"My Emily is full of them today."

"*Every* day! I just don't ask them all."

"Thank God for small favors!" Sue was smiling. We were playing now.

"You would have time for nothing but my questions!"

"And I might not know the answers."

"Oh, I doubt that!"

"Ask me your second question and we shall see."

I rose up on my knees. "Here it is. . . ."

"Go!"

"If there are many kinds of love . . ."

"There are. . . ."

"Yes, all right, there are many kinds of love, and if one shuts out one of these same . . ."

"Why do that?"

"Let's say that one does—just for example. If one shuts out one kind of love, does that shut out all the rest?"

"I think it does." Susie thought for a moment. "I would say it dulls them at the very least." I was quiet then. I had more to ask, but feared to ask it. My mind went far away. Susie's voice called me back. "Do you have another question?"

"How can you tell?"

"I can read your mind."

"You joke."

"Perhaps." Then in her teasing way, "Don't stop the questions now. You are in good practice!"

The dam broke. "I feel such love for you, Susie, I think my heart will burst! It scares me. I know girl friends love as deep as the Sea itself! Don't you think they do?"

"They do."

"When girl friends love it is a joyous adventure! Not only that, it prepares them . . ."

"Us . . ."

"Us! It prepares *us* for the future and we all know what that is!"

"Men!"

That stopped me. "I like many of the Whisker set . . ."

"I know you do . . ."

" . . . Emmons and Lyman, Gould and Cousin John and Ben—I love Ben!—but Susie, I think I shall never love another as I love you and what does that say for the future?" Carlo snaps at the fly. "Will I ever love a man as I love you?"

Sue is quiet.

"I don't *know*!" I sit up on my knees, no proper young lady here. "You know what Jane Eyre said about love!"

"Many things, as I recall."

"'To be together is for us to be at once as free as in solitude, as gay as in company.'"

"Yes."

"That is how I feel with you! It used to be like that with Austin, but no more. I feel it some with other girls, but not so much as with you. And not with any of the Whisker set! Oh, Susie that is how it *must* be with a man when I make my final decision! Marriage would be a sour thing without it held such Comfort!"

"Marriage is often sour."

"I would rather die!"

Sue looks at the ground.

"Do you think of marriage?" I ask.

"On occasion."

"What occasion is that?"

"On many occasions."

"Do you think of marriage to Austin?"

"I do."

"Do you feel such comfort with him as our beloved Jane describes?"

"Perhaps one day I will."

"I fear I shall never have it—not again—and never with a man to call *my Husband.*"

"Time will tell."

"Time will tell many things if we live long enough.

But it does trouble me, Susie, when I think of it—to give my Life to another! And that is what it is to have a husband nowadays. My deepest part cannot be lost!" Carlo turns to me, puzzled by the fervor of my tone. "I want to write. I *must* write! There is more to life than dusting!"

"I like a clean house."

"I don't like it *that* much!"

"I want to be a hostess."

"I don't."

"Most girls look forward to it."

"Since when have you cared what most girls do?"

"I comment merely."

"Well, I comment merely that most girls don't know which end is up!"

Susie smiles. I feel the warmth of her accepting Love. We sit in silence for a while. A bird comes down the walk, a wren, with plans of her own. I watch her timid steps. "Here is a question," I say.

"Another!"

I sit back down, no feeling in my legs after having knelt for such a lengthy spell. "Most all girls marry. You know they do. It's the chief thing nowadays."

"And your question?"

"Do you think they marry for Love?"

"Some do."

"Only some?"

"I surmise."

"Well, I have one thing to tell you. I will never marry *but* for Love, no matter how many hours I spend alone, no matter how many nights there's no one but me to warm my bed! Others do not feel as I do, but I am used to that."

Father and the Aurora Borealis

Temperance was all the rage that fall, and who should be lecturing on the matter but Father. It was very like him, despite our lovely decanter and four wineglasses—deep bloodred, clear stems, frosty chains of flowers encircling the Circumference—and despite his enjoyment of currant wine!

Father had been at Yale, then back to lecture me on the need for taking better care of myself, as he felt I was too thin. His constant harping on the matter only served to make matters worse. I was feeling none too well, but kept the matter to myself as best I could. Along with his health warnings Father made quite a point of not having been able to eat any bread while away, as he needed me to bake it. One can only assume that if he and his attentive oldest daughter were to be in a different location for any length of time he would die. I cannot say I hold this to be entirely implausible. The thought made me angry and quickly short of breath.

Mother was feeling better, thank goodness, and Vinnie was once again back in the bosom of the family, so the housework situation was considerably improved. Austin was gone to Sunderland to teach, however, leaving far less Hurrah about the house and a pining sister to boot. With Vinnie surrendering to the Arms of Christ in November, I was the sole impenitent sinner of my entire acquaintance—excepting my Shaggy One.

Ben's letters came regularly. Always, I would respond that very night, and me downstairs past 9, the others long asleep, Carlo at my feet and the oil lamp, my pen and ink, and the blessed paper that would carry my Words to my Friend! There you would find me, bent over the desk, describing in detail whatever creation I might be wrestling with, some ethereal vision demanding capture. Ben would always answer just enough—not too much—only what was needed to clear my addled brain, as too much closeness to one's verse may leave one without sight for what lives.

Father never again mentioned my fateful Valentine to Gould—*published*, no less, for all the World to see! But that would be the last, if I cared to retain my place in his Esteem. Mother shows little interest in my verses one way or the other, not a fearsome point of view yet not an especially encouraging one either.

Life was quiet. With Austin gone and so many of his classmates as well—done with college, off to the wilds of a larger existence—Amherst was carrying on in simple

Christian observance. Father was pleased with our lack of party invitations, although Vinnie and I could have done with a bit more in the merriment line.

And then—a surprise!

It was late. All respectable citizens of Amherst had begun the move to the pillow. I was in the kitchen over tea—and Carlo by the stove—when there came a furious clanging of the church bell. I ran from the house expecting to see the town ablaze, but it was no fire at all. It was the Aurora Borealis in all its majesty, lighting up New England!—Crimson, pink and gold!—Great streams of fiery light from out a flaming center like a Sun—and again the flash and again—repeating in a seemingly endless display its news of the Splendor of the Universe!

The street was full of people gazing up in wonder at the heavenly sky above North Pleasant Street. There were the loudest exclamations, great shouts of startled surprise and awe at the Glory of it all! Father was in front of the house, gazing up with all the rest, a huge smile on his face, eyes twinkling in what appeared to be almost mischief! It was *he* who rang the church bell! Father rushing out in the deep of night to personally ring the church bell?! Why, I never heard of such a thing! For a fire perhaps—he would stretch his comfort for that if the need arose—but to inform his neighbors of the chance to behold the beauty of Nature? I would not have thought so, but I would have been wrong!

Oh, what a mood he was in that night! I swear when Father is of a certain persuasion there is nothing grander in all Existence! Not even the Northern Lights! The Show lasted a full forty-five minutes! Mr. Trumbull gave the report in the *Express*, saying it was "one of the most splendid displays of its kind ever witnessed."

After the great display there were smaller flashes of the same, slowing in frequency and brilliance, until gradually the night sky returned to its familiar state. Slowly, the people went back inside their houses, some exchanging words for a time, as the event had to be shared. Father and Carlo and I remained outside to the last, Father in that enthusiastic frame of mind that charmed all. Vinnie returned to the house and bed, but Carlo and I remained in the road with Father.

Father was not ready to sleep, nor was I, and so we two sat in the parlor for the merriest time I can remember. We drank tea, while Carlo snoozed upon the rug. Father expressed surprise that we should see the Aurora here in Amherst, thinking it mainly a show for points farther north. I said that from what I had heard, such brilliant displays could normally be found in more northern regions, but lesser ones might be enjoyed in places like Massachusetts.

"Oh, yes," he said, "you're right, Emily. I have seen

those paler scenes. This was stupendous!"—I had never heard him use *that* word!—"I forgot they were one and the same. What a show!" He was not over it *yet*! I was not either, but as I tend to be quite beflown by even the simplest of Mother Nature's gifts, I would expect it might take some time for me to right my senses—but Father! It was a grand surprise! We stayed up together for hours that night.

"I'm sorry your mother missed the Lights," he said, "but she needed her rest."

We spoke of many things, of Mother's gentle nature, of Austin's superior mind, of Vinnie's flirtations. We spoke of Carlo and before you knew it we got to laughing over his obsession with squirrels and how if one were going to have an obsession at all one might choose a more interesting one. It may have been the best night in my Lifetime, although I suppose it's too early to tell. I do know it left me with an added sense of the warmth residing deep within Father's nature, which has been extremely pleasant.

Once in bed it took a long time to welcome sleep. I lay next to Vinnie, who miraculously was *not* snoring, and thought about Father.

He is so wonderful and terrible, so ALL there and NOwhere. Plain terrible would be a relief. One would know where one stood.

In the morning, Father rapped on my door. It was time to be up and doing. I wished he would leave me alone.

It was a Patchwork time. Beginning with Susie's arrival, my mind was a quilt of contrary squares, each one exclusive of all the rest. And where was Emily in all the jumble?! Most vexing was my huge love for Susie and the matter of religion. Susie was of fixed opinion. Nothing would do but that I come to rest in the waiting Arms of Christ, not the precepts merely, not the Glory of all Creation, not the knowledge of the Bible, or the wonder of Eternity. I must become a Christian in the traditional way. I must declare myself a Christian. I must go to church so many times a week—and it must be to the building called church, not to the woods or the meadow. I must pray so many times a day. I must believe in Original Sin, embracing the thought that we enter this world with evil thoughts and must be cleansed. I could not! I had another way. How unlike Susie to worship Tradition. I found the fact impossible to believe. I knew her. Tradition could fall flat on its face for all she cared—*should* fall if sense were to be appropriately served! But Religion holds a separate shelf in Susie's cupboard. Finding that we could not discuss the matter without unpleasantness, we decided *not* to discuss it. It was an uncomfortable arrangement.

Other Patches did not fit the quilt of my mind—Vesuvius joy and low spirits—verses published and not supposed to be—handsome Whiskers and Father's displeasure—precious friends and friends leaving—walks with Carlo and being too ill to leave the house—and on and on. I was sick much of the time, the ax in the chest, the cough, with eyes too pained for light. Don't look! Quilt overhead! Here is darkness, and peace, and rest! But here is loneliness.

I missed Austin terribly after he left to teach at Sunderland. It seemed to me that he would never again live at home, where he belongs. I wrote him several times a week and am happy to say that he did write back most usually, as a decent brother should. Susie was blessed with his letters as well. Romance was in the wind—a glorious coupling! Sound the trumpet! Beat the drum! Another piece of contrary quilt presents itself. The evil, selfish voice is heard. The news is grand but what of *me*? Discarded now? Out upon the heap?

Keep quiet, or someone will hear your thoughts!

That fall Susie and I and Vinnie were very much looking forward to attending a series of lectures that captured our fancy. They were to be given in Amherst by Richard Henry Dana, that brave Boston sailor, on none other than Shakespeare! The most special was the one on Hamlet, my favorite tortured Prince! In the morning of the *Hamlet* lecture I started out with Carlo to secure some medicinal drops for Mother. When I shut the door behind me I felt a familiar fright. Sometimes when I dream, or just before I leave for that enchanted land, I feel a start, as if I am on a wall and just step off. Nothing beneath. Such a fright grips me that all is lost! Heart racing—breath shallow—safety gone! That was my perception when I shut the door.

Wait!

Carlo looks up in question.

Can't leave!

Carlo sits.

Stove!

Carlo snaps at a fly.

Water boiling!

Another snap from Carlo.

Forget it. Not boiling.

I start off.

I just checked it.

Carlo follows.

But did I?

I stop.

Was it this morning I checked the stove?

Carlo stops.

Or yesterday?

Heart racing.

It was yesterday. Before church. Kettle cold. Did I check today?

My inside voice is stern.

You checked twice, Emily! Continue on!

I can't move.

Legs numb.

Terror!

Flames!

Terror!

The House will burn to the ground!

Mind stops.

Go back. Better safe than sorry.

I try to breathe.

Who says that? Father? Mother? Both.

I turn on pudding legs, Carlo behind, sure his care-taker has lost her mind. He may be right.

Once inside I see the kettle, quiet, stone cold. Exhaustion claims its victim.

Bloodless head. Can't think.

Up the stairs. Carlo watches but does not follow.

Stay with me, Carlo.

He doesn't move.

Please.

But no.

Please!

Into my room.
Safe.
I sleep deeply, dead almost.

When I wake up I feel unwell. I know straightway I will not go to the lecture. The World will pass me by. There I am, alone in my darkened room, forsaken even by my dog. The well-known words take their place in my brain.

> *How weary, stale, flat, and unprofitable*
> *Seem to me all the uses of this world!*

Shakespeare got it right.

Father Puts Out the Fire

I have met with many bouts of low spirits. I don't know what to do about it and so I go on singing and hope for the best. Hope is a bird, arrival unnoticed until there!—perched quiet on the shoulder. No, not on the shoulder, in the Soul! Sometimes the wind blows so cold and the night comes so dark, one thinks there will never be a single thing in this World to look forward to. And then, sure as Day, that little bird returns, chirping the sweetest melody, and all is well! I must write a verse about that.

I was quite ill during the months that followed the *Hamlet* lecture and the scare of the burning house—confined to bed, the reluctant partner of my pillow. Vinnie was often ill as well *and who would dust the stairs?!* The question burned within my breast. It was Mother did it. Pocket handkerchief ready! Duster in hand! Proceed! Somehow we were never all sick at the same time, at least there was always one of us well enough to rally to the charge!

Many left us that spring. It hardly seemed as if they

could, so many gone already. The usual round of mourners passed through the cemetery beneath the window, Consumption so often the cause. We had just lost Leonard Humphrey to the grave when others left by separate means. Lyman left in March to seek his fortune in the south. Vinnie was extremely vexed about it, her first serious romance ended. I did feel sorry for her pain. I was vexed as well, losing, as I did, an excellent reading partner. And did Austin return from Sunderland to the waiting arms of his devoted sister? He did not, but instead threw caution to the Wind and went to Boston to teach.

Ben married in June. It was a terrible leaving to my jealous mind. Was I to marry him? Surely not. The thought may have passed through my mind on a whisper journey. Ben was my Preceptor, my friend—and such he would remain—but that did not help *any*! Another had won his heart and that, to this miserable sinner, struck a blow to her own. Her name was Sarah Warner Rugg— now Sarah Warner Rugg Newton. And there the matter must be laid to rest.

When I was well enough to be up and doing, it was Susie and me all the way. Though she had visited during my bout of illness, she stayed not long for fear of tiring me. Now we were back in business! All matters, both inconsequential and Large, were covered in deepest deep by us two and always the feeling we could go on together forever! One evening, shortly after the news of Ben's marriage, we got talking of Europe. Sue would love to travel to that part of the world. I find it a noble calling, but for my part, I would just as soon go in reverie and spare the inconvenience of dealing with luggage. Mother's daughter after all! Sue's first stop would be Italy. She is especially fond of all things Italian in the art line.

"I must say, when it comes to books, the English are my favorites," I offer. We are alone in the meadow, only Carlo to tell the tale. He lies by my side, panting in the summer heat, a look on his broad face to suggest a smile.

Sue lies back in the grass. "The English books are good," she says, a compliment of high order. Sue is not given to curlicues. She says what she means and little else.

Hawthorne's *The Scarlet Letter* had just been published—a sad story—but very true. I mentioned how fine I thought it was. Susie had not yet read it but was planning to. "Name your favorite English books in order of preference!" I instruct. "Go!" And we are off, Sue first, then yours truly. Before you know it I am on to my most cherished topic. "One needs solitude for writing," I declare. "The mind must have space to receive those thoughts from Infinity!"

Susie agrees.

"And how do we get that space?" I give her no time to answer. "Where is the room when one is filled with chatter as regards the price of twine . . . ?"

". . . or what color should be worn in August . . ."

". . . or what the neighbor should have said . . ."

". . . or *did* say . . ."

". . . or did *not*! There is no room left for Glory! Oh, keep me free of such a Circumstance!"

A breeze comes up. Carlo lifts his chin, nose to the wind. All is well.

Up with the jib sail! Lay her a'hold! Currer Bell is a woman!

When the news reached Amherst that the extraordinary author of my beloved *Jane Eyre* was a woman, I felt a celebration to be in order! I had suspected as much—but to know! A woman by the name of Charlotte Brontë was the writer. A woman! I wondered how Father would have taken the news had Charlotte been his own. Who would have baked his bread had his beloved daughter gone about pilfering her precious time, penning dark tales of the moor, full of impropriety and unbridled Passion? Too horrible to contemplate!

I was considering these points on my way downstairs with Carlo one afternoon in July. It was close on three and awfully hot. I was looking for something, a thimble, I think. Father and Mother were sitting side by side in the parlor, Mother sewing, Father reading—nothing carnal, one can be sure. I suspect Father's tight rein and narrow mouth tell of unspoken interest, but cannot be sure on that point.

At any rate, there they were and Vinnie nearby, dusting—no surprise there—and the cats about her feet. As I reached the parlor there came an awful banging on the door, the cats all a'swish and Vinnie and Father and I rushing to answer the call. A neighbor's barn was on fire! All hurried out, and soon it seemed as if the whole town would burn to the ground! It was a shame Austin missed it, as he does so possess a taste for excitement. There was a terrible wind and all dry from no rain and *no engine*! I don't remember why. It was broken or away tending to some other disaster. The men were all heroes under Father's supervision, you may be sure. Together with buckets and more water than I have seen at one time, save as Nature would arrange it, they put the fire out!

When it was over Father sent the men off to Howe's for a grand time and returned home to his book, gathering whatever relaxation might be offered from so lifeless a tome. I put off my search for the thimble or whatever other small item I may have been missing, and giving in to exhaustion, bade Carlo follow me up the stairs and into my room, where I met with the comfort of my pillow. As I lay in bed waiting for sleep, my thoughts returned to the brave Charlotte Brontë, who wrote the great *Jane Eyre*, and how Father would have felt had she been his daughter. Soon closeness to sleep blurred my thoughts and the fire became one with how angry I was beneath my mind. Father would have been displeased—not proud, not happy for his daughter's good fortune, but ashamed of her indecent behavior. I dreamed I was the barn. Father was putting my fire out and there was nothing I could do to stop him.

Shortly after the fire Austin was home for a whole month. It was August, I believe. The House was itself again and all of us so happy to be together. Mother was feeling better, up and doing, and polishing a specially selected apple for her only son each and every day. It seemed to me that Austin's admiration of Susie was growing. Hers was for him. I know because she told me.

All things must end, or so we have been told. Soon the trees would be letting go their tenants. Soon Austin would be gone. Before I knew it, he was off to teach at Endicot in Boston. And that was not the worst of it. Sue had been called to teach at Mrs. Archer's Boarding and Day School for Young Ladies, in far-off Baltimore— Maryland, no less! It was a fine, sought-after job. I was happy for her opportunity, while at the same time found myself wishing the job did not exist. We were both so awfully vexed about the idea of our separation that we could not say good-bye. We decided to write each other notes instead. We left these—at different times so as not to meet—at the foot of our favorite tree in the meadow. I included a poem. It was for her and none other. I think I will not quote it here.

Ill health returned to the Dickinson girls. Vinnie was not so bad as I, but had a fever nonetheless. I felt certain my trouble was Consumption, lying in wait since infancy, but again said nothing of Consumption to anyone. I knew Mother was upset, as she became especially quiet. There is much Consumption in her family—in *my* family—which is never a good sign. Grandmother Norcross and her brother Hiram both gave their lives to that guiltless marauder the year before I was born. I have always fancied it my job *not* to do the same. I surmise it to be Mother's concern that causes her to be mute. Though she stays close, cools the fire from my brow and hurries to bring whatever I might need, silence is her loyal companion.

Father was determined that Vinnie and I should be cured. We had long been putting up with Dr. Brewster and then to Greenfield, but nothing could be done. It was decided that we should be treated in Boston. Aunt Lavinia's homeopath, a certain Dr. Wesselhoeft, would have the honor. Wesselhoeft. One would not expect the final *e*.

All in all, the trip passed without mishap. We made a stop in Worcester to see Uncle William and to offer our condolences as poor Aunt Eliza had just recently died. After that it was off to Boston to stay a fortnight with Aunt Lavinia and Uncle Loring, little Louise and Frances. It was lovely to see Austin—when free from teaching hours at Endicot—but awfully hot, which put me not in a mind to go out. The rush about city life is not for me and doubly so in such oppressive heat. I begged Austin to excuse me.

We saw Dr. Wesselhoeft, whose remedy proved useless; however, a certain Dr. Jackson saved the day! He prescribed the glycerine, which worked wonders.

Once Home, I felt I had never been so glad to see any place in all my life! Mother and Father had gotten on well without us. I had been concerned something might happen to them while away, so the sight of them at the door and Carlo at their feet was a welcome one indeed!

I would soon be twenty-one. It hardly seemed possible. I was not at all sure how one was supposed to feel at such a worldly age, but I was certain that however one was supposed to feel I did not feel that way. I imagined myself an "intelligent and thoughtful young girl"—certainly not a woman. I wrote of this to Susie in far-off Baltimore, who surmised that nobody felt the way they thought they were supposed to feel, but were disinclined to mention the fact. That helped some. However, as usual I secretly felt myself to be different from all.

In the midst of these weighty considerations came Thanksgiving! Susie was not at home, but in all other ways it was a grand time. Father and Austin arrived from Boston, Father having once again been a delegate to the "Bald Men's Society"—the Whigs!—and then the fun began. After church, where Reverend Colton spoke with pleasant sincerity on the nature of being a worthy Husband and other matters of essential propriety, we enjoyed a wonderful dinner. Mother left no stone unturned in the cooking line! After dinner Father suggested Austin take the Girls—Vinnie and me—for a sleigh ride! Abby came too, and didn't we have the most wonderful time, laughing and reading letters from Susie and taking in the fine New England countryside. Later at a party Abby sang her favorite song—that would be "Blue Violets"—in enthusiastic, ragged fashion, then I off to the hearth with Austin to muse. It seemed as if Life were back to where it should be—as if we were children again and always would be. I missed my Susie, but all else was in its proper place.

Professor Tyler's Woods

The branch of the quince tree scratched against the side of the house beneath the window. Jack Frost was moving at his expected pace, dropping not a stitch of time as usual. Winter's slant of afternoon light told of things to come—the heft—the foretelling—but of what? The branch *scratch-scratch*ed—the Angel's fingernail hinting—and all the while me thinking of Susie and when shall I see her and why must I wait so long? I thought I should be shut in a closet until a happier time. It was too awful, really!

To start things off, Pussy died. Vinnie was crushed. Now there were three cats in all, namely Roughnaps, Snugglepoops, and Tootsie. If you ask me that was plenty, but Vinnie saw it different. I did feel sorry for her. She was so close to the creature and loss is always hard. I know how precious a pet can be. I don't know how I will survive should Carlo die before me.

The branch of the quince tree scratched once more. I looked through the window at the narrow branches. I wondered if they were lonely without their summer tenants. Did they feel as if they had "themselves," brown and stiff only, no fruit, no leaves, no tender blossoms? Did they wonder if it would be so always, or did they know that spring would come? I told myself they knew, for it seemed as if they did, to me at least, and for whom else may one speak?

Spring will come for me as well.

It was a pleasant understanding.

I found myself with the pen more than ever. I think there was a difference afoot in my desire to write. Until then it had been a great joy, a blessed return to myself, a dream I would pursue forever, a help in times of fear. It was all that now and more. The "more" was that I *had* to write. I *had* to return to my Self or I would die. The writing of my verses had become nourishment larger than food or sleep or friend or any. Without I wrote my verses I felt I would slip away until I was gone. I could not be without my Self. I could not survive that Circumstance.

Each day the pockets of my apron received their guests—scraps of paper, shopping lists, envelopes, whatever might be used to carry my jottings—notes from Infinity—observations from the garden—the path of a bug—the death of a cat—the dependability of a star—caught until such time as could be considered afresh, put together in just form, my single lamp lighting the page to carry the Light past Death, should I die—I knew I would, though it seemed beyond a thing to contemplate—and should another come to read them.

Do I not seem the accomplished young lady, saving the world from behind my bedroom window? I have to laugh at myself, which is a good thing for one filled with so much self-importance! Most of my verses are slight, bits of nonsense, wisps of girlish fancy. The prime example being the poem published—without my knowledge, or consent—that very month in the *Springfield Daily Republican*. It was a Valentine to none other than William Howland, trivial, but not badly done and quite roguish, if I may cast a ray of praise upon its humble author. I was not pleased with the changes made by the editorial staff, not to mention the gray stare from Father. I do so wish he took pride in my writing. He takes pride in me, I know, but not in the literary line. His approval appears in matters concerning forbearance and the making of bread.

I sat looking out the window, as the branch of the quince tree continued to scratch against the side of the house. A funeral was passing—heads bent, dark coats and shawls. All was February gray—like Father's face when he saw my poem in the paper. He saw it there but read not a word—and was mute! I wished he had said *something*! A reprimand would have been better than nothing!

A squirrel darted across the stiff grass, past the

mourners, a nut between his anxious jaws. I thought of the bread to bake, the stairs to sweep. Vinnie could not be expected to do *all* the housework, though it would please my evil heart! Mother was sick again, with pains in the limbs. Much would be left to Vinnie.

"Time to go," I told my sleeping Carlo. He woke with a start, ready for whatever I had in mind.

That afternoon I got a letter from Jennie, my dear companion from the schooltime days—jumping on the bed in the extra room, composing notes to the cats to keep out. It came all the way from Ohio! Jennie said I simply must come and visit her and she would not take no for an answer. I was flattered to hear of such longing for my company, but the thought of leaving my precious Home caused quick concern. I was surprised by the force of it.

No, no. Mustn't do that.

Heart beating quickly. Breath thin. No air.

Dungeon Fear returned?

I quickly declined.

> *Thank you for your kind invitation.*
> *It would please me more than I can say,*
> *but I must be excused. Perhaps you can*
> *come to Amherst. Oh, I am hoping that*
> *you can! But leave my Father's House?*

*It would be as if to rip my heart from
my chest. Please understand and know
that I love you.*

Affectionately,
Emily

It was a time of many changes. It hardly seemed as if
there could be more and yet it was so. Some alterations
cause me to question the sense embarking on so flimsy
a Circumstance as living upon this Earth. I find that even
melodious changes are not always easy as they wrench
the Soul, only to drop it in the land of the unfamiliar.
The old ways are in the blood and a happy wrench is a
wrench all the same.

The first change was terrible. Death claimed my
dear former roommate, Cousin Emily, the selfsame who
had offered such support during my stay at Mt Holyoke,
another stolen from me by ruthless Consumption. Oh,
it is too awful a disease! And no way to stop it! Father's
sister Aunt Mary was next, or first perhaps. I don't recall.
Grief dulls one's sense of time—only blank—blank—and
more blank—until the blood is once more perceived in
the veins and Life exists for a while.

One change was easy. Austin had finished teaching
and was at home. How grand to see his slippers under
the chair and better yet to see him! It picked up all our

spirits. Mother's strength improved, which meant much fussing about—"did we have what we needed?"—and smiles and all that went with it! Father was most relieved to have us all "where we should be"—as he said many times—together! Oh, it did feel good! The Special Five! And I know Father was comforted, being so often away, to have Austin about the house. Vinnie enjoyed the parties with her handsome brother and his Whisker friends very much indeed. Vinnie loves any chance for a party. The attentions of dashing young gentlemen never fail to please her—and carriage rides with stars bright, moon low—forget the shawl!—Father will never know!

A week after my birthday—and me twenty-two!—Father was elected Representative to Congress for the 10th Massachusetts District. It was quite an honor but meant that he would be more often away. As if that were not enough, Austin left for Harvard Law School. Our home once again became a shadow of its former self—Mother and Vinnie, yours truly and Carlo carrying on as in time of war, the men gone, the women and the animals striving to survive each new day. Once again, I forgot the cats! I will not hold myself in terribly low esteem for the omission as the cats have never been uppermost in my mind. Another cat joined our merry band when Austin left for Harvard—not a fair trade in my opinion—by the lively name of Drummydoodles. Vinnie gets full credit for that merry bit of literary imagination. "Drummy" is a bit wild, a large tiger cat, possessing jungle ways. Birds beware!!

And then came March. The month brought the most awful death I had ever known. Two unacceptable words—

Ben. Died.

My Preceptor, my inspiration, alive no more! I had lost him twice already, once to Worcester, once to marriage, but that was not enough. I was to lose him again and this time forever in this world—and in Eternity, perhaps. How is one to know? It was too cruel! I felt had I loved him better, he would have stayed. I thought so many things, fanciful things—that he would appear at the door, be sitting in the parlor; that a letter would come in the mail from him, or a book, or some precious gift or other. I dreamed about him. He was so real and we were so real together. Then the awful waking up and he was dead. I felt I simply must know if he was afraid to die. The question troubled me greatly. I could not rest until I knew the answer. I thought to write a letter to Ben's Pastor to see if he knew what Death was like for my Preceptor. As I did not know the Reverend Hale, this took ample consideration as to the matter of propriety. I delayed initiating the correspondence for many months.

The very same week that Ben died, Sue went to visit Austin at Harvard and they became engaged. I had been waiting for just that, but when it happened I was not glad. I knew I should be happy for them, but could not be. It was loss all the way. Ben lost. Austin lost. Sue lost. And I alone.

It happened again.

New London Day. June. Hot. Father has been working for years to bring the railroad to Amherst and now it has come— "Amherst & Belchertown" to points unknown— Whistle hooting twice a day, and now the dusty time to celebrate—such heat—the earth parched to desperation. All of New London has come by special train to Amherst to revel in "progress" and to praise the grand accomplishment of a certain Mr. Dickinson, known otherwise as Emily E. Dickinson's Father, Chief Marshal at his day of Triumph! There is a dinner planned, refreshments prepared and the streets overripe with hordes of lively folk and shouts and carriages everywhere, proceeding at a pace better suited to the open country. I look out the window. The streets are filling. The noise is great. My Pleasant Street no longer belongs to me. It has been taken over by strangers, to be used as they see fit.

They didn't ask me.

A stern voice is heard in the other half of my brain.

Why should they ask you? Is it listed in the ledger as "North Pleasant Street, owned by Emily Elizabeth Dickinson"?

Mother calls. Time to meet Father at the station. Out we go, swept into the flow of assuming humanity. It is *so* hot, but they don't care for that.

They think the day was meant for them. Where do I come in?

Dust fills the June air. The heat is oppressive. I feel faint, head heavy, legs weak.

Not again!

I try to keep walking.

Walk straight.

Terror.

Stay in the utmost center.

Panic!

I can't breathe!

I try.

Breathe!

I can't.

Help me!

An "excuse me" to Mother.

Must get away!

Mother, worried, asks what's wrong.

Can't speak.

"Are you all right?"

NO!

"What is it?"

No tongue.

"Emily!"

I head for Professor Tyler's woods. I can see the trees, quiet, cool, waiting. I will not faint in their sturdiness, for there I know is Peace.

Lonely upon the Shore

I t had been some time since a Terror of such momentous proportion had presented itself. Now I worried daily about the future. When would the Terror come again? Where would I be? What would I be doing?

Summer continued despite my concerns. Austin was not well at Harvard. He carried on with his studies, but it was one cold after the next and several bouts of low spirits. We were quite the pair. I really did feel that if he could be at Home, all would be solved. I was convinced that my desire to provide every comfort from the garden of my love for him would make him well. But he did not come home. The law won out, as it had with Father.

Father Time—upon his silent rounds—continued to bring indubitable changes. I felt the punctual gentleman's work in my blood, proceeding its relentless way—too quick for such as I. Sue was back in Amherst and out of black. It seemed the engagement did it, not I. I must admit to no small amount of jealousy on that point. Her mind was on her marriage to Austin now. All the girls were wondering about whom they would marry. Abby and

Tempe could speak of nothing else. I exaggerate some, but not much. Existence as wife was the Cornerstone of their thoughts. My Cornerstone was Poetry—*my* poetry! Could "wife" contain a Circumference so Large?

It wasn't long before Abby became engaged. I felt a sense of foreboding. I wished I could have joined her in her happiness. She did seem very much in love. Her husband would be Daniel Bliss. She would be Abby Bliss. I prayed the name carried with it the infinite news of their future.

Once more my friends had entered a province I could not embrace. It had happened in the matter of religion and now again—each one—at sail in amplitude—and I a lonely girl upon the shore. I imagined joining them. My stronger part—or was it the weaker?—had pictured a new nest and I—Wife!—with all the glory and the dusting such title confers! Companionship forever and little Emilys all about! But even as I pictured the scene, savored its sweet nectar in my veins, a darker portion held its standard high. Poet! That voice was stronger than all the rest, held more of my Self. I could not but listen.

Days became weeks—weeks months—and all a'wash in my brain. Before I knew it, Sue was off for Geneva, New York, and then on to Michigan to see her brothers. We had been arguing—about religion mostly, specifically about my not becoming a Christian and not knowing if I ever would. Susie could not accept this. And there were other things. I think the engagement to Austin had some to do with it, though I can't be sure. She felt I had changed, that I doubted her love and was always trying to get her to prove it. She may have been right about that.

There were few letters after she left. I wrote, but Sue rarely answered. Soon there were no letters at all. The rift was widening more and more, until it seemed the very air became a stranger to my lungs. Blood cold, mind gone, heart sore—about to split my chest! When I could no longer bear the pain, I wrote to end our friendship. I told her I had been vexed over small things and should not have been, but that we could not go on arguing. We had always differed in matters of religion and that would have to be as it was. After some brief agonizing time Sue wrote that she did not care to end the friendship. I was deeply thankful and vowed to myself that the subject of religion would forever remain out of bounds for such as we. I opine Austin will have to become a Christian now that he has Susie's unwavering point of view on the matter to deal with. We shall see how long it takes.

Summer 1854.

Where had the year flown?

In July Austin graduated from the prestigious

Harvard Law School. We were all very proud. Though he did not go to accept his diploma—Mother had need of him—we had a celebration at Home. Father was overjoyed and said he was soon to have a new partner in the law firm. We all knew whom he meant. Austin got the point straightway. It was to be him! It seems Father had never asked Austin what *he* thought as regarded the arrangement—no surprise there! Austin was undecided as to what to do. I advised him to remain silent and make up his own mind as to what path his life should take. He took my advice for a time. I had been hoping he would return Home to stay upon the completion of his studies, but soon he and Susie were off to Chicago—leaving his devoted sister to fend for herself.

The New Year brought heavy snow and ice and a plan for "the girls" to visit Father in Washington, D.C. Not only that, as we would be coming home through Philadelphia, it was decided—and who can it have been who decided it?!—that we should spend some short time with our long-missed friends, the Colemans, in that Cradle of Independence so vastly admired. Eliza was the only daughter now—since the death of her beautiful sister, Olivia. We were set to leave in early February, the caprices of Old Jack Frost permitting. Carlo eyed the valises, head low, denoting curious concern. His mood mirrored my own.

It seemed to me that all was well enough at Home and that leaving might cause some unmarked danger. I also worried that the Dungeon Fear might return while I stood on some freezing train platform in the middle of nowhere and no place to hide. But we would be meeting Father. That fact served to get me on my way.

The morning of our leaving nothing could ease Carlo's mind save breakfast. Mother was in our room, fussing about with our luggage, being sure nothing had been forgotten that might save us from Death. I led Carlo downstairs. "Don't worry," I told him. "We shall be back and all will be well." I said this for my benefit more than for his own. He sat—Perfect Dog—waiting as I added the meat to the vegetables. When I began to stir, he stood up. All thoughts of desertion had flown. His drool told all. Eyes on his breakfast, he backed up as I put the bowl down on the wide plank by the oven. He quickly collapsed flat, his large front paws on either side of the bowl, rear legs out, ears in the food. I would have to wash his ears before leaving for the train.

Mother cried when we left. She said it was because she was so happy for us, but I believe it was more a question of her *own* Dungeon Fear—that she might never see us again.

It was a day's trip to New York City. It seemed we were forever asking for directions, changing trains and dealing with the luggage. As endless walking was required, I was extremely grateful for my decision to wear sensible shoes. The cars admitted much draft; however, the view was often pleasant. I don't believe I have ever seen so many cows.

Father met us in New York. We stayed the night in a hotel near the station, then off for the next round— a ferry to a place called Jersey City—and many more changes of trains, to Camden, another boat and the night spent in less than comfort at the Philadelphia Station! Father was extremely pleased with the efficiency of the railways, commenting several times about Progress and how it made the world smaller. I was none too sure a smaller world was necessary, or even advisable, but kept my thoughts to myself.

I was not overly impressed by our Nation's Capital. It's a lovely-looking city with large, stately buildings in which important decisions are made, but I could do without the bustle. The most wonderful aspect of the city in my view is its profusion of blossoms in the early spring. One is fortunate, indeed, if one is able to visit our Seat of Government at this time. Why, even in February the maples are in bloom and the birds announcing their delight and the sun on the green below, while in New England all is frozen and gray!

I was not well during a large portion of our three-week stay at the Willard Hotel in Washington, which may have altered my impression of the city. I spent much time inside, keeping company with my cough and resting from the rigors of travel. I did, however, visit the Capitol Building, where Father had been offering many fine resolutions on subjects ranging from the Territory of New Mexico to the Wilkes report. After my visit there, I made a drawing of Father approaching the building, briefcase in hand and a little bomb like an apple, its wick nearing extinction. It was not a bomb in the literal sense of the ability to explode a building, but only a stirring up on the inside, where the meanings are. It was meant to express the thought "Where Father goes—watch out!"

I have two principal memories of my stay in Washington and environs. The first, standing by the window in the room at Willard—the ax in my chest—and looking out at all the fine ladies and gentlemen in their fancy clothes, hurrying this way and that, and me wondering what I was doing there. I also wondered what *they* were doing.

The other memory is far more pleasant, glorious in fact! Mount Vernon!— The Quiet at the tomb of General George Washington, the beautiful Potomac and the charming painted boat we rode in! That was a day to lift one's hat to! Along the path on the way to the tomb a couple was "playing spoony," trading kisses beneath an arbor of blossoms. Vinnie was transfixed and didn't I have to pull her along by the hand?! I myself did not take a great interest in the scene, picturesque as it was. However, before I knew it I would be experiencing a longing for such pastimes one could not have thought possible! I will soon get to this extraordinary happening, but must approach the day in orderly transport.

After three weeks among the Society of Lawmakers, Father adjourned his Congressional duties and saw us to Philadelphia. It was grand to see the Colemans. They had been through such terrible suffering after Olivia's death. How can Consumption be so mean? How can *God*? There is much to understand in this life. I shall never know the smallest part of it, but must continue on despite my ignorance.

The house was grand indeed, three stories in all, with white shutters gracing the narrow cobblestoned street. And what conveniences—water inside and toilets! And a handsome bathtub! Why, it made one want to bathe incessantly!

I took advantage of the opportunity to rest, visiting with Eliza, talking for hours and lazing about. Vinnie took advantage of the shops. There were many fine stores on Chestnut Street, to be outshone only by the Hospital for the Insane. We did *not* visit there—thank God Father had not instructed us to inspect the dreary establishment!—

thereby missing one of the most depressing sojourns offered in the entire city. But one cannot have everything. We did, however, enjoy touching the Liberty Bell and tasting the finest ice cream west of Boston!

After partaking of our ice cream delight, Eliza mentioned that we must hear the minister preach at their church. The three of us were lounging in the parlor, after our traipse throughout lively downtown Philadelphia. "He is simply the best!" exclaimed Eliza, stretching out her legs and exercising her toes inside her stockings. Her shoes had long since been tossed to a nearby corner. "His sermons are better than anything!"

"Anything?" said Vinnie. Her mischievous tone suggested something in the carnal line.

Eliza sat up, serious now. "I mean it," she said. "Everyone wants to hear our Reverend Wadsworth." The next morning we had our chance.

It was a large church. I followed Vinnie, Eliza and Mr. And Mrs. Coleman into the pew, a few rows back from the pulpit. It was welcome to experience the quiet, as my brain had been addled by the fluster of city life. I sat a moment, then retrieved my hymnal from the rack on the rear of the pew in front of me. The hymnal had a dark blue cover. I opened it. The pages were gossamer thin. I looked down. The letters were finely rendered, as in some ancient manuscript. I touched the page, enjoying its gentle feel.

I looked up and he was there.

Time stopped.

There he is again.

What did *that* mean?

A charge passed through my body.

He was slender, with dark hair and eyes—gentle, sad eyes—touched by the beauty of Life—and the pain—humble, intelligent, dynamic, inspired, shy. All this I knew before he spoke. I knew him—and Centuries before—and always and ever.

There he is again. The way he stands. The way he holds his hand at the side of his robe, feeling bursting within that hand—shyness and a bold reserve in one. Man and boy, innocent and wise, compassionate and hurting, tender upon tender, consoling and knowing of pain—consoling because knowing of pain—and more. I will know more and more of him and remember more, as we shall be connected for life. And after? Let there be no after! I could not bear the parting!

"That's him," whispered Eliza.

My Philadelphia

His voice was deep and warm, in his words and in the silence between, with space for contemplation. I had heard none like it in all my life and at the selfsame moment had known it always. I knew the point he was about to make, the flow of what would follow. Not only that—I knew the mental attitude with which it would be spoken.

I am wrapped in the depth of his vision, the compassion, the originality of thought, the boldness, the sense of humor—that attribute without which all is lost! Never had I heard a minister put things that way. Innocent Christians and pitiful impenitents alike are forever and everywhere being subjected to a Religion resembling the terror of Bears! Original thought?! That is proposed to be almost as sinister a contemplation as Original Sin—and we all know how sinister *that* is! This Reverend Wadsworth speaks of Love—how intellect is useless without that most crucial of qualities—how affection is the noblest attribute of beings. He means Carlo too, I know. My loyal companion is not excluded from this man's care.

He continues. Clarity, Common Sense, Wonderment, Daring—all reign supreme! And such power to console!

He knows pain. He is hopeful in spite of the knowing.

My thoughts tumble end over end.

His spirit is large from overcoming. He admits the tiny bird that comes again and still and never fails to come.

"Help comes in many forms," he continues. "We must only look for it."

Yes.

"We find it in the sunrise, in an unexpected kindness, in a poem."

My blood runs cold.

"Poet means Creator."

My tears come over the dam.

"The poet can heal."

Handkerchief to brimming eyes.

"The poet can light the way."

He tells a joke. The congregation is laughing. He pulls a severe face, mock disapproval at such inappropriate expression. Silence. No one stirs. And then—a smile to light the Heavens! The congregants are laughing. My Soul is inside out.

I love him!

The thought shoots through my body.

I love this man!

My "other self" attacks.

You think of him as a man?!

My scolding voice is after me now—

He is a minister!

A surer voice declares—

One and the same.

My thoughts are giddy now, heedless, with a voice of their own.

I love this Dr. Wadsworth—this Charles Wadsworth—this Charlie!

My heart stops.

You call him "Charlie"?

My truer mind answers.

Yes, I call him Charlie! Helpmate, Protector, Lover!

Breathing stops.

How dare you call him "Lover"?!

The voice is unforgiving.

He is not your Lover! He is a minister!

A timid challenge from my boldest part—

And so?

My being opens wide—at Home! In Port!

Who is to say whom I shall love? My loving is my own!

"Kindness matters," I hear him say.

317

Yes.

He speaks of the value of independence, of freedom, of the need for contemplation and a faith matched with common sense. He praises a bond with Nature, the "nourishment of reading" and the value of "looking as children look." He closes his eyes. Moments pass before he speaks. "We must remember it takes courage to have Life." He looks up. "Life is given to us by God and yet it is for *us* to take it. We must pray for the courage."

The service is over.

"What did you think?" Eliza whispers. "Isn't he great?"

I cannot speak.

"We are so lucky. Everybody says so."

I look down to adjust my shawl. When I look up he is gone.

I did not meet my love that day. He did not greet his congregation, as I thought he might. No handshakes, no pleasantries, no mulling. My Shepherd was gone. It may have been just as well, as I cannot imagine in the wildest portion of my brain what I would have said—Heart pounding, head spinning, knees weak, breath Nowhere! I would have cut quite the caper and would have been fortunate not to swoon in a dead faint at his feet!

Once back at the Colemans', I questioned Eliza,

enlisting as much propriety as could be employed. "I quite enjoyed the sermon," I said in apparent calm demeanor as we adjourned to the parlor after dessert.

"I told you," said Eliza. "The entire congregation has never been so pleased with a minister, ever!"

I did not care about the entire congregation and almost said so before catching myself, and not a moment too soon! I had nearly released the cat from the proverbial bag, and we all know what disaster that can lead to! It was hard to frame my questions. I did, however, obtain a small number of facts. I was told by Eliza that "her" minister had suffered in life, although she did not know what had caused that suffering. He was a Poet— be still, my Heart!—or had been a Poet, she wasn't sure which. He was a deep thinker—well, *that* I knew—and he always took great care to console members of the congregation in their times of difficulty. *That* I assumed. And he was shy. I knew that too, although I'm not sure how I knew it. Last came the bit of truth too horrible to bear. He was married, "happily married," I believe was Eliza's way of putting it—a knife in my jealous heart!

On the trip back to Amherst I was filled with the sensation of moving in the wrong direction. As always, a force drew me to the sanctity and peace of Home. Yet, even as I was being drawn steadfastly to the nest, at one and the same moment I felt I was being torn away from my Life. I felt I belonged with this man forever, my Protector, my "understander," my Charlie—this Soul I had known for eons of time, this one who had given me a Place to land! Religion and I could be one—*were* one! He was certainly religious and his thoughts on the matter were the same as mine—the same as those I had held for as long as I could remember—thoughts of faith and common sense, independence and freedom, a sense of humor and kindness, the importance of Nature and reading—and the writing of Poetry! I loved this man with the All of all I had ever loved, or ever would love! I wanted to cling to him forever! I decided straightway I would do just that.

It is fair to say that since the day I beheld My Philadelphia I have not been the same. I daresay I shall never be and that is all to the good. Oh, there is an ache in my Heart, but I don't care for that. The joy of my Love is a gift I would not trade for any manner of riches, any place on this Earth.

Home

s we set our valises down in the hall, Carlo bounds about in delight, welcoming us Home, where we belong. Mother is there with her warm smile and tears of joy that we are *not* dead—and all the questions! Are we thirsty? Are we hungry? Are we more hungry than thirsty? Are we more thirsty than hungry? Are we both thirsty *and* hungry? Do we want dinner straightway? Vinnie and I smile at each other, enjoying Mother's familiar fuss. Vinnie asks about the cats.

"They're fine," says Mother, although she has not a clue as to where they might be. Trapping innocent sparrows, no doubt.

Vinnie and I are just about to go upstairs for a rest when Father, briefcase in hand—home some time ahead of us—enters the hall, a serious expression on his face. "Well, girls," he says. "What do you suppose?" I of course have no idea what to suppose, nor it appears does Vinnie.

"We are moving back to the Homestead."

Father made additional pronouncements after that,

but I heard nothing. I was numb. If blood did indeed flow through my veins, I was not aware of the fact. I hesitate to consider why a return to my birth house should strike terror in my heart, but it did. My mind leaped instantly to my first move—I but nine and very much afraid. It seemed no different now. That same fear was in my blood. Had I learned nothing from Life's experience in fifteen years? The question was vexing to me, making my current circumstances all the worse.

I discovered myself on the stairs, Carlo behind, hurrying up to my room, in my mind a desperate wish that I might reach the door before fainting and causing all manner of commotion. How could I explain myself to others when I couldn't explain myself to myself?

We reach the door—cut glass of knob reflecting colored light—hand to knob—shafts of crystal rainbow—reached! Turn knob—open door—bed—fall—pillow—soft—cool—quiet—safe. I cry many tears, Carlo at the side of the bed, wondering.

Life is too formidable a business. I am ill equipped for such a journey!

Each new thought brings more alarm and more until I feel I will surely expire.

My Protector, my Shepherd, my Charlie—in faraway Philadelphia! How can he comfort me? How can he love me when he does not know I exist?

And more thoughts, terrible, frightening, lonely thoughts and nothing to stop them!

Susie! Will you forget me now that you and Austin are one? I need you! I must have you!

After some time the tears stop. I am too exhausted to be their host. Carlo is asleep now. I can hear his even breathing, sure, comforting. I think of Charlie. I will write to him. I will tell him how I heard his sermon, how I know he could help me. I will speak of my distress. Eliza will deliver the note.

No. I will write him one day, but this is not the time. I will wait until I have a need so great, I cannot but ask for his help and he will give it!

Then more water over the dam and longing like to overtake me!

Oh, I want you to come to Amherst!! Oh, please to come! Oh, will you come?

Carlo shifts position on the mat. Tears subside. Steadier thoughts claim residence.

Perhaps one day you will come. Would it not be grand? And we could walk with Carlo in the fields— just us three?! I love you, Charlie!

I think of Susie and how I felt I should never love another as I loved her. One thing is for sure. I need not worry about that.

A knock on the door. Carlo sits up. It is Mother in to

see if I am all right. She sits on the bed, strokes my hair back as when I was a child and sick. A little bird calls. "A whip-poor-will!" says Mother. We are both amazed, as one rarely hears them. They sleep their days away on the forest floor, hardly ever making themselves known. "Listen," says Mother. "I've heard them in Monson, but never in Amherst. It's a good sign."

I hope she is right.

The next morning I heard another friend of feather. This time it was a robin. Carlo and I were walking in back by the woods, and there she was, perched on the limb of my Elm tree. It was a glad report. We watched her awhile before she flew off to spread the news of Spring, then continued along the edge of the woods. I stopped to look at the hill behind the trees. We would be moving over that hill, starting a new life. No Elm tree. No front door stone.

The first line of a little poem came to my mind. As I had nothing to write it on and no pen to write, I led Carlo back to the house to catch it on a scrap of paper.

I take my strength from Robin—
Perched high upon the tree—
With nothing more than stick bones
To hold her chemistry—

She traveled far—
From places South—
That I shall never see
If she can make so long a trip—
A hill's not much for me!

There are times when one must rhyme. It helps to tie the senses on.

By October, when the leaves took on their red and flaming gold, plans for the move were well in place. Mother's neuralgia was worse and her concern about the wallpaper did not help one bit. Mother enjoys change less than I do, if such a thing is possible. It was good neither Vinnie nor I was about to be married, as Mother needed all the help she could get.

Father was cheered by the impending move. He had convinced Austin to join him in his law practice and move onto the grounds of the Homestead. Father would be building a new house for him and his new wife—my soulmate sister! Susie wrote expressing concern about the advisability of the arrangement, but added that she was delighted with the plan to hire an Italian architect. It is my opinion that Austin did not want to join Father's practice, desiring rather to settle in Chicago. I hope all works out smoothly. Austin is easily swayed by Father's wishes, which I take not to be a good thing. I suppose the same could be said for yours truly, though I make every effort that it *not* be so. I walk a careful way with Father. In many ways I have pleased him without meaning to. I am well educated, yet do not use this education outside his House. I have strong convictions, but keep to myself all those in danger of falling into that dreaded territory of opposition to his own. I am at Home—in his House—where I long to be, with those I love—available to cheer his heart and bake his bread. It is, I suppose, a good arrangement, though in some ways it is just that—an arrangement. Not a very passionate way of life. And yet I have my Poems! Therein explodes my innermost life! My All! At the end of the day I assemble the fragments of my Self, gathered on scraps amid my daily labors. And who knows? One day my poems may reach outside his House. That will be—or not—as the wind decides. To be alive is so chief a thing! I do believe that is the truth—and we all know Truth is the thing that lasts.

Author's

Notes

Phrases

These are some of Emily's own words that found their way into my attempt to capture her voice.

PHRASES FOUND IN THE POEMS

This list uses the first lines of the poems, along with their numbers, as they appear in R. W. Franklin's *The Poems of Emily Dickinson* (see page 345 for bibliographical information).

p. 8, "but what of that?": *I reason, Earth is short* (Fr403)

pp. 21, 120, "a wooden way": *After great pain, a formal feeling comes* (Fr372)

p. 33, "a dreaming laid": *I cautious scanned my little life* (Fr175)

p. 39, "docile and omnipotent": *I like to see it lap the Miles* (Fr383)

p. 54, "strive at recess": *Because I could not stop for death* (Fr479)

pp. 54, 186, 311, "where the meanings are": *There's a certain slant of light* (Fr320)

p. 56, "tell it slant": *Tell all the Truth but tell it slant* (Fr1263)

p. 61, "the first league out from land": *Exultation is the going* (Fr143)

p. 97, "my first well day": *My first well day since many ill* (Fr288)

p. 206, "I heard the buckle snap": *He put the belt around my life* (Fr330)

p. 214, "narrow hands": *I dwell in Possibility* (Fr446)

p. 232, "dimity convictions": *What Soft—Cherubic Creatures* (Fr675)

p. 314, "Centuries before": *After great pain, a formal feeling comes* (Fr372)

PHRASES FOUND IN EMILY'S LETTERS

This list uses the letter numbers assigned in *The Letters of Emily Dickinson*, edited by Thomas H. Johnson (see page 345 for bibliographical information).

p. 11, "address an eclipse": (L261)

p. 18, "in all my glory": (multiple)

p. 37, "culprit mice": (L202)

p. 66, "obliged to write": (L6)

p. 79, "found my Savior": (L10)

p. 82, "How Large they sound": (L6)

pp. 117, 259, "same old sixpence": (L260)

NOTE ON GRAMMATICAL USES

Emily's phrasing, and occasionally spelling, were idio-syncratic. For example, she spelled "don't" as "do'nt," and "skunk" as "skonk" (although this may have been only twice as a child of eleven in a letter (L1) to Austin). She used "do'nt" instead of "doesn't," as in "that do'nt bother me any," added "ly" to adjectives as in "the forsythia looked finely," and sometimes omitted verbs from her sentences. She used many dashes. To help make her more approachable to the modern reader, I have kept these usages to a minimum.

Basic Facts about Emily Dickinson

Emily Elizabeth Dickinson was born in Amherst, Massachusetts, on December 10, 1830. She died in Amherst on May 15, 1886. Although the cause of death was listed as Bright's disease (a kidney malfunction), she is considered by many to have succumbed to severe hypertension.

Emily had one brother, William Austin Dickinson (Austin) (1829–1895). She had one sister, Lavinia Norcross Dickinson (Vinnie) (1833–1899). Her father, Edward Dickinson (1803–1874), was a prominent lawyer who served a term in Congress from 1853 to 1855. He was also treasurer of Amherst College for thirty-eight years. Her mother, Emily Norcross Dickinson (1804–1882), was a homemaker. Emily attended Amherst Academy from 1840 to 1847 and Mount Holyoke Seminary from 1847 to 1848.

What happened to Emily after this book ends? In a nutshell, Emily became one of the most famous poets of all time. But what was her life like after the age of twenty-four? How did she spend her days? She remained living in her father's house, the Homestead, in Amherst, where she was born and where she died at the age of fifty-five. She helped her mother and Vinnie with the housework; cooked; baked bread, black cake and gingerbread; read books; played the piano; wrote letters; tended her garden; walked with Carlo (until he died at the age of sixteen) and wrote her poems. Emily continued to suffer debilitating bouts of anxiety and suffered what appeared to be a severe attack of anxiety and depression in the fall of 1861. However, then began an extraordinarily prolific period for the poet. In 1862 she wrote close to a finished poem every day. From that time on she became increasingly housebound, rarely leaving the Homestead. She did, however, keep up a lively social connection with friends and relatives with copious letter writing, in which one could see her thriving sense of humor.

In the years following the end of this book Emily corresponded with Reverend Charles Wadsworth (My Philadelphia). An intense relationship developed between the two. In the spring of 1860 he came to visit her in Amherst. He left for San Francisco with his family in May of 1862, when Emily was thirty-one. He visited Emily again in the summer of 1880. He died in 1882. Emily referred to him in a letter (L765) the summer after he died as "my closest earthly friend." It had been a long friendship. He was clearly important to her throughout her entire life.

Emily never married. She is said to have been enamored of several men, all of them married. In addition to Charles Wadsworth, the names most often discussed in this connection are Samuel Bowles, a family friend and editor of the *Springfield Daily Republican*, and Judge Otis Phillips Lord, a business associate of her father's. After her father's death and the subsequent death of Judge Lord's wife, he and Emily were said to have had a romantic relationship, nearly becoming engaged.

Emily Dickinson wrote over seventeen hundred poems. Only ten were published in her lifetime. Most of these appeared in the *Springfield Daily Republican*, and were submitted, for the most part, without her knowledge. Three were published in the Civil War publication *Drum Beat.* She initiated the publication of none of her poetry. Emily bound her poems in small hand-sewn booklets called fascicles, which she kept in a drawer of her bureau. She sent copies of some of her poems to friends and relatives as gifts and condolences. In 1890, four years after her death, the first edition of some of her poems was published, entitled *Poems by Emily Dickinson*, edited by Thomas Wentworth Higginson and Mabel Loomis Todd.

Emily Dickinson is considered by many to be America's foremost poet. As I write this, all one thousand seven hundred and eighty-nine of her known poems have been published in *The Poems of Emily Dickinson*, edited by R. W. Franklin. There are countless editions of her poetry in the United States and in many languages around the world. *The Dickinson Electronic Archives* (www.emilydickinson.org) is currently in the process of publishing Emily's poems and letters on the internet, the largest known audience in the history of recorded time!

I was introduced to Emily Dickinson in 1976 when I saw my acting idol, Julie Harris, on Broadway in William Luce's *The Belle of Amherst.* I was astounded by Julie's magnificent performance and overwhelmed by the spirit of Emily Dickinson. Some years later, when my publisher suggested I write a book based on the young life of a strong, original, accomplished woman, Emily came to mind.

I had previously written about the young life of Joan of Arc (*Young Joan,* HarperCollins Publishers, 1991), and being an actor as well as a writer, I had approached the writing of *Young Joan* much the way I approach an acting role (I had played Joan of Arc twice). I decided to embark on my research for this book about Emily in a similar manner, though I haven't had the privilege of playing her. Not yet, anyway!

Here's how it went. Emily grew up in the mid-1800s. That meant, for starters, I needed to study the time period. What did she wear? What did she eat? What was her house like? Her town? I had to learn about the

337

religious expression of the period, the transportation, school life, hobbies, furniture, plumbing, medicine, habits, customs and on and on. How was it different then? And how was it the same? My acting teacher, Uta Hagen, had stressed these two questions equally. Exploring how we are like people from other centuries and other countries helps us feel closer to them. The answers to the second question (how was it the same?) are similar for most periods of time and in most countries. Young girls have birthdays and get their periods. They have crushes, girl friends, parents, siblings, relatives, pets, holidays, colds, moods, fears, joys, boyfriends and so on. I didn't have to research the similarities, but the differences were another matter. My work took several forms. And several years.

I began by reading the letters. Emily was a prolific letter writer. *The Letters of Emily Dickinson*, edited by Thomas H. Johnson, contains over one thousand letters written from the age of eleven until a few days before her death. It is an extraordinary resource for immersing oneself in the poet's voice. Not only did I read the letters over and over for several years, but I also spent endless hours listening to a two-tape set of readings of the letters and poems by Julie Harris. Hearing her speak Emily's words was an invaluable gift.

Early on I joined the Emily Dickinson International

Society. With the help of several Dickinson scholars I studied Emily's life and work. With biographer Polly Longsworth (who wrote *The World of Emily Dickinson* and *Austin and Mabel*) I explored her life. With poet-professor Joy Ladin I studied the poems, deep and spare, containing razorlike thoughts of insight and inspiration. Many of them are funny, too. Some are hard to understand; some are simple. But they are always nourishing. Both the poems and the letters gave me a realization of her wonderful sense of humor.

I did a lot of reading. Biographies, reminiscences, essays and books about nineteenth-century New England all added to my understanding of this extraordinary woman.

I spent a great deal of time in Amherst. The Emily Dickinson Museum became my second home. The museum includes the Homestead, where Emily was born, lived for most of her life and died. I spent many hours in her bedroom, her parlor and her garden. The house in which Emily lived during most of the story of this book no longer exists. It has been irreverently replaced by a Mobil gas station! I checked it out, though. The cemetery Emily used to see from her window is just behind the gas pumps. Emily, her mother, her father, and Lavinia are buried there. Her gravestone says "Called Back." Austin is buried with Sue and their children in Wildwood

Cemetery, about a mile and a half to the north.

It was interesting to visit Amherst in all seasons—exploring, taking pictures and making notes in the heat of summer, the joy of spring, the grandeur of fall and the snow of winter. I walked Emily's walk to school at Amherst Academy. (The location is now a parking lot with a plaque stating that the school used to be there.) I walked her walk to church and along the road she so often walked with Carlo. I visited Mount Holyoke College (Mount Holyoke Seminary in Emily's time). I felt like a detective, searching for the truth, a grand adventure!

I spent days in the archives at the Jones Library in Amherst, poring over endless bits of material, including letters written by Emily's father; sermons delivered by her adored Reverend Charles Wadsworth; prescriptions ordered from the local pharmacy for the Dickinson family; records of the eye doctor in Boston who treated Emily for a mysterious eye condition in 1864; articles on tuberculosis (at that time called consumption), Bright's disease, hypertension, conditions of the eyes, lupus, anxiety disorders and depression. Best of all, I held an original of one of her poems, "We play at Paste/Till qualified for Pearl" (Fr282). At the Frost Library at Amherst College I held her Latin book (a gift from Austin, shared with Abby) and saw a lock of her hair. It was like spun gold. At Harvard University I saw the bureau in which she kept her poems, a sampler she made when she was ten, her piano and her tiny writing desk. That was a surprise. How could a desk so small launch that grand outpouring of poems?

Perhaps the most enjoyable part of my research was my investigation into the habits, appearance and history of Newfoundland dogs. I got an added sense of Emily's spunk, knowing that her constant companion for sixteen long years had been such an enormous, bearlike creature. A question among many that I never found the answer to was "Where did Carlo sleep?" I checked the letters, the poems and the biographies, but could find no answer. I started asking around. I asked the curator of the Archives at the Jones Library, I asked Polly Longsworth and Joy Ladin, Cindy Dickinson (Director of Interpretation and Programming at the Emily Dickinson Museum), the scholars at the Emily Dickinson International Society and the guides at the Homestead. No one seemed to know. One of the guides sent me a copy of an article about pets in nineteenth-century New England. It said that pets were usually kept in the barn or in the house. The choice was a personal matter. I would have to imagine where the Dickinsons might keep an enormous dog like Carlo. This ended up being a fun supposition! As with every choice in writing the book, my plan was to find out everything I could about what actually happened. If I couldn't find out, I was free to imagine what *might* have happened in Emily's world in Amherst, Massachusetts, in the 1800s.

Writing this book in the first person was a bold choice. It would be as if Emily were talking. That way I felt I could get "inside her skin." I had written *Young Joan* in the first person, but Joan's voice is nowhere near as well known as Emily's. With Emily Dickinson we have her poems and letters, not to mention college and university courses throughout the world, exploring her individual voice. Expectations would be high. I hesitated at first. Still, I ended up feeling that writing in the first person was the way I could best express my sense of what growing up might have been like for Emily. I figured that after studying the facts and the numerous opinions of others, this was what I had to do. And as Emily might have said, my own way is all I have.

My work ended up taking nearly ten years. I hadn't expected it to take that long. And I hadn't expected to form such a deep relationship with Emily. I know without a doubt that she will be with me for the rest of my life, and perhaps beyond. As Emily would say—*did* say—*"This life is not conclusion."*

My biggest hope is that after reading *A Voice of Her Own* you may want to read her poems and to find out more about her. This book is my sense of what it was like to grow up as Emily Dickinson. What is yours?

I have many people to thank. I want to thank Julie Harris, my constant inspiration; Judith Schmidt for her endless support and love; my editor, Anne Hoppe, who guided me in countless ways to be far better than I thought I could be; my former editor, children's book author Charlotte Zolotow, for her belief in me and for sharing her books and her love of Emily; Joy Ladin for her help with the poems and with life; Cindy MacKenzie for her invaluable *Concordance to the Letters of Emily Dickinson,* the wonderful bonding over Emily and for the laughs; Cindy Dickinson (Director of Interpretation and Programming at the Emily Dickinson Museum—no relation to Emily) for her welcoming support; Polly Longsworth for the endless information and for her spot-on understanding of Emily; Betty Bernhard for her meticulous reading of the manuscript, her fierce dedication to Emily's mother and her warmth and advice; David Garnes for his help with Carlo's sleeping arrangements; the members of the Emily Dickinson International Society (EDIS) for sharing their expertise and for so quickly accepting an actor/writer of fiction into their midst; Shulamith Oppenheim for her love and generosity throughout my long journey; Pamela Newkirk for seeing Emily in me and not giving up; my family; and, of course, Emily—for being herself.

Further Reading

Dickinson, Emily, selected and with an introduction
by Joyce Carol Oates. *The Essential Dickinson.*
Hopewell, N.J.: Ecco Press, 1996.
——— . *Essential Dickinson.* A CD recording read by
Julie Harris. New York: Caedmon Audio, 2006.
Available online at LearnOutLoud.com.
Eberwein, Jane Donahue, ed. *An Emily Dickinson
Encyclopedia.* Westport, Conn., and London:
Greenwood Press, 1998.
Franklin, R. W., ed. *The Poems of Emily Dickinson.*
Cambridge, Mass., and London: Belknap Press of
Harvard University Press, 1999.
Habegger, Alfred. *My Wars Are Laid Away in Books: The
Life of Emily Dickinson.* New York: Random House,
2001.
Johnson, Thomas H., ed. *The Letters of Emily Dickinson.*
Cambridge, Mass., and London: Belknap Press of
Harvard University Press, 1986.
——— . *Emily Dickinson: Selected Letters.* Cambridge,

Mass., and London: Belknap Press of Harvard University Press, 1986.

Kirk, Connie Ann. *Emily Dickinson: A Biography.* Westport, Conn., and London: Greenwood Press, 2004.

Longsworth, Polly. *The World of Emily Dickinson.* New York and London: Norton, 1990.

——. *Austin and Mabel: The Amherst Affair & Love Letters of Austin Dickinson and Mabel Loomis Todd.* New York: Farrar, Straus, 1984.

Luce, William. *The Belle of Amherst.* New York, Hollywood, London, Toronto: Samuel French, 1976.

MacKenzie, Cynthia. *Concordance to the Letters of Emily Dickinson.* Boulder: University Press of Colorado, 2000.

Sewall, Richard B. *The Life of Emily Dickinson.* Cambridge, Mass.: Harvard University Press, 1994.

Author, playwright, and actor Barbara Dana spent over a decade researching Emily Dickinson for this book. Her award-winning books for children include ZUCCHINI and YOUNG JOAN, a novel based on the girlhood of Joan of Arc. She is also the coeditor of WIDER THAN THE SKY: *Essays and Meditations on the Healing Power of Emily Dickinson* for adults.

Ms. Dana has three grown sons. She lives in South Salem, New York, with her yellow Lab, Riley. You can visit Barbara Dana on her website at www.barbaradana.com.